Found By You

The Spring Rose Bay Series. Book 1

By K. L. Jessop

FOUND BY YOU
Copyright 2016 K.L.Jessop

Najla Qamber Designs - Cover Design.
Lindee Robinson Photography - Photo Image.
Book formatting by White Hot Ebook Formatting

Disclaimer: This book contains references and scenes of a sexual nature and strong language.

~ Dedication ~

To those who guided me through the tough times.

Chapter One

Amelia

For the love of god someone get me a Tequila! This woman gets more intense each day. Commanding at me down the phone as I wait for the next instalment of planning her wedding, when I'm not even a fucking wedding planner. Last time I checked I was a semi-reclusive red-head that lost her way in life. Now suddenly I'm taking orders I don't need from a celebrity rich bitch I'm yet to even meet.

As soon as I pushed the speakerphone button my body shuddered with the unpleasantness of her high pitched Botox trapped voice, throwing demands at me down the phone like she was the queen of Hollywood. She's nothing more than a bratty little rich girl on the cover of magazines because daddy has a healthy bank account. She wouldn't know a day's work if it slapped her across the face.

"Are you aware of the wine glass fountains I want? My crew will bring them over for preparation the day before, I do not want anyone to enter the function room during the time they're there and after. Is that clear Miss Weston?"

I rolled my eyes at Andrew who's sat across from me looking ridiculously handsome in his grey suit as he listens to our call. "I completely understand Nadia. Although *my* crew needs access to the function room at all times. The room cannot be prepared to the high standards you're asking if you refuse them access. And as part of Management I can't stand by knowing they're not doing the job in hand, regardless if it's to your needs."

I brace myself for another Bridezilla moment, this woman doesn't do understanding or compromise, everything is about money and status and if nothing goes her way everyone knows. Nadia Lenton is the daughter of one of the country's high flying business pricks that thinks by clicking fingers everything and everyone within touching distance will stop and bow down to their needs. Not so long ago her and Andrew had a full blown argument because she wanted the entire hotel on shutdown and only accessible to her wedding guests.

The Grand Hotel is a high class seven star affair located along the west coast, being a tourist attraction is one of our main forms of earnings as well as business associates whom use our building for conferences, closing it off to *her* people would lose us a great deal of income and popularity.

"Fine! But make sure you only have the same team at all times. This is no ordinary wedding Miss Weston, this is our wedding. James and I have people to impress in high places!"

"Stuck up bitch," I hiss ending the call.

"The only reason I'm gritting my teeth and letting that dragon use and abuse us-or you, is because of the hefty payment we are going to receive once done. That's all that matters."

"Even if she has me in therapy in the meantime?" I sigh, resting my head in my hands. Andrew is aware of my stress and anxiety levels. Just after I started working here he had to come to my aid after having an argument with a very angry guest. That was the day we had our break though and talked for hours about how shitty life can get. Not many people take to Andrew, his dark mysterious attitude can leave people hanging with unanswered questions as they try to work him out. He is a great guy but I swear he's often more hormonal than I am at times.

"You're already in therapy, Amelia," he grins, standing. "Besides Matthews can sort her out when he arrives, he'll love that."

Mr Matthews is the Managing Director of The Grand that Andrew and I run, he comes to spend his summers here at Spring Rose but had to cancel his visit last year. "When is he arriving?" I ask, shutting down my computer.

"When he decides to let me know. The little prick just turns up when he wants."

Grabbing my bag I head out with him, knowing that even though our work day has finished, Andrew will still be here for hours yet. He lived and breathed this building.

"So what are your plans for the evening?" he questions, taking the keys to lock my office door before handing them back.

"A secret love affair with a small blonde." I smiled.

"Ah yeah, the Reception girl?"

"Her name is Megan, Andrew. You know I think you

should get to know your staff a little more or at the very least learn their names."

"And why would I want to do that, when I have you to tell me who they are?"

"Because it's polite. Besides you might find enjoyment out of the office. Fifteen hour days and no play time aren't healthy for a grown man." I teased.

His deep chuckle radiates through the corridor as we walk towards his office. "Christ what are you, my mother?"

"Fuck, no. That would be some challenge. See you tomorrow Mr Mysterious."

I leave him chuckling as I head down the hall, the need for an over calculated glass of wine and a cool shower was calling. This is only my second summer in Spring Rose Bay and this year's humidity and sweat is greater than the last. I loved it here. It instantly felt like home when my feet touched the sand and cool water of the ocean. But it was my job that kept me going. As Assistant Manager I have the daily duties of organising and directing all hotel services, as well as working alongside Andrew who has overall say in Management. The wide six story building is exquisite. Grand staircases, glass chandeliers and marble floors provide it with elegance and beauty and oozed expense. Its three hundred guest rooms provided the luxurious comfort while the very top floor was primarily for the staff, providing offices and accommodation for workers over for the season.

Rounding the corner into reception I'm greeted by a wide smile belonging to a pure blonde in the form of my best friend Megan. "Please tell me tonight's plans are purely alcohol based and swooning over hot guys on the internet," she asks as I hang up my keys.

"Sounds like heaven."

"You look stressed everything alright?"

"Nadia-fucking-Lenton."

"Ah, that explains the face. You heading off now?"

"Yes, I need a run, loosen this frustration."

She gets up to file some papers, looking gorgeous as ever in her black pencil dress. "You know there's better ways to relieve frustration than running babe," she replies with a wink.

I rolled my eyes and turn on my heels. "Goodbye Megan."

"You know I'm right though!" she shouts, making me chuckle as I head out the building. I've known Megan for seven years, we met working in a Hotel in London and from the moment I met her I knew I needed her in my life, she transferred down here a little while before I did and eventually help secure the job I have now. She's forever trying to hook me up with any hot guy that walks through the hotel doors, desperate to get me back into the world of sexy times and playful fun. As far as I'm concerned men are purebred assholes that think only of themselves, I don't want a man in my life and I certainly don't need one.

***

My feet pound the dust track as I run the coastline. I was always drawn to the coast; it brought fond memories of holidays as a kid. If the sun was out you wore the swimsuit, if it rained you had it on under dad's oversize jumper. It's a place of freedom, washes through my veins taking stress and unwanted emotions with each wave that ebbs out.

Growing up in the London lifestyle was a different

world to the one I live in now. Mirrored buildings stood amongst the streets of endless traffic while suited men delivered another account of high speed living to their day. Then before you know it everything changes. Life has a way of fucking you over when you least expect it. I had great experience, fought each day to stop myself from going under but ended where I couldn't fight no more.

As I reach my porch my phone vibrates against my ass that's zipped in my back pocket.

Megan: If you're still trying to run off the fact you have a bad case of sexual frustration, you've left it too late. I'm heading to yours and ready to get intoxicated. Xx

Me: Just got back and need a shower, smell like a wet cat. Xx

Megan: I hope that's your way of referring to just been given a 'wet pussy' Ha!

Me: Dirty minx.

Megan's sat on the kitchen counter swinging her legs when I enter the room. Her eyes going wide at her phone. "Check out this bad boy," the screen is bursting in muscles and curves of a half-naked guy I don't recognise.

"Do you know him?" I question, pouring us both some wine.

"I'd like to know him."

"You want to know every man with abs and muscle," I chuckle. We head out to the patio to sit under the evening sun. "So are we going to Felicity's party on Saturday?"

Her eyes shoot up from her phone. "You want to go?"

There was a time when going out never interested me. But since moving here with Megan I'm starting take back control of my life again. "Yes. Although I do need a new dress."

"And shoes. I need new shoes," she grins.

"Why? You'll only end up taking them off, why buy more when you hardly wear the ones you own?" The first time I met Megan was at a party, a table was in the corner of the ballroom and up on top bare foot and a short black dress was Megan dancing to her audience.

"I've told you, a new pair of heels makes the walk of shame seem better."

I shake my head grinning at her. "Will you ever learn Miss Simmons?"

"Not when Tequila and tables are involved. It's an easy pass to hard muscle and the ride of your life. You should try it; give your vibrator a break."

"I have. It broke weeks ago."

Her mouth falls open as her eyes spring wide. In a flash her phone is out searching web pages for sex toys, alarmed with the fact that not only is it broken, I've not had an orgasm in over a month. "Fuck, no wonder you run," she giggles.

God I love this girl.

***

"Is it on yet?" Megan shouts from the other side of the cubical. I take the purple dress from the hanger and slide it over my body. It did nothing for me, I looked ridiculous.

"Oh, now that is *so* you," she says sarcastically, sticking her head in threw the curtain.

"I look like a twelve year old in a prom dress. Plus the back is too low." I turn my body to view my behind in the mirror, revealing the low cut dress that opens down to my lower back.

"Hmm true, try the next one." She disappears and starts a running commentary of what she's trying on whilst muttering to herself. Without looking, I know she's probably stood with one hand on her hip and a forefinger to her mouth as she looks at what to try first.

"I don't know which to try first." See what I mean? It's uncanny how we know each other so well.

"The green one." I suggest, trying to fight my way out the dress but failing. "Ugh shit, can you help me with this stupid zip please?" I huff.

She flings the curtain back and spins me round tugging at the zip just above my ass to unfasten it.

"What do you think about this?" The pastel green dress hugs her body perfectly, sitting just below her ass and showing off her tanned legs and a chocolate coloured birthmark on her right knee.

"Little short isn't it?" I'm moved aside so she can admire herself in the mirror.

"Not short enough if you ask me," wiggling her brows and handing me my next dress. "Try this one."

I slip into the black lace tight fitting dress with a sweetheart bust and cupped shoulder straps.

"Now that has sexy written all over it." Megan says as I twist to check the back.

I always think people talk shit when they make comment about what I wear or how I look-purely because I

8

don't see what they say they're seeing.

"You don't think it's too much?"

She rolls her eyes. "Uh uh, if I saw you out wearing that, I'd defiantly fuck you."

There were only ever five people in my life that I loved, trusted and worshipped the ground they walked on. I put my heart and soul into those five, stood by them when they needed it, helped out when I could and thought nothing of taking on their problems because in return I'd have that love and support back. I was wrong.

Out of those five, one left me for a place in the stars and the other two betrayed me in the worst possible way. My mother died when I was eighteen and everything changed. Wrapped up in his own grief my father become a part of the betrayal when he decided to take sides with the enemy-my second betrayal, which just so happened to be my first love. Hurt and fear is all I know. What only makes it easier to bare is the beauty that's hugging the shit out of me right now. Megan and her brother Lucas are my everything and I love them unconditionally. There are no words big enough in which to thank them for there forever love and support. However, I may be able to plaster on a smile and laugh with others but in reality I'm still suffocating.

Chapter Two

Marcus

I lean my arms against the metal edge of my balcony, which overlooks rich colours of turquoise and deep blue. Small figures of movement along the golden sands as sea birds dive into the water near the rugged coastline. I longed for this, dreamt about it and craved it for months. Missing out on this place last year felt like an eternity, it's like a drug you feed off and last summer was the biggest fucking come down ever.

I threw myself into work, worked every hour of the day to keep one thing in my life worth living for. Many a time I was so close to jumping in the car and getting away from the never ending shit I was surrounded in but I knew that would be wrong. I needed to put everything I had into keeping some things from falling apart, no matter how much effort it took.

Now I'm done with all the shit that was or has been thrown my way, done with people for caring nothing more than themselves, taking advantage, your self-respect, regardless of the consequences and laugh in your face whilst doing it. I wasn't prepared to deal with that and most certainly won't be doing it again, right from when I found them. Trust plays a big apart in humanity and when you walk in on your best friend banging the shit out of your girlfriend that trust is ripped to shreds. Years of brotherhood wasted, a union of love and respect sabotaged by their cheating stupidity, while I'm left in a pool of humiliation and self-loathing.

That was then, and within minutes of being in this environment away from the craze of city lights, daily traffic and entourage of people, it all disappeared. Forgotten. All I can focus on is this tropical foreground in front of me that embeds in your mind and will be my home for the next four months. Less work and more surf. I needed it, search for the real me again, fight back at those thoughts and forget everything and everyone beyond these borders.

Nothing hurts more than being kicked down by the person you thought would never hurt you and I got it from both barrels. I hope the guilt rots them for the rest of their days knowing in the back of their minds the disloyalty they caused and how it affected those around them. My mind may not always remember exactly what happened, what went wrong or how it even got to that stage, they are questions I ask myself often enough, but I sure as hell know the heart will always remember the feeling of being sliced apart, and it's that feeling I need to escape from.

I never told anyone I was coming or that I'd even arrived other than my Mother; there are not many people to inform. My Dad's an asshole who only cares for money and status, my sister is a spoilt daddy's girl and neither of them ever approved of me coming back here. In their eyes I was losing focus of what was important and letting my fortune fall. The way I see it is completely different, I own my company, have various properties around that keep the bank balance healthy and have a great team around me who I can rely on.

Maybe if my dad got his head out his ass he would see just how far I'd come and the investments I've made. His experience in business over the years has paid off when it comes to my work ethic but that doesn't mean I have to follow suit and be stuck in the office from first light till dark. I'm a people person and like to explore the world around me, see life outside the four walls of a high classed fucking building. I craved clean air and communication and if I can't come here to enjoy my summer it's a bad fucking job.

***

Rubies. The familiar building that provides dance floors, bars and an outside seating area, everyone hits this place after work and at weekends once the doors open. I loved it. The club was a regular stop once I landed in Spring Rose and one I grew up with. In my recent visits so much had changed over the years and the deterioration was noticeable. The spark was lost and its reputation took a nosedive. Once it was on the market I snapped it up and proceeded to bring it back to the life it once had. Ripping out the interior and putting my own stamp on it with the help of the best designers out there.

The buzz of club music and sweat hits me as I head in through the door, adjusting my eyes to the dim-lit lighting I head to the bar. The idea of wanting a quiet drink on the way down here has now shifted to soaking up the atmosphere as numerous party goers gather around me. Women dressed in short skirts that left little to the imagination danced around in spirals, as their partners or local pussy cravers leant against the oak wood bar drinking them in. Sometime ago I would have been one of those men and thought nothing of taking them home, sex was nothing more than a physical act that needed feeding so I went all out and fed the damn thing. Now though, after pulling that rope one to many times it frustrated the shit out of me as each woman is just like the last.

I ordered a beer and sit in a far end booth, taking it all in as I wait for Jack-the manager on duty. The new guy behind the bar caught my attention immediately. I knew from the staff's information sheets who he was but never saw him in action, and if he didn't know who I were then he'd soon find out. He drank more drinks than he served and eye fucked every female in the bar, before diving his tongue into a woman's mouth while his hands disappeared up her skirt as she sat on the bar stool. The group around them cheered and after he released her they both down a shot. This fucker was on my watch, who I pay and he's acting like the local man whore.

"Hey, big boy."

I cursed inwardly at the sight before me, a wannabe model dressed like a hooker sits down at my table and I wondered how she's not been arrested yet through indecent exposure.

"What's your name?" she asks through her cheap red lipstick.

I smile, trying my best to be polite. "Marcus."

"And does Marcus work out? By the size of these biceps I'd say so." She squeezes my muscle and her eyes light up. I wouldn't say I'm a hard ass bodybuilder but I like to keep in shape. There was no better feeling than hitting the gym after a long day in an office.

"I do work out yes."

"Hmm I thought so." Suddenly she went all giggly and immature which only heightened my suspicion, behind all the thick makeup there was a look of youth about her.

"How old are you?" I ask, taking a swig of my beer as frustration lined my veins.

"Seventeen."

What the fuck!

I'm a thirty year old guy sat drinking with a fucking toddler. I'm up and out my seat in a flash.

"Hey, if you're going to the bar, I'll have a double vodka."

I spun round and leant into her so only she could hear me. "I'll buy you a double vodka on your eighteenth birthday. Now get the fuck out my club before I call your parents." I headed out the back to the office in search for Jack, I did not leave this place in the hands of others to encourage teenagers to start underage drinking and take regular trips to the sexual health clinic.

Waiting for Jack I checked over emails from back home and the latest developments of my new projects. Spring Rose bay was my home town and I loved everything about it, when I first returned back after leaving as an early teen it was like I'd never left, everything was untouched and

15

stood tall as I last saw it. The only difference was kids my age had either left for a new life or become untraceable. It took a lot of adjusting to learn that my best friend Victoria Foster was no longer around. The strong minded girl with puppy fat and buck teeth I spent most my childhood with. Her obsession with fashion was crazy and saw herself as a designer for the rich and famous. All contact with Victoria broke a few years after leaving, she'd obviously hit it off in the big wide world as I couldn't track her down for love nor money.

Putting my own stamp on this place now is something I never thought was possible due to disagreements with the local council. Those assholes certainly like to hold a grudge even if you were a mere part of the events that took place. Still set with their heads in the 1950's, the thought of the local rich boy whose father destroyed a good family name-whilst balls deep with a married woman-was a disaster waiting to happen. When I first announced my plans for this coastal town and how I wanted to modernize it with the times it was like saying I was placing them all with a death penalty. Thankfully with the help of my mother, she used her charm and explanations of my reasons. Christ knows what she said but I had them eating out my hands by the end of the meeting. Now I have properties developing right where I want them to and businesses that bloom more each year.

"Marcus, my man. Shit me it's madness out there. Good to see you." Jack said, entering the office with summer heat peppering his brow and his body humming of club nightlife.

"Likewise." I stand for our normal man hug and slap on the shoulder before he sits opposite me on the sofa.

"So how's city life?"

"Busy, dirty and stressful all balled together in a deep pile of pollutant shit. How's the coast?"

"Clean, hot and buzzing with chicks in bikinis," he chuckles. "Bet you're glad to be home huh?"

"Like you wouldn't believe."

Jack and I go back a long way, hitting the town and on the lookout for pussy whilst crawling our way through bars was mostly how we spent our summer. We met one season after his parents embarked on a new life at the coast, packing everything they owned in a camper van and hitting the road to wherever it led to. Working every hour they could wherever they could to stay in a coastal zone that warmed their hearts.

"So tell me more about the fucktart behind the bar that's mouth fucking punters and drinking my booze like his life depends on it?"

He sighs shaking his head. "His name is Nathan, as you know he started just over four months ago. Then suddenly the bar was swamped every night, it'sbeen buzzing for months, so he must be doing something right."

I shot him a look. "Like serving underage girls?"

"What?" The thought of some punked up ass treating my club like the playground grated my nerves and the fact the guy sat across from me didn't realise pissed me even more. "Marcus, everyone is checked on entry."

"Well then clearly the door staff's authorising has slipped. As for Nathan I've been here five minutes and I'm already looking for his replacement."

Jack stands with his hands out as if in surrender. "Look, I get your pissed, but trust me when I say he's good at his job. Let me have a word before you kick his ass."

The noise from the club threads its way through the office door, stating the fact nightlife has picked up and near on ready to peak. I stand, grabbing my jacket to head back out. "Fine, but get it sorted and fast. I do not want my club turned into a fucking crèche of underage drunks."

"I'm on it. You sticking around for a beer?" he asks, following me out.

"Yeah, right after I've made some calls." I head out in need of air and shit me it felt good once it hit my skin. The nightlife of the town oozed electricity and vibe, the sound of laughter, music and high heels hit the streets. And the air that was filled with sea salt and hot doughnuts engulfed me. Instantly draining the frustration from my veins as a smile ticks my lips. I've missed this place and fuck me it feels good to be home.

Chapter Three

Amelia

"You can't wear a Maxi dress to a club; you'll come out looking like you've borrowed Cinderella's rag dress." Megan stated, painting her nails on my bed. I hated getting ready to hit the town and meeting up with others. My mind is a permanent paradox. I like to go out but it's getting out the door that's the problem. The anxieties want to come out to play and won't fuck off till you're half way through a mini bar.

"What about the black dress you bought the other day? That looked gorgeous on you."

"Hmm I'm not sure, it maybe a little to… um-"

"Fuckable?"

"Exactly." I like to feel comfortable in clothes and not look like half my outfit is missing. That causes the wrong kind of eyes to peer your way and get the dick monitor twitching.

Megan rolls her eyes with a huff. "Well while you keep searching for floral skirts and twin sets, I'll get the Tequila."

I go back to the task in hand and dive into the wardrobe only this time searching for a pair of heels to go with an outfit. On her return and looking incredible as ever in her pastel green dress, Megan places two shot glasses on the dresser along with a bottle of Tequila and fills them before handing me one. Throwing it back I let the sharpness burn my throat and chest as I head back to the pile of clothes draping over the chair.

"Maybe I'll go for jea-"

"Maybe you'll go for the black dress," she interjects putting on the stereo. "The black dress and only the black dress. Trust me."

I rolled my eyes and dig it out knowing she won't back down till I'm wearing the goddamn thing. "I'll feel like the local slut if I wear it."

"Ha! Please, a slut that's dried up more like. I really think you should get yourself checked out. It's unnatural to lose your libido this long."

"Fuck you." I giggle as I jump into my dress, getting her to zip me in before she heads back to the stereo. Seconds later Katy Perry's-Last Friday Night pours through the speakers. Megan dedicated this song to us a while ago; she thinks it suit us down to the ground. Although listening to the words, it's more her song than mine. She's the one that post's drunken pictures online and wakes with a stranger in her bed while examining the hickeys on the neck. I'm more the head pounding and black out blur. Either way with the volume up high and singing deep from our lungs it always gets us in the mood and allows my nerves to settle.

The thud of the music hit my chest as we entered Rubies. People consumed in conversations and cocktails took up the large space as the clatter of glasses and beer bottles echoed through your ears.

"Happy Birthday, Felicity." I smile, giving the chocolate haired beauty a hug.

"Thanks babe. Love the dress. Where's Megan?"

"The bar. Wow there's a lot of people here tonight." I scan my eyes around the dim-lit room and the large number of bodies that have took over the dance floor.

Megan heads towards us, a wicked grin on her face as she says, "Holy shit, have you seen how many hotties are here?"

"I know right. And on that note I'll catch you ladies later on the dance floor, I'm off to find my birthday treat in the form of muscle."

Megan hands me two Tequilas before we head towards the back of the club, following her like my second shadow. I'm twenty-six for fuck sake and I feel incredibly anxious without her near until my blood in swimming with alcohol. Self-confidence can be a bitch when you lack it, people don't realise the damage they can cause with their hurtful actions and vile words, and it makes you look at life, human nature and yourself differently. It suppresses you from having normality and brings you down to your knees at the slightest thought. Without her I feel as though the world closes in on me and I'm wide open to every dark and dangerous situation out there while everyone looks on laughing at my stupidity.

Having Megan gives me a cocoon of shelter and eases me back into the flow of society; washing all my fears away and knowing I just have to give her a look and she'll be right there to say fuck them all. However there are times she throws me in deep and I'm thankful for that. By leaving me it makes me do things outside my comfort zones - leaves me if she has to but is always there when I need her, and will drop anything to come to me. She will even sleep in my bed if I ask her to. She truly is my lifeline and the best friend anyone could wish for.

"Hey, Wild Weston," Jack smiles, rounding the bar with empty glasses. "How's it going?"

"Hi, handsome, very well thank you."

"Glad to hear it." He says, with a grin as he prepares a few drinks and places them on the bar. Jack is Manager of Rubies and a fine figure of a man, the tips of his dark slicked back hair finish at the rim of his ears and the muscle he carries on his body was coated in a tribal design that cascaded down his right arm. He is one of the nicest people I've met and always greeted me with my nickname of Wild Weston. It makes a nice change from Ginger Spice that Lucas calls me.

"So where's your sidekick?"

"Right here lover boy and we'll have two margaritas when you're ready."

"And where have you been, Miss Simmons?" I ask Megan as I bite the tip of my straw.

"Babe there's a whole lot of fuckable in here tonight; I just had to weigh up my options on which I'm going home with."

I giggle as Jack shakes his head grinning whilst handing us over our drinks. "Jesus, Megan, you never fail to amaze me with your sexual antics."

Leaning in towards the bar she gains his attention.

"You know, Jack, my door is always open if you want to learn more of my antics. I have great assets too," she winks, taking her drink.

"I'll bare that in mind."

Her pure angel like face and big ice blue eyes was enough to make any man weak at the knees. And I envied her at times. I wished she'd find her dream prince but her wild imagination and love for a good time showed no sign in settling any time soon. Men to Megan were only for the use of sex and lots of it, she showed no desire to have a permanent fixture at her side and with the witnessing of my own history and how life can be destroyed, I think it opened her eyes more to a life that is much better off as uncomplicated sex and parties, rather than a happy-ever-after. Maybe Megan's way of life was in fact the right one, I certainly didn't find my prince when I ran into the arms of a wrong man and from my experiences with him I most definitely didn't have a happy ending. Instead I was just surrounded in a huge pile of bullshit and pain. Maybe Megan's outlook on life was the only true one that existed.

My body was floating with the relaxation as the alcohol had finally taken over my thoughts. The music drums my chest; heat prickles my body as the coloured light dance circles on the walls, bodies twist and twirl along the dance floor as women provide entrainment to onlookers with their seductive moves.

"You want to dance with me?" I ask Megan, brushing my fingers over her shoulder with a wink. "Work our magic together on the floor?"

"Are you going to keep your hands to yourself, or do I have to restrain you from my sexiness?" she questions with a glint of devilment in her eye.

"I can't promise anything. How about a little grinding?"

"Deal," she jumps off her stool and takes my hand. "But I'm not fucking you at the end of the night."

Laughter bounced between us as we worked our bodies to the music. My nervous energy was now replaced with a rush of adrenaline as we twisted and grinded against each other, consuming the watchful eye of onlookers while they encouraged us with cheers as we teased them with our moves. Swaying our hips and running our hands through our hair, interlocking our bodies to the beat that hummed its way inside us. This is what I miss, this is who I use to be and only get it back when I'm with her and my veins running with Tequila. Megan brings out the girl I once was, the girl I yearn for and the girl I once loved.

The dance floor slowly picked up with semi intoxicated bodies thickening with heat. In need of a drink I escape between Felicity and Claudia. "I'm going back to the bar." I shout to Megan just as a guy takes hold of her hand from behind and spins her around to face him. I watch them as I sip my drink. Teasing him with her moves she sweeps her body down his, swirling her ass with bent knees before pushing back up to grind against him. Her arm braces his neck as she rests her back to his front, closing her eyes and loses herself in him. I can't help the chuckle that escapes my throat at her naughty behaviour. As soon as their mouths connect and his fist is in her hair, I knew I'd lost my girl date for the evening.

"That girl's a live wire," Jack chuckles, collecting a glass from the bar.

"Looks like I'm sleeping on my own tonight."

After what felt like an eternity Megan sways over with

her new fuck buddy and says her goodbyes, making sure I was alright getting home. Once I finished my drink I was heading home anyway. All I wanted was my bed and the pleasure of removing my new heels that burned my feet.

"We'll don't you have a sweet ass." I froze as hot breath pounded against my ear and the stale smell of alcohol prickled my sense. Grabbing my arm I'm spun around and faced with a stocky guy towering above me with lingering eyes, grinning like he just won his primed piece.

Fucking great!

"Can I get you a drink?" His eyes were everywhere but my face and his hand still firmly on my ass.

"No, thank you."

"Come on just one drink."

"I said no."

"Why not?" he steps closer. His sex filled eyes have now turned dark and the look on his face suggests he doesn't like the word no as his hand now runs over my body.

Just breath Amelia, stay strong.

"Because I've had enough." I move to pass when his hand grips my arm pulling me back, his heavy body pushing me up against the bar. My chest becomes tight as the panic starts to build. Looking down the bar for Jack to come to my aid.

"Please let me go." I plead, my throat thickens from the proximity as his fingers dig into my skin with his squeeze.

"I. Want. A. Drink." He growls.

"She said no!"

Everything happened so fast, a tall figure swoops in front of me forcing the asshole back. His features are hidden but the structure of his body is double the size of the other, causing his shirt to snug perfectly to the muscle that lies underneath. Conflict from the two men electrifies between them as the heat from the back of the unknown stranger hits me full force. All I can do is peer around the bicep that's barricading me in place and protecting me.

"Who the fuck are you asshole?"

"I'm the asshole that's been watching you harass this woman and through lack of hearing ignored her dismissal of a drink. So unless you want me to rearrange your face then by all means stay here. Otherwise, step the fuck away!" he demanded. Fists clenched, his upper body solid as he spoke through his teeth. My heart was pounding in my chest, only now I couldn't work out which man it was for. With a snide remark thrown my way the drunken asshole backs off, leaving Mr Intimidation in front of me as we watch until he staggers out of site, and then I'm suddenly feeling a new level of anxiety.

"Are you alright?" his voice was deep and husky.

I look up and in a split second all sense of breathing and mobility are shattered as I fall into a tunnel of magnificent attraction.

Holy fuck he's gorgeous!

Chapter Four

Amelia

Everything stilled around me.

It was as if a switch had been flicked and all that's happening is the pounding of my heart and the flutter of his lashes that coat his big brown eyes. His short fair hair threw off a slight soft spike, his unshaven jaw provided him with a look of perfection, and his body was over all stunning. His locked gaze on me is unnerving yet I can't draw my eyes from him. It's foreign to me and as much as it scares me shitless I like it.

Goosebumps pepper my skin when his fingertips brush down my arms, making me snap back to reality as his smile grew wider. "Are you alright?" he asked softly.

"I-I… um… I." Jesus Christ my vocabulary is mush as the nervous energy comes back to hit me. I need a drink!

"You're shaking," he looks around the bar before grabbing my hand. "Come with me."

If I were in *my* frame of mind I shouldn't be agreeing to this, but I'm not thinking clearly. It's mind blowing and frightening in equal measures and if Megan were here she'd be screaming at me to jump on him and enjoy the ride, if she hadn't already done so herself. It's dangerous to be with him but I find myself not wanting to leave as my hand locks with his.

"Stay here, I'll be right back." We're at the other end of the bar and I follow his orders as I watch him manoeuvre around others. His self-assurance is intriguing as he cruises his way through the crowds, providing the odd handshake to on goers and smiles to the ladies that swoon around him. He's clearly a well-known man and my questions are answered when he steps behind the bar and talks to Jack, causing them both to look in my direction. I need to go. I can't be here, I don't even know why I'm following his orders. Mr Sexy-Intimidation grabs what looks like a bottle of whisky and heads back, gracing me with his smile and retaking my hand as he guides us through a side door of the bar. The heavy fire door shuts, making the echo bounce the walls of the abandoned staircase as the music becomes muffled on the other side. I'm halted to the ground as I watch him stride the stairs, wanting to follow when really I should be running.

As if he knew of my hesitation he turns and looks down at me with furrowed eyes. "Everything alright?"

"Um… I'm not sure."

He slowly steps back down with a look on his face that I can't work out. The crispness of his white shirt hugs his firm body while dark washed jeans rest perfectly on his hips. He oozed magnetism, profession and intimidation but as he stepped closer it was his eyes that struck me. In the brighter light the honey hazel colour had flecks of gold. They were warm, inviting. Trusting. Something I've not seen in a man in a long time. A man of his sculpted structure was all the more confusing. His entire body unnerved me but work your way up to his eyes and everything changed. It was as though they didn't belong to the framework they rested in. They sucked me in and captured me, like he saw deep within me. Like he could read my every thought.

"Talk to me," he coos.

"I'm not one for doing things like this." I admit, feeling dazed as to why I feel able to be so open with this stranger. However true it may be.

"Like what, having a drink with a guy?"

"Having a drink with a stranger whose expectations are clearly different to mine." I focus on my black heels, and like the comfort that soothes the anxiety my fingers fumble with my ring as I begin twisting it around my finger. He steps closer, lifting my chin to make me look at him and causing a shiver to cascade down my spine.

"Would it help if I told you my name is Marcus, and I have no expectations other than a few drinks with a beautiful woman so she can calm her nerves?"

Don't run Amelia, just try. You'll be stupid to run. But probably more foolish to stay.

We enter through the glass doors and I'm taken by surprise for two different reasons. The layout is beautiful, but it'sempty-only us swallowed up in the wide open space.

"Where is everyone?" I question as my eyes glide over the exterior. The tanned colour decking is terraced out, full length mirrored panels and plants coat the outside edges as fairy lights lace along the beams above us. Marcus heads towards the seating area placing the glasses and whisky on the table and begins to pour.

"This is only rented out for private functions."

"Sooo why are we here?" The strong scent of whiskey hits my senses as he hands me a glass with a knowing look on his face. My eyes-widen as his words become clear. "Wait a minute. Are you saying you rented this, so we could have a drink, when we could of easily stayed downstairs?" My voice was a little high than intended which induced a chuckle from Marcus.

"If you put it like that, then yeah," casually bringing the glass to his lips as he watches me. I'm speechless at his generosity and at the fact he can just click his fingers and hire a large terrace of a busy building at such short notice, before splashing out on one of the most expensive whiskeys that even my dad can't afford. Then annoyance washed through me at the thought of being at someone's expense, just to calm my fucking nerves that consume me. He doesn't owe me anything and I certainly don't want his charity.

"I need to go." I place my drink on the table and head for the door. My breath caught when his hand made contact with my waist to stop me, providing delicacy and warmth as it rests softly on the thin fabric of my dress.

"Wait, Amelia. Stay please, it'sjust a drink." Confusion and anticipation blind me, my head is saying leave while my gut is screaming at me to not be a fucking idiot and just try. I've not been in situations like this in years, I've not wanted to be, but the longer he has hold of my waist the more I'm enjoying his touch.

"How do you know my name?" I whisper, flicking my eyes back to his.

"Jack told me. Please stay."

Taking my drink I sit down, letting the expensive amber liquid funnel through and soothe my nerves. A short silence falls between us and my body comes alive at the intensity of his gaze. In normal circumstances I would be near on panic with his intense stare, but I find myself comfortable-if not liking his presents on me which is difficult to comprehend.

I wish I wasn't the girl with two personalities. Confident business woman who takes no shit from others and loves her job, then next I'm a messed up anxious fruit loop that's afraid of her own fucking shadow. There'd be a time where I thrived on confidence and attitude. Now I'm just a lonely woman who relies on her younger best friend and therapy sessions to help get her shit together.

"I must say, it's rare to find a woman who enjoys her whisky. You're regular?"

"Only when emotionally off balance, I never use to like it but the older I get the more I've become acquired to the taste. Usually Tequila is my weakness."

He nods and shifts in his seat, turning himself towards me as he rests his arm on the back of the cushion. "So, Amelia, do you work and live in Spring Rose or are you here for the season?"

"I'm a permanent fixture. I'm the Assistant Manager at The Grand Hotel. You know it?"

His hazel eyes throw off a look of surprise as they hold mine before the corners of his mouth curved into yet another heavenly smile. "I'm familiar with it, yes."

"I've only been living here a short time, this will be my second summer here and I love it. It's a beautiful place."

"Seems it has beautiful people too."

I'm unsure whether it's the alcohol that's hit my cheeks or the words he's just spoke as I'm presenting a nice colour of rouge. It's only been a short encounter but he's already having a strange effect on me, my nerves have settled and I'm not having irrational thoughts about what could happen. Right now whatever this is, I'll happily bottle it up and take it.

"So, what brings you to the bay, Marcus, business or pleasure?"

"Both. I've got a few days of business to attend to then go from there I guess."

My eyes roam as he talks. He truly is handsome, through his smart evening wear there's an air of beach life in his appearance, the tanned leather braid band on his wrist shouts surf life, however I can picture him ordering people around as he strides down hallways in tailored suits dripping in confidence.

"What type of businessman are you?"

"Property developer, I'm Director of my own property and development company and currently in the process of new developments here at the coast before heading back to London."

"Oh, so you are an office man. Damn, you've just ruined my image of you in board shorts and a surfboard under your arm." I giggle as a wicked grin plants his face.

"I'm sure it can be arranged."

The waves of the ocean crashed against the cliffs drowning out the nightly noise around us. After four rounds of drinks and comfortable chatting, Marcus kindly walks me home. His company to escort me brought a mixture of feelings. After a battle of telling him I was fine on my own he grabbed my hand and was made to walk with him. The warmth of his hand moulds perfectly to mine which caused butterflies to take flight. He's not let go all the way home and its surreal how at ease I feel around him.

"Well this is me," I gesture, walking through the gate. Anxiety kicks back in, I don't want this to be any more than what it is no matter how he's making me feel. It can't be anymore.

"Amelia, I really enjoyed tonight, can I see you again?"

"Yes, I'd like that." The words were out my mouth before I had chance to realise and I hated myself for letting my guard slip.

"Great, then I'll arrange something for in the week."

"Sounds great. Good night, Marcus, thank you for walking me home." The generosity his provided tonight is alien to me, yet for the first time in so long my demons have been forgotten and pushed aside for a few hours, leaving me completely winded by the unknown feeling that lies within me. He can save me from a drunk any day of the week if it makes me feel like this.

My body loses touch with my mind as I reach and place a soft kiss on his cheek, fingers dust over my hips as we make contact, instantly liking the closeness of our bodies. His light touches become stronger once I go to pull away, leaving me to stop dangerously close to his lips. His musk and cinnamon fragrance engulfs my senses as hazel eyes make me drunk with a need I've not felt in so long. I want him to kiss me. I might even need him to kiss me. Tingles cascade my spine when he tucks my hair behind my ear and cups my jaw.

"Amelia," he whispers. "Can I kiss you?"

"Yes."

I don't even have to think twice. My heart races a mile

a minute and with a quick glance at my lips he's captures them with his. They're like silk. Soft, gentle, and once our tongues made contact a spark shot through my body like I've never experienced. I'm pressed against the door as we entwine, both his hands now cup my neck, brushing the pads of his thumbs lightly over my jaw, like he knew of my reaction if they'd trail any further south. My fingertips trail the covered muscle of his chest as I fall further into his seduction. Good god this man can kiss. The desire in my lower belly is electric, my knees weak. But I'm not this person, I'm not supposed to feel. My mind is a blur; my whole body's woken by his touch, while the world around me seems to spin. I've not felt this good in years. I've not felt anything in years and I don't think I want it to end.

"Fuck, Amelia, I've been wanting to do that all night," he murmurs.

"Thank you for tonight Marcus."

He smiles, running the back of his hand softly over my cheek. "I didn't do anything."

"Believe me, you did more than you realise."

Chapter Five

Marcus

She kisses like a goddess.

The sound of my bedside clock fills the room as I lay stirring into a darkness. All I can see is Amelia. She fills the space around me. Consumes my every thought. Never in my life has a woman stolen my breath like she had. It's scary and electrifying and I'm unsure on which I prefer. I never come here looking but I can't help but think she's going to be hard to shake off.

Upon my return back into the club I grabbed a beer and headed to the far end, letting the atmosphere wash through my veins. Groups gathered for night vibes as others enjoyed the company of beer and laughter. The dance floor was swamped of couples, and women in excessively short clothing swirled around each other. But there was one woman who stood out from any other, and as soon as my eyes fell on her I was captured from that very second.

The way her body moved to the beat was intoxicating, the way her hands laced through her hair was sexual and the more I watched the performance of grinding her body against her friend, the more I craved to be near. Long legs, tight curves and a slim waist, all wrapped up in a black lace dress as her red hair waved off her shoulders in loose curls. She was the sexiest thing I'd seen. The heat and strong scent of vanilla and honeysuckle ricocheted off me as she made her way to the bar, oblivious to the lingering eyes of male sex that caught her attention and followed her every move.

The anger that roared through me as that asshole demanded her attention was something I've never experienced. Her distress was visible-forever looking over her shoulder and like a magnetic force I felt myself moving towards her. I wanted to rip off his fucking head as he grabbed and pinned her to the bar. His greedy hands played her ass, causing me to act like an over possessives boyfriend as I pushed him from her.

Amelia's body trembled but it was her eyes that told a story. Crisp cornflower blues that sucked you in and hypnotise you making it difficult to look away. They hold untold emotions that are screaming to be released. I wanted to wrap my arms around her and secure her to my body to keep her safe. I knew at that point I couldn't let her leave and I took that as an opportunity to hold on. I told Jack I was taking her to the balcony to calm her nerves. According to him when Amelia's upset she likes a whiskey as it settles her. It was only then at the mention of her name and her job roll that all the puzzle pieces connected.

Amelia Weston-Assistant Manager of The Grand

Hotel. My Hotel. And the latest employee I'm waiting to meet.

Andrew mentioned of a fine redhead that's took over the role impeccably and improved the dynamics of the Hotel, I never imagined our first encounter to be storming towards her like some nut fuck and coming to her rescue. I don't know why I didn't tell her who I was, maybe I just wanted to forget about who she was professionally and get to know the person she truly is. And as the drinks flowed, the more her personality began to shine through.

I never planned on kissing her. A few drinks was all it was meant to be. Maybe all it should have been. But those beautiful blues once again locked me in and all means of self-control were lost. I need to feel those lips again. I want to run my hands over her body, along her jaw and kiss the hairline scar that threads her chin.

I can smell her sweet vanilla scent on my clothes, still feel her mouth on mine and I'll give anything to have her in my bed laid next to me right now.

"Fuck me; I'm in so much trouble."

***

"Hey, Mum." I just got back from the gym when my phone flashes at an incoming call. I wondered how long it would be before I heard from her.

"Marcus, darling how are you?" her elegant voice had a smile behind her words. I can picture her now sat behind the large oak desk sipping on her morning coffee while she scrolls the internet news and passes comment on which celebrity had another round of cosmetic surgery.

"I'm good, why the early call, is everything alright?"

"Yes fine, I was just checking the web news and I wanted to hear from my best son and see how life was down under."

"I'm your only son and Spring Rose is hardly down under." I say dryly.

"It is in my world. It feels a million miles away let alone a few hours," she sighs. "So how is the wonderful coast, does it miss me?"

Mum loves this place as must as I do and it crushed us both when we left. Knowing dad was the reason behind it made me even more determined to come back. Never once did he have a good thing to say about the coast and never saw the potential. I thought this was part the reason he often lived in his office working every hour available. At the time I had respect for him providing a good income for his family, little did we know that his late night stays at the office was with a Councillor's wife.

"The coast is missing you dearly. Are you still planning on coming down in a few weeks?"

She gasps with a hint of disgust, "Marcus Matthews, I'm surprised you even asked. I can hear the sand screaming at me to have my toes on it from here."

I chuckle at her frustration. "How's things back there, everything in order?"

"Yes dear. You don't have to worry when your mother is in charge." This is true, Mum runs the business for me back home taking over secretarial roles and ordering people around while I come to the coast. She knows more than anyone the shit I've been through with Sadie and Sean and her words when I left to come here was 'take as long as you need' she's been my rock these last eighteen months and I will be forever thankful for her support.

"How's the weather?"

"Oh what can I say, it's hot, the sand is still beautifully golden, the air is clean and the sunshine makes you want to bask in it all day."

"Stop it. Are you trying to send me into a depression, it's raining here… again!"

I can't help but chuckle. She hates the rain and the cold weather and often talks of taking a six month holiday abroad. That's until I remind her of her fear of flying.

"I will never make you sad mother. I'm your best son." I grinned.

"You're my only son."

I pull up to the latest of my ongoing creations and come head on with construction materials, machinery and men in yellow hard hats-all striding around a formation of rich red bricks and unfilled windows. When I saw that the area up on Fitzford Hill was up for grabs, I knew it would be the perfect location to build luxury apartments. High ceilings, large bay windows and balconies overlooking the clear blue ocean and golden sands. It was an opportunity not to be missed and one I knew would work well.

Taking a safety hat from one of the guys I head into the mass of ongoing workers as they continued the work while wires and cables hang unattended in rolls.

"Mr. Matthews, always a pleasure." Derek said, heading towards me and providing a firm handshake. He's in charge of the construction work.

"Derek, how are you?"

"Good man." We walk back out into the sunlight, taking in the wooden beams that support the ceilings and floors above me as it's prepared for the next level of work.

"So, what have we got?"

Derek rolls out the building plans placing the paper across his car bonnet, giving me the low down of the latest development and further plans to go ahead. His company is one of the best around; his highly experienced team develops properties of luxurious standards that bring skill and quality to their work. Over the years his team have provided award winning styles that result in excellent customer satisfaction and this is why I always hire him, where ever the grounds may be.

"The inner structure is looking great and to the requirements that you asked. Ventilation and air con are being put in place as we speak so the electrical side are soon good to go for the next stage."

"Fantastic, so the designers will soon be able to get in and work their magic?"

"All being well yes, I'd give it a few more days but as you can see we are way ahead of the schedule."

As well as Derek's manual workers his company also provides a team of highly qualified interior designers that has an eye for clean crisp décor that screams modern and class as soon as the plans are laid out. I've used them numerous times over the years for new builds and refurbishments and have no doubt that the plans for this latest project will look just as spectacular as any other.

The need for coffee was calling and Rock Waves Diner was the only place I knew would provide a decent mug. The coastal style décor was white washed walls and pale blue booths all thrown together with canvases of the ocean. On my way back to my car I catch a glimpse of rich red down on the shore line, kicking the water with her feet as she strolls along, standing out from the noise of the crowd that gather on the beach.

Today was the first time in over a year my feet touched the hot sand, the glare of the sun on my bare legs and arms radiating its warmth through me and finalizing the arrival of being home as my feet sunk into the golden treasure beneath me.

Lost in her own thoughts I place my hand on the small of Amelia's back causing her to jump feet and shoot round to face me. "Marcus!" she gasps, holding her hand to her chest with flushed cheeks. Her hair is wrapped up in a high messy bun as light wispy bits sway with the breeze, while her strapless sundress shows off a graceful guardian angel tattooed on her left shoulder.

"Sorry, didn't mean to make you jump. How are you?"

"I'm good, thanks," she says softly. Her eyes are covered with her shades and I'm desperate to see them.

"So this is how you spend your days when you're not at work, walking the length of the beach?"

"I come here when I need to think."

"Can I walk with you?"

We continue to walk along the shore line in a silence that's killing me. For the first time in my entire encounter with women I find myself at a loss of what to say. And I have no doubt Amelia is finding it difficult as her fingers twist her silver ring, a sign I'm beginning to recognise she does when nervous.

I cut in front of her, noticing her stiffen slightly. "Take off your glasses, I need to see your eyes." She rewards me with the bright blues that take my breath away. Jesus how did I find this woman? Looking over the water she breaks the connection that I instantly want back. Lifting her chin I make her look at me. "Amelia, I meant what I said the other night, I really would like to take you out."

Her cheeks and neck once again coat with pink but she doesn't look away this time. "But why? Why not any other woman?" she murmurs.

"Because they're not you. You're beautiful and I like being around you. And if I'm honest, I can't stop thinking about you." I tuck the wispy strands of hair behind her ear, not missing her sharp inhale of breath. "Please say you will?"

"Ok," she whispers on a shaky breath.

I place a kiss on the corner on her mouth. I can't seem to control myself when I'm around her. I want to touch her in every way possible but I don't think it's going to be that easy, her guards are up and don't appear to be shifting anytime soon. "Did you like the flowers?" I had a large bunch of wild flowers delivered to Amelia's door first thing this morning.

"Yes, thank you, though you shouldn't have done that?"

"I wanted to. A beautiful lady deserves to be treated well." Her smile vanished and her eyes become unreadable as she looks away; again lifting her chin they flick back to me. As much as I want to stay I'm getting the feeling she needs space. "I'll see you soon."

I'm heading back up the beach when I turn on the sound of her sweet voice. "Marcus, you don't have my number."

"Already got it." I grin as her brows narrow, and the fact I know where she works is another matter altogether.

Chapter Six

Amelia

Ok just Breath.

Apprehension flows through me like a swollen river. My mind is a mixture of excitement and bewilderment as I think back to the times I saw Marcus. Ever since, my nights have been restless, my days wasted as I think of him-those eyes, his charm. From his kiss that still tingles and his tender touches that gave me goosebumps. In the few hours with him he reminded me of how caring a man could be and how even in my anxious state he made me feel safe and completely at ease. Which clouds my judgment in a way I cannot even begin to comprehend.

I've tried to push those thoughts of him into the memory box of my mind but it's not been easy. No man has ever bought me flowers. My ex Daniel thought it was a waste of time so I never received any nor was I allowed to buy them. Flowers were my life line that still connected me with my mother, they brought fond memories of her and seeing the newly fresh flowers filling my room in blossom brings comfort inside of me.

The sound of porcelain clatter's from behind the counter as the scorching of the espresso machine fills the air, leaving the heavy scent of coffee. I beam as I see Megan striding through Rock Waves door, looking professionally hot in her black pencil skirt, white blouse and red heels. That girl could make wearing a paper bag look sexy. Underneath her 'I am fabulous' act she plays daily, she really didn't have any idea just how flawlessly sexy and incredible she really was. That's what was so innocent about her and one fragment of her personality I adored deeply.

"Hey there sexy lady, how are you?" her arms stretch out to hug me. Ever after all these years, the closeness that I have with her never ceases to amaze me, just one hug can relax my overactive mind.

"Good. I've missed you."

"You too, have you ordered?" She throws her bag on the seat next to her and bounces her ass down.

"I wasn't sure what time you'd be here, so I waited."

Her ice blue eyes study me as she searches my face. Her brother Lucas always referred to us as his blue eyed girls, as we each provided two different shades of colour.

"What's wrong? And don't give me everything is fine shit." She's like my mother-sister-agony aunt and best friend all rolled into one and knows with just a look if there's something wrong. "And quit bouncing your fucking leg, I can feel the vibration from here."

I can't help but chuckle. Megan gets easily irritated by

my quirky ways of how I control my nerves. "Ok, right. When you left Rubies the other night, I never went home like I said I was going to."

"Rrrright," she says inquisitively with a little squint of the eyes.

"I was about to leave when some guy made a move and I freaked out a little. Then like lightning this other guy springs from nowhere and steps in to help me, and holy fuck he is gorgeous, like heavenly. Everything happened so fast and the next thing I knew we were sat on the terrace of Rubies drinking whiskey and talked for ages before he walked me home and-"

Her hand come up stopping me. "Wait a minute back the fuck up. You let all that happen?"

I nod, knowing as well as she does that that's not happened in a long while. After one failed relationship I refused to enter into another, I don't chase guys I run from them. "Wow. What have you done with my friend? You know the one that stays in after eight with coffee and cookies."

I threw her a look. "There's more."

"Oh my god, you fucked him!" she shrieks. I literally could have died as my cheeks shot red and Megan holds her hand to her mouth with a giggle as heads turn towards us.

"Shout a bit louder I don't think they heard you down the back! No, I didn't." I lowered my voice. "But I kissed him, like *really* kissed him…and loved it." Her mouth drops open and she leans forward, slapping her hand on my forehead. "Megan, what are you doing?"

"Checking for a fever."

Batting her hand away I roll my eyes. "Be serious." Her face is like a kid that's just been given a bag of Bon

Bons, all excited and high on sugar, while I'm still trying to focus on the seriousness of this and work out what the fuck to do, as that all too familiar feeling for apprehension creeps in. "He wants to see me again."

"And your face looks like someone's died because?"

"This is me remember, I don't do relationships, I don't do dating and as much as I'm dreading the whole thing, a part of me can't help but want it. And that scares the fuck out of me, Megan." I sigh, leaning my head back against the cushioned seat of the booth. I've had the same mixed feeling since that night, even more so since earlier on the beach.

She reaches over taking my hands in hers, planting that 'here it comes' smile on her pure baby skinned face. "You want me to tell you what I really think or some bullshit we both know is a lie."

"The truth please, and be harsh." I knew she would, Megan tells it straight no matter who's in front of her.

"It's understandable that you're scared. This is a massive step and I get that. But wherever this leads, maybe you just need to bite the bullet and go for it. It's been a long time since London and you have come so far in your recovery. They aren't all like that fucking piece of shit and you can't continue on letting him ruin what you do in the further, you just have to try babe."

I swallow looking at the same words on the menu that I've been looking at for the last five minutes, knowing in my heart that she is right. Megan and Lucas are forever saying those two words to me, 'Just try' and I do. But for a long time I've fought hard to keep my shit together and by doing it on my own was the best way possible. However the thought of getting 'back out there' causes my stomach to churn. A lonely life isn't looking at all pleasant and in all honesty isn't what I wish for. But if it means protecting myself, state of mind and heart then I'll do anything within my power to make sure I'm not broken again.

"He sent me flowers this morning."

"Uh, shit me he's a keeper!"

***

Shit!

I dart out of bed and rush around my house like a mad woman, frantically trying to get my things together and my eyes out of sleep mode, but failing miserably as another night of restless sleep and nightmares takes its toll. Today was a massive day for me as the owner of The Grand was arriving to spend his summer at the coast. Jumping out of the shower to do my hair and make-up, I dive into the wardrobe and pull out my grey fitting dress and finish it off with my high black heels. Grabbing my bag and keys I hit the road in record timing.

"Miss Weston, the meeting in the conference room started fifteen minutes ago." Felicity states, peering her head over the computer in reception.

"I'm aware of that thank you. Is Mr Matthews here yet?" I asked in a hurry, grabbing my office keys from the cabinet.

"Yes, he's been here since seven this morning and Andrew's tried calling you."

"My phones dead!" I shout, heading down the hall.

I peer my head through the door causing everyone to turn as Andrew stops talking. Embarrassment flushed my face with everyone's focus on me, instantly wanting to stick my head in the sand and disappear. Once a month,

Management and supervisors of different roles of the Hotel get together for a general meeting and heads up on the latest information and upcoming events. Today was no different.

"Nice of you to finally join us Miss Weston, can I ask where you've been?" Andrew asks in his deep voice and a cocked brow.

"Sorry, I had a phone call from Nadia Lenton, you know how it is when she's on the phone."

He nods with an 'I know you're lying' look in his eyes. I sit next to Megan at the back, oblivious of the others in the room as my head needed a reprieve from the morning hustle and bustle to get here.

"So what did the celebrity bitch want this time?" Megan whisper's as Andrew continued his speech.

"Nothing I just said that to stop his third degree."

She grins. "So why are you late?"

"I had a nightmare and overslept." Megan gives me a pitied smile and a look of concern, knowing my suffering of nightmares and the ones her and Lucas have often witnessed. "So what have I missed?"

"Not much, staff rotas. Oh and the meet and greet of Mr-Sexy-CEO-Matthews, who noticed of your absence by the way."

"Damn it! He's going to hate me already. Is he still here?"

"Indeed I am." I swirl my head around to the deep voice coming behind me and freeze. Leaning against the desk, dressed in a charcoal tailored suit is the piece of perfection that's brainwashed my mind since that very night. The colour drains my face as I wide eyed him.

"Marcus," I whisper barely moving my lips.

His smile beams as he pushes off the desk and leans in

over my shoulder. His musky fragrance and body wash hit my scenes like a freight train as he whispers, "Good morning Amelia, pleasure to finally meet the other person who helps keeps this place running in my absence. And no, I don't hate you. Even if you had overslept and told your co-worker different."

Great so not only have I made a complete ass of myself in front of him, he also knows I've lied. "You're him." I whisper again, swallowing hard and looking directly over his shoulder avoiding his eyes. "You're Mr Matthews."

"Surprise!" he whispered. He makes his way to the front, smiling at the staff as he turns to face us all. My head spins with questions and answers, heat sours my body and I'm unsure if it'sthough panic or pleasure. He really was an incredibly sexy man but at the same time fury started to creep through me that he's lied about who he was, given the fact he's had plenty of opportunities to tell me. I sink down in my chair, wanting to escape his gaze and lose myself from others.

"I can't believe this, this can't be happening." I says quietly to myself but Megan picking up every word.

"Can't believe what?"

"It's him."

"Who's him?" she whispers back with a tilt of her head, her eyes solely locked up front.

"Marcus, he's the guy."

"What guy?"

"Jesus Christ, Megan keep up," I sigh. "Mr Matthews is the guy. The guy I kissed, the one who brought me flowers. He's. The. Guy!"

Her eyes spring wide and her mouth drops open, it's not often Megan is speechless, I feel exactly the same on the inside right now. "Whoa really? Check you out hitting it off with the local rich boy." She grins nudging my shoulder. My chest starts to tighten and palms sweat as panic sets in. Megan like always clocks it straight off and grabs my arm. "Babe, you really need to stop freaking out. Everything will be fine."

To make me even more on edge, Marcus sits directly opposite me for the rest of the meeting, never taking his gaze away which only heightens my nervous and frustration to point of overload. As soon as the meeting was over, I was out the door in a flash. The more he stared the more I did, and the more I did the more irritated I become with the fact he's taken a hold on me that I never wanted him to grasp onto.

Chapter Seven

Amelia

I pace my office floor like a crazy airhead thinking about Marcus and that I'm likely to now see him every-fucking-day. Now what? Which is likely to encourage him to be around me more. Then what? If only I had just stayed in. Curled up on the sofa and watch shit TV whilst munching on a family size bag of pretzels, none of this would have happened. I wouldn't have encountered his sexy charm and I certainly wouldn't have the mixed feelings like I have right now. Angry, hurt, confused. It's all going on. Most women would have just thought 'fuck it' and moved on, not let it bother them. Probably even got off on the thrill of kissing the shit out their panty-melting boss. But I'm not like most women. Trust is like glass-easy to break, impossible to put back together. I've learned the hard way and even the slightest thing of not telling me who he truly was, hurts. I was still striding out my frustration when the office door opened and Marcus casually strolls in like he owns the place. Oh wait, I forgot-He does!

"Afternoon, beautiful."

"You lied!" I shot at him.

The corners of his mouth tick in amusement as he stands with his hands in his pockets.

"Nooo, I just didn't tell you who I actually was." His cockiness only infuriates me more as he stands there with his care free fucking attitude.

"How the hell is that any different? I told you who I was, where I worked. I asked you what form of business you were in. You said you dealt with properties, Marcus. You. Lied."

He straightens, taking his hands out his pockets to tap them as he spoke. "I said my name was Marcus-fact. I also said I was here on business-fact. I own properties, Amelia-fact, this Hotel and Rubies being two of them. You never asked and I never told. Where's the lie?"

My jaw hit the floor with his statement. "Rubies? You also own Rubies? Oh my god now it all makes sense. Anything else on your list you failed to tell me?"

"Believe it or not I own a house too." He smirks. His cockiness of trying to win me over is doing nothing for me.

I can't think straight. I turn from him, overlooking the shore from my window and rest my hands on the desk. I feel his eyes burn into me from the other side of the room before he's up behind me; I straighten folding my arms as he steps close trapping me against the oak desk. My heart races with his proximity, butterflies take flight in my belly as his hot breath brushed over my neck, lowering his voice and dancing his fingertips over my hips. "Have dinner with me, we can talk."

My head falls into my hand as the sarcastic laugh leaves my throat. Is he for real? "No."

"Why not? You said you would before you kissed me."

I turn quickly, causing him to step back. My confidence climbing like I've never known it before as I stood in front of this beautiful beast of a man. "That was then and I was drunk. I may have seemed like a desperate woman to you then, Marcus, but believe me I'm anything but."

"You often kiss the shit out of men when drunk?"

If looks could kill he'd be on the floor right now. As much as it was slipping away from me and his presents were causing my body to react in the way I didn't want, I couldn't let my guard down. I had to fight, if I've learnt anything from my history with men it's not to let them walk all over you. Lifting my head and look directly into his hazel eyes. "My first rule of business, never get involved with employees."

"I don't work here, Amelia, I just own the bui-"

"You have an office with your name on the door, you work here." His powerful eyes suddenly begin to make me uncomfortable, I slide passed him needing space. "My second rule. Never lie, to which you've failed already. You could have prevented that by telling me straight."

He sighs and cocks a brow, clearly enjoying every second of my flustered state. "And is there a third in this rule game of yours?"

"Yeah-" I stride over and open the door, raising arm length to hold it while my other hand places my hip "-with all due respect Mr Matthews, this maybe your building but this is still my office. Close the door on your way out."

Ok so that's technically not a rule.

He takes two strides towards the door and I'm feeling a little triumphant that I've won this battle, only it's short lived when he slams it shut and thrusts me against it, our lips a breath apart as he locks his eyes on mine, placing his arms either side of my head to cage me in. My body stiffens instantly. His voice low, "Do you have any idea how sexy you are when flustered? The way your neck turns every shade of pink and your eyes dart everywhere."

"It's people like you that make me flustered."

His brows furrow as his eyes search over my face. "Do I intimidate you, Amelia?"

"What do you want from me?" I whisper in a rush.

He studies me for a few seconds before he speaks. "I have rules too. First I never lie. Giving you wrong information about me and not telling you the whole truth is two completely different things altogether. And second, I go out with who I want regardless of who they are or where they work. You intrigue me Amelia, there's something about you I want."

"You're a man. All you want is a free pass to a woman's panties." I hiss. My mind is in spirals from his words and the proximity is too much. My own panties are most likely ruined as my body fails me from loving every goddamn part of this. I'm craving his lips to touch mine. To whisk me away from normality just like they did the first time.

"If a free pass was on offer right now, I'd rather have it to get to know you. I think you'd want that too. To be freed from whatever lies behind those eyes."

"You don't know anything about me!" I snap. My legs

now quivered as my body fought hard against my emotions. I'm clearly easier to read than I thought and if he knows of my want for freedom what less does my body language tell him.

"I know enough. I want to know the real Amelia Weston," he murmurs as I swallow down the ball of tears that's on the verge of spilling.

"Well you're out of luck. She fucked off a long time ago."

"Then I'll do whatever it takes to find her." My guard finally falls the moment his lips touched mine, and just like before that unexpected shock shot through my body as the gentle whispers of his finger caress my neck, making the hairs stand tall. His velvet tongue playing with mine caused my insides to melt and butterflies to soar. Every fragment of dread vanished in an instant just like it did the very first time I laid eyes on him at Rubies. Consuming my every thought with a feeling I don't recognise. A feeling I don't understand.

"You really need to go." I whisper.

He runs his thumb along my bottom lip, sweeping it over the scar on my chin and studying it before flicking his eyes back to mine that are now glassed over with unshed tears. "I'm not giving up on you that easily, Amelia. I want and will get to know you, however long it takes." With that he's gone leaving me a hot mess and wondering how the hell I'm going to get out of this stupid situation I've got myself into.

***

"I kissed him again." I announced, bursting through

Megan's door.

All I get is a huge grin before she removes her outstretched body from the sofa and comes to place a kiss on my cheek. "I'll get the Tequila," she whispers, leaving me standing in the oversized room.

I plonk myself down on the sofa as she hands me a drink. Looking up at the ceiling like I always did when my head needed to focus. Megan's house is amazing, all open planned and stylish; originally belonging to her uncle before he moved abroad. It was rented out as her parents aren't beach lovers and her brother Lucas worked away. Her neighbours were thrilled when she moved in as the previous tenants were a bit of a rowdy bunch, so having a young respectable member of the Simmons family take on the premises they welcomed her in with open arms. I'd love to know their opinion now as she's one for causing her own rowdiness.

"So, what are you going to do about Marcus?" she questions, joining me and curling her legs behind her.

"Nothing." I lean into the armrest all the while she gazes right at me with raised brows. "Why are you looking at me like I'm insane?"

"Probably because you are," she places her glass on the coffee table, "Look, you've been out with him already and by all account enjoyed it. Clearly he made you feel at ease within yourself so I don't see the problem. He obviously doesn't think there is one so why not go for it. He's is a good guy."

I shoot her a look. "Your point being?"

"There not all like Daniel babe. Marcus sent you flowers for Christ sake that in itself says a lot. Forget about who he is and think about how he made you feel when out with him. What have you got to lose?"

"Everything I've rebuilt over the last few years." I let out a deep exhale and close my eyes. "But what if he wants more, Megan? I mean are his dates the same as my kind of dates? Not that I go on them but still. He will see me, all of me and I don't know how I feel about that. I can't let that happen." My eyes and chest become heavy with emotion at the thought of what could be. I never wanted to be found by another because I knew what the possibility of that meant for the future. I've never exposed myself since Daniel and it scares the shit out of me.

"Babe, you're freaking out again, stop it. Marcus is one of the nicest guys I know. He won't push you into anything you're not comfortable with. Just have faith and promise me you'll try. You know you need to do this and in your heart, we both know that you *can* do this. By not doing it, you're still letting that fucker win." She's right I can't let an asshole from the past ruin and run my future. Yet the thought of letting someone in is a whole new level of fucking scary.

"Huh, who needs a therapist, when I have you and self-help remedies in the form of Tequila." I smile.

"Well as your home help therapist, I'd like to end this session with one last question, if I may?" she gets up heading toward the kitchen and grabbing the Tequila to refill our glasses.

"Ask away,"

"Is he good with his tongue?"

"Fuck yeah. I dread to think what else he can do with it." I chuckle.

"Well if he's that good let me know, I'll be happy to help him out with his requirements." I choke on my drink as our giggles filled the room, falling into our world of our own giddiness. I blast out Katy Perry while Megan loads up the internet for our nightly searches of hot guys and celebrity gossip. Its times like these that are precious to me, having someone close that's there to talk my problems through. To know that no matter what they always had my back. Times like that were when I wished my dad was here to hug me and my mum was still here to guide me in the right direction.

My only direction now was with a sassy blond who loves Tequila and when on holiday her older incredibly hot brother, Lucas who I now looked up to as my own. I didn't want anyone to spoil what we had, because they were all I ever needed. But somewhere in this crazy subconscious of mine there's a little voice of my guardian angel that's saying that same thing as Megan.

Just try.

Chapter Eight

Marcus

"Are you listening to anything I've said?" Andrew asks, with an irritated look across his face. I scroll over the web page of the latest news not paying one bit of attention to the headlines in front of me as my mind plays over the information I read earlier.

"Sorry, I was just…why is Lenton's Daughter wanting her wedding here?"

Henry Lenton is a very powerful man, his Theatre Company is one of the largest organisations which travel worldwide, he's a hard and ruthless man who worked his backside off to be where he is today and I give him credit for that. The fact he's a complete asshole is another matter. That said he's also the former husband of Sylvia-the woman my father was fucking in his office when they decided to destroy two families.

"This is a seven star hotel on a glorious coastal resort. She's a celebrity with money. Do the math."

"I know that dickwad, but why here?" His brows narrow in confusion and I can't be fucked to go into detail. "And why is Amelia practically organising the damn thing when her job role doesn't involve wedding planning?"

Andrew chuckles, rubbing his hand over the dark scruff on his jaw, "Yeah, she's been trying to get out of that one since the entire thing started. But she seems to be the only one Nadia listens to. She has this calming effect on people which is a surprise considering she lives on her nerves."

My eyes dart up from the computer screen. So it's not just me that makes her anxious, I thought to myself. "And she manages to work here…with you? Jesus that takes some doing." I chuckled.

"Watch it asshole."

"Can you tell her I want to discuss this with her when she has a minute?"

"No problem." Andrew stands, stretching his tall thick body and heading for the door. "By the way, it's good to have your grumpy ass back around the place."

"Who the fuck you calling grumpy, you're the one that walks around looking like Scrooge's brother most days." His deep laughs fills the space as he leaves. I've missed this guy and it's good to hear him laugh again, he's had it tough.

A soft tap hits my office door and it slowly opens to Amelia peering her head around before coming in. "Hi," she whispers. Her fingers twisting around her ring as I take the opportunity to run my eyes over her body.

"Amelia, please sit." Nadia Lenton was a strong

powerful woman who has ways of bringing people down regardless of her actions, and I didn't want Amelia to be a victim of that. Or anyone. "Tell me about the Lenton wedding."

"Would you like me to be professional or personal?"

"Let's stick with professional."

"Well, she wants full access of the hotel regardless of what she's actually paying for. No change in staff members during her time here but has asked to for us to re-interview them before the day, which I'm not prepared to do. The function room out of bounds two days prior to the wedding. Red carpet on entry and my head on a stack if nothing goes her way."

I nod once she'd finished. This sounded like Nadia perfectly, she demands full attention at all times and thinks she's fucking god. "And your thoughts personally, don't be afraid to hold back."

"She's the biggest bitch I've worked with, that's got a stick so far up her ass it's dislodged her brain from thinking clearly and processes shit to fall from her mouth."

My laugh roared through the office which encouraged Amelia to join in. There she was, the women I was with that night at Rubies and one I was so desperate to know. "Couldn't of put it better myself." I rounded the desk and leant against it in front of her. Her body language changed instantly and reverted back to the anxious girl with worried eyes. "While we're still on personal mode, please let me take you out. And don't give the 'But you're my boss' crap because that shit never bothers me. It's just a drink."

"Our one drink led to one bottle last time," she coos as her cheeks pinked.

"Then this time I'll bring two." I grinned. Even with

her wall of defence yesterday, I knew it wouldn't last long, she tries hard to fight but whenever I touch her or get close I feel her melting under me like warm butter.

"Pick me up at seven." She says just above a whisper, collecting her notes and diary and heading to the door. My eyes focus on her ass as she strides across the floor, all snug and perfectly curved in her tight black skirt as her hair of fire cascades down her back. *Fuck me*.

"Amelia, wear something comfortable. I'll be taking you to the beach."

A few hours later I left my office and the buzz of the hotel to hit the gym when I received a text from Megan.

Megan: I believe you're taking my girl out tonight. Look after her, don't fuck with her head.

What the hell? I'm a man but I'm not an asshole, I have no intention of playing her.

Me: I don't intend to.

Megan: She's special, Marcus. You hurt her I'll feed your cock to the gulls.

Within days of being here I've done a complete turn around to what I said I would do and found the most beautiful woman to which I can't get out of my head. I want her for reasons beyond my control. Her body yes, but more importantly the more I'm around her and witness the way she closes herself off, hides herself from the world the more I have this powerful need to save her, and that is something I'm determined to fix.

***

"So why the beach when there's all the other places?" Amelia questions as our feet sink into the sand. "Not that I'm ungrateful, just curious."

"You wanted to see me in shorts and with a board right? I thought we'd strip and go for a swim." I clock the flash of fear on her face as she looks over my shoulder to the water. "Relax, Amelia, I'm just kidding. We won't do anything you don't want. However, I do want you to sit over there and try to enjoy yourself." I point to the red blanket that's laid out between the sand dunes surrounded by lanterns and chilled wine.

"Wow, Marcus, that's beautiful. Nobody has ever done anything like this for me before." Her expression is priceless. It's just a blanket with wine and nightlights yet she's acting like I've giving her the world.

The sun is downing to set and the sky becomes illuminated in vibrant oranges and reds as we sit against the dunes drinking wine and talking about our childhood memories. Even though there's still an air of hesitation, Amelia's more relaxed to when I first picked her up earlier, and moulds perfectly beside me. "Tell me something true," she murmurs, twirling the stem of the glass between her fingers.

"What?"

"It's a game me and mum played when I was a kid. It can be anything. Big, small or completely ridiculous as long as it'strue."

I take a sip of my wine and try to think of what truth I could possibly say, there were so many things that ran through my head when it came to this woman. "You're beautiful."

"Ugh, I'm serious."

"As am I. Your turn."

She thinks for a little before a cheeky grin forms her face. "I had a slight crush on Andrew when I first moved here. Everyone think he's an ass but he's just a pussy cat behind a mysterious mask."

"My favourite colour is blue."

"I hate my laugh, it sounds weird."

"It's sexy," I replied, finishing my drink. "When was the last time you slept with a guy?" *What the fuck did I say that for?*

Her head snaps up to look at me, a flicker of anger and pain in her eyes. "There aren't questions in this game, Marcus, just truth."

"Exactly. So tell me." I request softly, unsure if this was right of me to even ask. She's already closed off; the last thing I want her to do is freak out and run, yet as she searches my face I see her anger subside. Exhaling an unsteady breath and closing her eyes for a moment before her line of sight is fixed solely on the ocean.

"I don't know," she murmurs. "The last time I recall being with a man and feeling anything was around seven years ago. The last time I had sex with him was a little over five, and by then all feelings had died."

"You stopped loving him?" The silence was icy as her eyes glassed with unwanted memories and sorrow.

"I stopped loving him long before that. By then I'd stopped living."

Lifting her chin I cup her cheek, smoothing my thumb over her soft skin. How can anyone as beautiful as her feel so low they needed to stop being who they were. More to the point how can anyone make her feel that way to begin with.

"Then we need to make you feel alive again." I could tell by the pleading look in her eyes she didn't want this conversation to continue, so I diverted back to the original topic and went for the something ridiculous.

"Seagulls scare me shitless."

Her laughter was like music to my ears, making me join her with my preposterous but true confession. "You're so weird."

"Am not. Have you seen their eyes?"

"It's just a bird," she says through the breaks of her giggles. Clearly finding my phobia amusing I jab her in the waist to stop the teasing, making her jump with a squeal.

"Oh, I've found a ticklish spot it seems." My grin was a mile wide as I raise my brows in devilment.

Her eyes-widen as she chokes out her words. "Don't even think about it." She retreats and was up on her feet in a flash, backing down towards the beach as the grin still plastered my face. "Marcus...you wouldn't dare!"

"Oh I totally would." I'm up and charging towards her as she sprints the sand in high pitched squeals and laughter. Turning her head to catch my approach as her red hair flies high in the wind as she heads across the beach. "You can't run from me that easily." I'm behind her in seconds, grabbing her hips and pulling her to the sand as she shrieks. Straddling her she twists her body begging me to stop with uncontrolled breathing and laughter as I tickle her ribs.

"Stop! Marcus...I can't breathe!" she pants as the air leaves her lungs.

"You want me to stop? But you love it." I chuckle.

"Stop...*Please!*"

Taking her hands in mine I pin them above her head, both breathing heavy from our hysteria, our eyes hold each other's heated gaze yet hers show a trace of apprehension. She's so fucking sexy. "I have a powerful urge to kiss you right now, Miss Weston."

"I don't think that's a good idea," she exhales.

"Why not? You might enjoy it."

"That's exactly why it's not a good idea."

My lips curve with her honesty as I place them on hers, coaxing them open to slip in my tongue. The taste of cherry wine and her sweet scent of honeysuckle and vanilla is intoxicating, making my stomach tighten with our connection. Her hands twist under my hold and when released they fly to my jaw and hair letting me know she wants this.

"Christ your mouth is amazing, I could kiss you all day." I pull her bottom lip between my teeth.

"Then don't stop," she gasps, bringing us back together as I deepen the kiss. Her soft moans are enough my tip me over the edge as I press my arousal against her, making her feel exactly what she's doing to me. The need to touch her is torturous but my head is screaming it's too soon.

"Shit, Amelia, I think I'm in trouble."

"Told you it was a bad idea," she giggles.

Even in the low lit sky her brightness radiates. Every man and woman on earth could be stood on this beach right now but all I see is her. "You really are beautiful."

"And you really need to stop saying that," tapping me on the shoulder.

"Hmm nope, sorry. I'm going to tell you every chance I get. Starting with breakfast when I come to yours with bagels and coffee in the morning."

"Oh really? And what if I'm not there?"

I peck soft kisses over her skin trailing across her jaw and neck, "I know where you live. I know where you work and I also have your number." I finish with a soft kiss on the silver scar on her chin. "Failing that, I'll hunt you down via Megan."

"Oh god, I really do have a stalker don't I?" she chuckles.

"Absolutely, and one that plans to spend as much time with you as possible." I help her to her feet before scooping my arm under her legs to carry her across the beach. "Now *beautiful* let's get you home, a *beautiful* lady needs to sleep before her big breakfast."

"Ugh, enough with the beautiful already," she chuckled as I head back to the dunes.

Chapter Nine

Marcus

"Oh my god, I've always wanted to come here." Amelia squeals with excitement as the car enters Primrose Lodge. The large country grounds set twenty miles in from the coast, acres of land filled with every flower you can imagine and a maze that goes on for hours.

The past two weeks I've pushed further into Amelia's world and brought breakfast of bagels, croissants or savoury cupcakes to her door followed by sweet kisses and wrapping her in his arms, consuming her thoughts and house space in every way possible. She is still yet to open up fully but I know trust is what is needed when it comes to her and even though it's killing me wanting to touch her and be balls deep, I needed to show her that she could have faith in me. Today was a new challenge for her, taking her out of her comfort zone of the coast and away from the watchful eye of others-Megan.

"You love flowers and you've never been to Primrose Lodge?"

"Never," she smiles as her eyes scan the surrounds.

"Well you'll be in for a treat...let's go and explore."

Primrose Lodge was a stately home owned by the Dartman family who ran the estate for over a hundred years. Creating a fairy tale secret garden that shouted both mysterious and romance. Endless hideouts and trails, water features and wildlife filled the yards around us as the grand house stood centre stage amongst the veritable forest of colour.

Amelia's eyes are everywhere as she darts around in excitement, taking in the vast grounds and historic building as we head up the granite central stairs.

The house inside was a magnet of attraction, open fireplaces, wood flooring and large windows with thick heavy curtains, all under the high ceilings and golden chandleries as brass ornaments consumed the living space. It oozed history and adventure and left a lingering smell of hard graft and polish as you entered each room.

"This place is breathtaking," Amelia gasps, taking in the rustic décor. "Mum would have loved to have seen this."

"She liked her history?"

"She was a history teacher and of course loved anything medieval or historic. When I were a little girl as well as exploring the beaches we'd hunt down the castles and stately homes in and around our area and spend hours soaking it all in. Dad hated it; he was more of a sportsperson and liked his race horses. Mum was the one that got me onto obsessing over flowers, and if the gardens where as good as the homes we were both in our element." She smiles, digging out her camera from her bag and snapping away at objects around her, secretly taking a shot of her myself with my camera phone. Amelia was like a kid at Christmas all wide-eyed and speechless with a big ass grin on her face. I can't help but chuckle as I watch the breath of fresh air in front of me sink into the environment.

"Oh, Marcus, look! We need this for The Grand."

I follow her direction of sight and drew my brows. "We already have golden chandeliers."

"I know but we don't have those ones and they look so pretty and sparkly."

I chuckle taking her hand and pulling her away as she looks over her shoulder one last time. "Come on, there's more to see. This is just one of many rooms."

"How many are there?"

"Another thirty."

After spending the morning exploring the house in great detail we head out into the summer sun to experience the wildlife and gardens. Lengths of flowers beds and features displayed the grounds with elegance and chic as tourists gather in groups to share their experiences. "How did you know I'd like it here?" Amelia asks as we lay facing each other amongst the flowers in the garden, the sun illuminating the vibrant colours that sways with the gentle breeze.

"Because you always have some sort of flower in your house and I saw the photo of you sat amongst the tulip field. I thought this place was perfect."

"Very observant, Mr Matthews," she grins. "It was a family holiday in Holland. Three hours I spent amongst the tulips field. Just laid there absorbing the sweet fragrances as

I got lost in my dreams while the world carried on around me. Dad was about to send out a search party and went all over protective on me when I walked through the door, while mum just laughed it off with a wink as she knew where I'd been hiding. That was our last holiday as a family...everything changed after that." Her eyes were focused on the grass and the sparkle that was there a few seconds ago had vanished along with her enthusiasm. After spending time with her at every opportunity I got, I've become to read Amelia through her eyes. She doesn't have to say anything for me to know what she's feeling, and right now like many a time her eyes were telling me she was hurting. I just wish she'd open up and fucking give me something that enabled me to comfort her in the way I wanted. But like a closed book, she never did.

"Come on, let's go get lost in the maze." I smile, pulling her up and stretching.

Primrose Lodge maze was enormous. High hedges of pure green twisted and turned every corner creating its own lost world, while the footsteps of shoes on gravel was all you heard as people tried to find their way out. On collecting our tickets at the entrance we were given a map of directions to the exit, but after a few wrong turns and Amelia realising I had the map upside down we were a little lost. Only now it seems I've lost Amelia, clearly taking a wrong turn when she was checking her phone for a way out.

"Marcus, where are you?"

"Come find me." Although I couldn't see her, her voice was telling me she was close. "Whoever finds the other one first has to kiss the shit out of them." I shout into the air so she's hear me.

"Yeah, because the other person's not going to shit out

on that one are they?" she giggled. This was true. I couldn't get enough of kissing Amelia and I know she felt the same regardless whether she said or not. "What if I don't want to kiss you?" she shouts across the gardens.

"Then I will make you pay. There are plenty of options for punishment." Like tickling. I like how she has no control over her laughter when I get my hands on her. It's pure, sexy and I'll never tire of hearing it, each time she laughs her face and eyes come alive. I rounded the corner following her voice but find a dead end. "Amelia, are you close?" Nothing. "Is this where you jump up on me and give me a coronary?" Another dead end and still no answer.

She's playing me. I chuckled softly to myself, liking the mischievous side of her coming out. A few more turns around the hedgerows and shit loads of dead ends, I caught sight of her and froze. Up ahead she's sat on the bench staring into space, frantically twisting her ring around her finger as her leg bobs. "Amelia?" she flinched when I touched her. Her pale skin is ghostly, eyes for the first time unreadable and she was clearly lost in another world, the world I didn't like her in.

"Are you going to punish me?" she whispers.

"What? No I…wh-why would you think that?" I kneel down in front; shocked the thought has even crossed her mind. Her eyes dart all over my face but I still can't read them.

"You said you'll make me pay."

I felt like the world's biggest asshole. If I'd of known my words would have put fear in her like they have, I'd never of said them. "I meant like throwing you over my shoulder. I'd never hurt you, Amelia." Pulling her up I wrap my arms tight around her and rest my chin on her head.

Minutes pass in silence and the relief that funnelled through my body was welcoming once I slowly felt her relax against me. "Do you want to go home?"

She shakes her head, her eyes now full of a silent apology. "No, I'm sorry. I want…I want you to kiss the shit out of me like you said you would if you found me first." She smiles.

Who am I to argue? I kissed her senseless, running my hands down her back to playing with the rim of her top. As my fingers begin to trail under she stops me, grabbing my wrist in force. This isn't the first time and I want to groan in frustration with the need to feel her body in my hands. Flashing her lashes at me she grins, her lips red and swollen. "Come on. I want chips and a train ride."

***

"Have you seen the size of this thing?" I chuckle as I stand looking at the train Amelia insisted we go on. When I become aware of one that took us around the gardens I expected it to a least be adult size. Not some ridiculous small contraption that you knew full well wouldn't be a pleasant ride.

"Shit my ass is too big for the seat. You'll have to sit behind me." Amelia giggles, getting on the train that's clearly meant for children. "The last time I was on one of these was with my dad and I was sick from too much candy floss and doughnuts."

"I've not been on a train like this since I was a seven year old boy. The leg room has certainly altered."

Amelia turns round and burst into a fit of giggles at the state of my lack of room. "Oh my god you're practically eating your knees." The eight short carriage train that travels around the outskirts of the gardens to view the wildlife is occupied by hyperactive children and two adults-the adults being us. As the conductor in a brown waistcoat makes his way along the carriages for tickets, he stops and cocks a brow clearing his throat.

"Excuse me sir, there is a train to the west of the gardens for adults if you're wanting more uh…room."

I look at Amelia who's trying her hardest not to laugh and look back to the man stood in front of me handing him our tickets. "We're good thanks, we're reliving our youth."

"Ok, well enjoy the ride kids."

The journey through the gardens was pleasant, capturing the scenery with the naked eye while Amelia captured it through the camera lens. I can't keep my eyes of this woman, her creamy skin, big blue eyes and long red hair of fire, she's addictive. Working my way down her body I become locked on the small area of skin that's exposed between her vest top and shorts. My breath halts as an unknown feeling rushed through me, leaving my skin with a cold sweat. A glimpse of deep red sprung out between the separate pieces of fabric that covered her body, heightening against her pale skin with a silver shimmer. I wanted to rip her clothes off right then to discover what lie underneath. Have her blank canvas in front of me so I could paint my own marks on her body and not ones that no doubt created pain or haunts.

"Marcus." A nudge of Amelia's hand presses against my arm, snapping me out of my thoughts. Her blues eyes crinkle at the corners as she looks with a wide smile. "Enjoyed the ride that much you don't want to get off?"

"Huh?"

"The train has stopped. Are you ok?"

"Yeah." With a duck of my head I step out from under the train roof, stretching my stiff body from the cramped journey and confusion running through me.

"Thank you for today," she smiles, leaning into my chest for an unexpected hug. It'snot often Amelia makes the first move in the connection between us and each time she does I can't help but notice the hesitation.

I kiss the top of her hair. "Will you stop thanking me every time I do something for you. I do it because I want to. I do it because you deserve it." I'd hand her the world on a platter if I could. This woman is doing things to me and making me react in ways I never knew existed. I wanted to protect her from the good the bad and the ugly and I'd be damned if anyone stood in my way.

Chapter Ten

Amelia

A suited muscular man always pushed the right buttons for me and the one currently ogling me over his coffee cup in Rock Waves was no different. He's making my libido rocket, his hazel eyes complete with sexy grin and day old stubble is too much and I couldn't take my eyes away. Not once has he made meanings to take whatever this is between us further and as much as it's killing me, unbeknown to him I find it one of the greatest gifts he'll ever realise.

Men were off the radar. They were nothing more than heartless vultures and never cared of the hurt they cause in the process. Megan disagrees and will think nothing of a quick hook up to satisfy her needs. There are no such stories of happy endings when it comes to men, not for me. No white knights or heroes, just hurtful monsters waiting in the wings of a dark world to inflict pain. However the man sat before me like a lightning bolt came from nowhere and captured my mind and is slowly making me realise that maybe all is not what it seems when it comes to men. He's winning me over with his charm and possessiveness, forever bringing me flowers, skipping work hours for day trips and treats me with care whenever we're together.

I'm brought out of my thoughts when Marcus waves his hand in front of me. "Where did you go just then, want to talk about it?"

"No, I'm fine." I brush him off stirring my Latté. If I've learnt anything these last couple of weeks it's that Marcus is becoming incredibly good at reading me, watching me closely and his eyes never far from me. "So what are your plans today?" I ask, trying to divert onto something new. His brows rose as he sat forward clearing his throat.

"I go to work, boss people around. Then later I have a date with a beautiful red head."

Ugh there he goes with the beautiful. "Is that right?"

"Yep, and she's coming round to mine as well so I can show off my hugely expensive mansion and all the properties I own." He beams as I roll my eyes, reminding me of the fact he has properties all over and is incredibly wealthy yet he looks so…ordinary. Surely a man with his work ethic should be in skyscraper buildings with letters after his name, not sat in some beach diner drinking coffee with a woman constantly living on the edge.

"Hey, my little sex kittens," Megan calls, planting kisses on both our cheeks while her body is clearly screaming for sleep. "Marcus tell me. Is it in my contract to work nights when I'm a Front of house?"

I chuckle answering for him, "Afraid so babe, you do

have Night Auditor on your CV."

She huffs, "Ugh well it sucks. You know, Andrew is an asshole; I swear he has some kind of device up his ass that programmes his moods. I spoke to him this morning and shit me if looks could kill, I'd be the walking dead right now. I mean have you ever seen smile? The man's a beast."

A deep laugh rumbles from Marcus as he stands. "He only smiles when no one's looking. I'll get you a coffee." He heads towards the counter as my eyes follow him.

"Sooo, how are things?" Megan questions, darting her eyes between me and Marcus.

"Good. Great."

"Christ you're really convincing me with your forthcoming information here."

I sighed and sit forward so only she could here. "I'm freaking out about what happens next. There's only so much kissing you can do before things get frustrating and before you say it I know I just need to try."

"You'll be fine, trust me. Don't hide yourself from him babe." She squeezes my arm and kisses me on the head before heading over to Marcus, who's just called her. I watch the pair of them deep in conversation waiting for their orders, I can tell by the look in Megan's eyes she's doing her 'don't mess with her talk', it's only confirmed when Marcus glances at me, running his eyes over my body causing goosebumps as he stands with such efficiency and poise. How in the world have I got into this situation, a stunner like him not hiding his desire for my body, while I'm doing everything within my power to hide it from him. My only concern is how he will actually feel once my clothes are off, because in my eyes I'm anything but beautiful.

***

"My god this place is huge." My eyes scan the interior of Marcus's house. The spacious kitchen/dining area, is light and airy with a fridge big enough to throw a party in. Floor to ceiling windows that overlook the ocean were the main feature in the dining room while the oak table filled the space around me.

"Come, I'll show you the rest," he chuckles, handing me a glass of wine.

Beach wood furniture, cream sofas and vaulted beams that run across the high ceiling were the features of the living room. One width of the outside wall had more floor to ceiling windows letting in the perfect amount of light as two wide doors opened onto a large balcony surrounded by rattan seats and mid-height glass panels that ran along the outside edge of the balcony wall. It was simply breathtaking.

Marcus stands behind me wrapping an arm around my waist and resting his chin on my shoulder as we overlooked the sands below. "There's a place to the right of those rocks called Marbles Cove, it's the most stunning beach, and not many people know it's there."

"I've never heard of it. I often go to Preston Bay." My place of peace, where I go to collect my thoughts. Golden sand and a deep pool of blue water that lay untouched.

"Marbles Cove is spectacular. Glittering sands and shells in every colour you can imagine. I'll take you there one day."

"I'd like that, thank you. Your house is beautiful, Marcus."

Dinner was a delicious meal of some fancy style chicken with fresh vegetables, washed down with a bottle of white wine. I had no involvement in the kitchen, I was forbidden and had strict instructions to relax and make myself at home. So I took the opportunity to scoot into the world of Mr Matthews. It seems he's very successful with properties and developments. Several gold-plated and glass awards lined the high shelves of his library whilst plans and sketches coated the large mahogany desk. Heavy photo frames capture his beamed smile along with a beautiful elegant woman who I can only assume is his mother. The love that radiates around them brought a smile to heart along with a sting of hurt from my own memories of my family I no longer have.

The soft glow of the balcony lights fill the space around us with a yellow-orange hue as the rumble of the ocean plays its music in the distance. My legs curl behind me as we sit out in the night air; Marcus trails his fingers over my knee whilst he checks his phone as I study him, no matter what he's doing I always have his attention somehow, the little signs of wanting me in his presence rather than making me feel like an outcast. I don't understand what he's doing to me, it'sconfusing. I've never felt this way before. I should be afraid of him but I find myself breathtakingly fearless and wanting more. And that scares me.

"I believe you're staring, Miss Weston?" Placing his phone aside he takes my arms swiftly moving me to straddle him. "What are you thinking about?"

"That you should've let me help with dinner."

A slight curve forms his lips. "Well I didn't want you too. Now tell me what you're really thinking."

Exhaling I take my eyes from his, focusing on my fingers that fidget with his shirt and give him my admission. "You confuse me, Marcus," I murmur. "I should be running from you to protect myself yet I find myself not wanting to. I'm not use to that. And I'm certainly not use to being treated with such kindness."

He straightens so our bodies are pressed against each other, raising my chest into him as he cups my neck and smoothed his thumbs over my jaw. "You deserve all the kindness anyone can give, Amelia. I don't want you to run from me either, but if you do I'll be right behind you bringing you back."

"I've never been treated this way before, Marcus; I don't know what to do."

"Just do what you feel is right."

He kiss was silky. Relaxing my body like he always had a way of doing. Falling into him like a feather floating to the ground and freeing me from worries with each stroke of his tongue. His fingers are laced in my hair and I tip my head aside so his lips pepper over my neck, nipping tiny bits of my skin and causing me to whimper. My body's on fire, the flesh between my thighs aches for him as his own arousal pressed against his jeans. I need to go. I shouldn't be here, it's not fair that I'm putting us both through the same undeniable torture, knowing it can't be any more than what it is because of what I am.

His hand slips under the front of my dress as panic runs my body. "Marcus, I ca-" I begin to push back but he grips my hips firmly, my eyes-widen with the intensity to keep me in place.

He loosens his hold but his hands never leave my hips when his voice was just above a whisper, "I'm not going to hurt you, Amelia. But I really need to touch you." Lust coated his eyes as I stare back at him, trying to connect my mind with normality. "I want to show you I'm not like the others. That I'm not like your last. You don't have to be afraid."

"I'm not afraid." I breathe out in a whisper.

He pulls me close to his face, his breath brushing against my lips. "Your eyes tell me different baby. Let me make you feel good, Amelia. Let me touch you." His words were filled with empathy and yearning and I couldn't deny my need for him even if I tried.

I nod as all sense of reason banish.

My pulse quickens when his fingertips run along my lace panties to shift them aside, I ache for his touch yet my body it thick with trepidation. A low moan escapes me, and my eyes slam shut with the welcome invasion of his fingers in my slickness. I drop my head to his, holding the firmness of his shoulders once he pushes a finger inside, then another, awakening and relaxing my body. "Oh god, don't stop!" His thumb circles my swollen bud, electricity shooting through me in pleasurable waves. It's been so long since I've been touched by another; I feel I could explode any minute.

"I want to be the one that makes you feel alive, Amelia," he murmurs. "I need to be that person."

I feel intoxicated, paralysed by his touch, while my mind becomes a cloud of emotions as tingles increase in my lower belly. Never in my life have I felt anything like this, it opens up a complete new world to the one I've lived in, and to the one I knew. No man has ever made me feel this good. With or without intimacy. Even in the time of working me with his fingers Marcus makes me feel safe, cared for. Wanted. Sparks soar up my thighs, tantalizing me with its intensity as I begin to tighten around him. "Marcus," I whimper.

"Don't be afraid baby, just let go. I've got you."

I came hard, shattering around him with an orgasm that took my breath and ripped through me, muffling out my cries with his deep kiss and wrapping his arm around my back. Unwanted emotions try to fight to the surface of my mind but I push them aside and enjoy the closeness of our bodies as mine hummed in satisfaction. "Thank you." I whispered, burying my head into the crook of his neck and wanting to stay there forever.

"Stay with me tonight."

I froze at the four words I didn't want him to say. The four words that in one way meant much more to what just happened. My instant pleasure was suddenly crushed as my head shakes in response still buried in his neck. "I can't. It's too soon."

He pushes me up to meet his gaze, his eyes showing both disappointment and plead. "We don't have to do anything. I'll sleep on top of the covers if you need me to?"

"You'll do that?" my brows narrow. "Why would you do that?"

"I'll do whatever it takes to make you stay. I want to wake up beside you. You need to trust me." For the first time in so long I pushed away everything that was screaming at me and decided to go with my gut. And even though there was apprehension there was also that big ball of 'just fucking try' bouncing around inside me. "Amelia, do you trust me?"

"Yes. Yes I trust you."

"Then stay with me."

If I want the second chance I've longed for then maybe

this is it, maybe it's looking right at me. I have to move forward, I have to try and let people in. To let Marcus in and in all honesty I don't want to be on my own tonight, because like every other year that passes tomorrow marks the day I face unwanted reminders and melancholy, and for the first time in years waking up alone was something I didn't want.

"I'll stay."

Chapter Eleven

Amelia

My lips curved as a soft kiss dusts my nose and awakens my body from its slumber. A pleasant mixture of strong coffee and body wash hits my senses and even with eyes closed I can feel Marcus's gaze on me. Last night for the first time in so long I let somebody get close and sleep beside me. He made his promise and started out on top of the covers until I invited him in. A strange feeling of being more vulnerable with him on the outside come over me. He could of easily bind my body and trap me if he were to of straddle me. I needed to know of his movements and by inviting him into his own bed was the only way.

"You need to wake up beautiful,"

"And as before you need to stop saying that." I groaned, burying my head into the pillow. Once I peel open my eyes I'm smacked in the face with a half-naked man in work trousers topped with sculpted curves and hard lines that I want to run my nails along. "Oh wow, good morning!" I grin, causing him to chuckle.

"We need to get going or we'll be late."

"Why didn't you wake me?"

"You looked so peaceful. Oh and that's been buzzing for the last half hour." Pointing to my phone that was flashing up a reminder of a message. Scooping myself to sit up I grab my phone, sliding my finger across the screen. I suck in a breath as I'm hit with the date I wish to forget, June 2nd.

Lucas: I am thinking of my beautiful blue eyed girl today and wish I were there to hold you. Stay strong. Someone needs to keep an eye on that crazy ass sister of mine. Love you Ginger Spice and no matter what each day brings, just try. Forever proud of you. xx

Melancholy washes over my happy state. Today is one of the hardest days I face, a reminder of what I have and haven't got in my life.

"What's wrong?" Marcus asks, coming to sit on the bed and brushing the back of his hand over my cheek.

"Nothing, I'm fine," providing a fake smile. His gaze searches my face for answers I'm not willing to give before a look of disappointment comes followed with a sigh.

"Get dressed, we'll be late."

I grab my clothes and head to the bathroom, making sure the shirt that Marcus leant me covers my body from him. Last night I slipped into bed and made sure the shirt was twisted tight against my body so no desire fuelled hands could make their way underneath. Exposing myself was a whole new level of unwanted territory I didn't want to go down just yet.

"Amelia, I'll give you privacy if you want it, but don't lock the door like you did last night. You need to know that you're safe around me."

I'm yet to tell Marcus any part of my past. The extreme cold love from my ex, and the fact my dad now hates me because my mum died. It's not every day you ask your Daddy to step in and help you break from a volatile relationship you saw no way out of. I thought he'd save me but it turned out to be Megan and Lucas. I can only imagine the reaction Marcus will give once I tell him I'm dependent on therapy sessions. And once he finds out, it won't be me running-it will be him.

***

The heavenly vision of a naked chest from this morning has now become a distant memory along with a crap filled day turning sour by the second. Everywhere I looked June 2nd slapped me in the face on every turn. Megan spotted my depressed mood as soon as I walk through the Hotel doors and enveloped her arms around me, she's put up with a lot of shit I've thrown her way over the years- we've talked, cried and screamed at each other as I become a bitter broken mess, it's unthinkable to imagine what hell I put her through. She didn't have to stay-no one else did but she has and I will be forever thankful for that.

"How you doing?" she asks softly as we hid ourselves in the restroom.

"I stayed at Marcus's last night and before you ask we

never had sex."

"We'll it's a big step and a great one, but that's not what I meant. How are you really doing?" she bats her sympathetic lashes.

I sighed, resting my head on the wall and briefly closing my eyes. "Ok, I can't wait to get home and shut the world out. I had a text from Lucas this morning."

"Yeah I spoke to him last night. Are you seeing Marcus later?"

"No, I cancelled our plans earlier. I'm not great company right now."

She wraps her arms tight around me as we hold each other. "I love you, you know that right? If I didn't have to work I'd be right with you."

The ball of emotion thickens in my throat with her words, knowing she's hating the fact she can't be with me on a day that brings a truck load of haunted memories and emotions. "I know. Come on let's go, I've still got room attendants to yell at before I leave."

***

The tears that I've fought all day roll down my cheeks as my finger glides over the glass frame that holds the photo of my mother, her sharp blue eyes and rich red hair that cascaded down her shoulders cocooned her pale complexion as thin pink lips show off her remarkable smile.

Today would have been her birthday and eight years since her death. This day alone brought emotions for so many reasons and no matter the years that past, it never got easier to bare. I felt the need to celebrate for her, yet I mourned for her dearly. Whatever I felt on this day was never the right feeling to have and that alone was a massive head fuck.

The morning of her birthday was filled with flowers, gifts and classical music. The all-female musical ensemble was mum's favourite girl crush and dads annoying ear piece that he pretended to enjoy. Whenever they were on T.V endless conversations were held as we talked about their stunning prom dresses that dazzled in beads and lace.

We were so alike it was uncanny. Yes there would of course be a resemblance, she was my mother, but to those who didn't know us they'd think we were twins as our similarities and mannerisms were off the chart. She was my best friend, my world and some drunken fucker that thought it was safe to get in his car took her from me. She never made it home for her birthday dinner.

Like every year her memory box comes out and invades my mind as I scan over the endless photos of a strong family unit that's now turned to shit. Piles of glossy cards and photos that show the celebrations we shared together laid out on the carpet as bright smiles and her laughter come alive in my mind.

In the bottom of the box was the CD I kept of all her favourite songs. Placing it into the stereo I drink in the words that play out from the speakers, closing my eyes as I drowned in the music with a tearful smile. Picturing her twirl around the living room with Dad to the melodies as her skirt fanned out around them. Amazing Grace was our favourite and over time the words meant more to me than they did the very first time I heard them. Grace was my mother's name and I believe through all the shit that's been thrown at me, her spirit and the words to this song saved me from a lost world I was once blind in. She became my angel of hope. My angel of guidance.

Throughout all the photos and memories my mind betrays me from thinking of her and begins to focus on the other person I lost since that very day.

My father.

Our relationship was strained after mum died and that was like swallowing a bitter pill. Each day he laid eyes on me he was reminded of her. The relationship and home environment that a father/daughter once shared had soon become hostile and unbearable to be a part of.

Despite everything we have both been through and him betraying me in a brutal way I still loved him, why would I not, for many years he was my hero, the man I ran to when he arrived home from work. The man that picked me up when I fell off my bike and the man that secretly held back my hair when I first rolled home drunk and told me not to tell my mother. I still hope that one day he would wake up and realise I'm still here and that I need him more than anything. I needed him than, I needed him after and I need him now.

After three rounds of whiskey, throwing caution to the wind I pick up the phone and dialled the number to my childhood home. Uncertain as to whether he still lived there. Anxiety churned my belly but I know I needed to be heard, enough time had been wasted between us and I wanted to make him realise I'm suffering just as much as him.

"Hello." His deep voice froze my thoughts as I stared at a picture of him and mum in my hand. His voice made a million thoughts and feelings ricochet within me as the life I once had now stole my breath.

"Hello. Who's there?"

"Daddy?" I whispered as the tears fell. The silence that

ran through the receiver was chilling, sending a shiver down my spine as I crawled my knee up to my chest.

"D-Daddy it's me, Amelia-" I was hit with the dull tone of begin hung up on.

He cut the call. The bastard cut the call. Frustration hit me and I slammed the phone down beside me, as I continued to drink. If mum knew what he was doing she'd not be proud.

With a deep breath I rang him back, this time it went to the machine. If he didn't want to talk, he could at least fucking listen and I had to get out what was lying heavy on my chest.

"Dad, I knew you don't want to talk to me and as much as it hurts I understand. I just wanted to hear your voice. I'm not in London anymore, I'm on my own now. Please don't shut me out anymore, I need you. I miss her too dad, more than you will ever know. Even though it's difficult for me to understand I don't blame you for hating me and I'm sorry if I've hurt you in any way. I love you daddy. I lost you both that day and I don't think for one minute that mum would be-"

He picked up and growled through the receiver. "Don't you dare speak of you mother, Amelia-Gra…" *Grace*, he couldn't even say my fucking name as it reminded him of her. "You shouldn't have called."

"Please, dad can't we move on from this. I need you." I choke, my tears become uncontrollable through his cruelty.

"It's too late, we're different people now. *Don't* call me again, Amelia."

His voice moved me in a way I never experienced before, behind his stubbornness there was no emotion behind it. But that only ignited my fury more. "No, dad I…I'm your daughter for Christ sake!"

He'd gone.

Pain, loss and rejection roared through me, gripping my gut with a twist while my heart ached in agony. I knew it would happen and I don't even know why I put myself through such torture by phoning him. Maybe after all this time I hoped things had changed. It only caused my broken soul to be shattered a little more.

In the depths of my deepest melancholy I reached for the one form of comfort that would numb my soul and wash all memories.

The whiskey bottle.

I want her here with me. To tell me it's alright and that I'm loved no matter what has happened over time. That I'm not alone. But she's gone and all I have of her is a small box of photos and a fucking CD.

I pressed auto-repeat on the stereo, turned the volume up full to drown out the agony of my despair and throw the remote across the room. Drinking straight from the bottle like some trashy hobo I hugged my knees as I cried myself into the world oblivion.

Abandonment was now a new form of torture.

Chapter Twelve

Marcus

My head hurt, my shoulders ached and a large whiskey was calling.

Today was a bedlam of paperwork, emails, calls and site viewings. It was almost as if everyone got word I was finally back and wanted to have me at their beck and call as soon as their eyes opened. I hadn't even had chance to see Amelia since we left my place this morning and the need to have her near was driving me crazy. I don't know what it is about this woman but I need her close to me every chance I get.

I've notice a change in her over the last couple of weeks, her anxious state has become less apparent and she beams every time I see her, radiating the room with her big eyes and smile and making me want her more each and every time. I'm not going to lie, the crave to have her fully and make her mine is becoming unbearable. My balls have never felt so tight. I want to feel and kiss every inch of her pure white skin as she lies under me. To feel her lips pressed against my neck and have her calling my name as she comes undone around me, reignite the spark in her that died all those years ago.

Yet I know in my heart what she needs more then everything from me is trust and time, all the signs are there and I'll do whatever it takes to give it. I knew from our time on the beach that there are demons in her past, her eyes are a story of a thousand words she never needed to say. Fear runs through her gorgeous blues often, suffocating in her own thoughts as her face drops with sorrow from wherever her mind may have taken her.

I was just about to leave for lunch earlier to find her when I got a text which had me stopping in my tracks and confusion flooding my brain.

Amelia: I need to cancel our plans for today. I'll call you.

Me: Everything ok?

I had no response. Even when I rang I got nothing. She's so closed off it frustrates me, she needs to know I'm here for her, that she can trust me, that I'm willing to take the pain away if she'd just let me.

Last night was a breakthrough letting me touch her and how her body quivered around me as she came, agreeing to stay and waking up beside each other like I've longed to do for weeks. Then that all went to shit when she locked herself in the bathroom for half an hour before climbing into bed with my shirt wrapped so tight round her it was as if it were her second skin. Hiding herself from me and laying tense so far away from me, I even felt uncomfortable.

Scrubbing my face in my hand I head to her office for answers only to find it's locked so I head for the next one. "Where's Amelia?"

Andrew looks up from his desk, brows knitting together in confusion. "I sent her home."

"Why?"

"Because she's all over the place today. Didn't she tell you she was leaving?"

"No."

Calling it a day at the Hotel I pick up a takeout and find myself sat outside Amelia's house, debating whether to get out. She's running from me and I wanted to know what the fuck was going on. Everything seemed perfect this morning until she checked her phone, then within a split second I lost her.

Women are so fucking confusing at times.

I'm out of the car heading up her drive when I'm hit with classical music. I instantly recognised the strings and vocals to 'Amazing Grace'. It struck me odd that she liked this kind of music giving the fact her and Megan were suckers for partying hard and grinding against each other. Knocking was ridiculous as there was no way in hell she'd hear me through the racket so I went in anyway "Amelia?"

There was no sign of her in the kitchen as I place the takeout and keys on the counter, and I could hardly hear my own voice as I called. I found the remote to the stereo and hit mute as I made my way further into the living room. The silence was deafening but was immediately hit by harsh sobs coming from the floor in front of the sofa. Rounding it quickly I find a mass of photos, a half empty whiskey bottle and a desperately fragile woman curled in the fetal position hiding her face with her hands. My chest tightened as concern filled me. Kneeling, I brush away the hair from her tear stained face. "Amelia, baby?"

"He hates me, Marcus," she cries. "I can't do this on my own."

Scooping her in my arms I hold her tight to my chest and walked us to her bedroom, wanting to take her away from whatever reason for her distress. I hated to see her this way and knowing she turned to the whiskey and not me irritated me a little.

"He can't even say my fucking name without hating me. I'm so alone."

"Ssh, I'm here now." Placing her on the bed I lay down beside her, pulling her close as she cries against my chest. I feel helpless and at a loss of how to console her. She seems so broken.

"Talk to me, Amelia."

"I'm so lost. Damaged. A fucking screw up and I hate what they've done to me. What *he's* done." She gets up off the bed, stumbling around the room crying and ranting through her drunken sobs that I try hard to understand.

"It was never meant to be like this. It should never have been this way. It was perfect, then everything changed." She catches herself in the reflection of the mirror, gritting her teeth in anger as she spoke. All I could do was watch as she let her pain roll off her tongue. "*He's* made me this way! Megan got me out, my best friend found me and the others left me to rot by myself. Just try they all say and I do, every fucking day but it's not easy. It never happened to them.

They weren't there when he done those things. He never loved me! None of this would have happened if she hadn't left me!" She turns now and looks at me, pain drowning her beautiful face as she sniffed back the tears. "What did I do to deserve this, Marcus? What did I do to end up this way?"

Her body shredded with grief and fear as she stood before me like a lost soul. I'm by her side in seconds, providing the comfort and protection she so desperately needs as she grasps the muscle of my back as those she would slip away if she faltered.

"Please don't hurt me like the others, Marcus," she choked. "I don't want to hurt anymore. I don't want to be this person anymore."

"Ssh, I'm not going to hurt you, Amelia," I sooth her hair, placing a kiss on her head and hold her tight as her clung to me. "I promise, I'll never hurt you."

A few hours ticked by as we lay on the bed, reassuring her she wasn't alone. Amelia's tears had now subsided, leaving her breathing pattern to dart out a silent hiccup that shook through her ever so often. We laid in the twilight filled room tight in each other's embrace as my mind snowballed with every scenario possible. "Is this why you cancelled on me today?" I murmured.

"Yes. I didn't want you to witness the ugly side of me." I didn't want to press her but at the same time I wanted to know what was going on in her head, what hurt laid behind her eyes and what fears made her tremble so badly.

Lifting her chin I make her look at me. Unshed tears pooled in the corners of her puffy red eyes, the lightly dusted freckles across her nose had an undercoat of pink that matched the colour of her neck. Even emotionally exhausted she was sexy. "You are anything but ugly. Don't ever say that, you hear me."

"I can't take this anymore, Marcus," she whispers as her voice cracks. "I feel like I'm suffocating."

"Then let me in. Let me help you."

She nods, sniffing back her tears and playing with the button on my shirt. "Today is my mum's birthday, as well as the anniversary of her death. I've not spoken to my dad in years and for some stupid reason I decided to call him. I just wanted to hear his voice as I miss him so much. I thought this time would be different, maybe after the years of not speaking he'd be pleased to hear from me. But I got what I'd expected. Hurtfulness and hatred when I mentioned her name."

"What happened to her?"

"She was driving to work when the car forced her off the road. A drunk driver heading home from an all-night party, she died at the scene. My life changed that day and I slowly lost everyone around me. Dad found the grief too much to handle and with me being the spitting image of my mother and a constant reminder of what he'd lost, his love for me slowly died. Even though I needed him, I gave him space. I thought he just needed time to come to terms that she had gone and eventually he'd come back to me. But that never happened. I was eighteen and I felt so alone. So when I saw the open arms of another man I ran into them without hesitation. Then one day I needed my dad more than ever as I was going through new nightmares as well as losing mum and he slammed the door in my face. Megan and Lucas are the only family I have now, without them I'd have nothing."

It angered me that she had been going through this grief alone, abandoned and lost. My relationship with my mother is strong, close and loving. Amelia's lost all of that and the thought of losing that myself with my own mother is unthinkable. I can't even begin to comprehend what she must be going though. But there was one thing that still played my mind from her saddened admission. '*I was going through my own nightmare.*'

I couldn't help but think there was a bigger painful picture to this story and I had no doubt that it involved the guy she ran to. She opened up and told me so much already I didn't want to push her further, I knew I had to be patient.

Tucking the hair behind her ear I stroke my knuckles across her cheek. "I can't even begin to imagine what you're feeling right now and I don't think any words I say will change the hurt inside. But no matter how lost you may feel in this world you're not alone, Amelia. Don't ever think that. You are an amazing woman and what's so remarkable is that you don't even realise how incredible you actually are. There are people who love you, need you and care for you, and that's something you need to hold on to. You may feel damaged and broken but that's easily fixed."

"You can't fix what's already broken, Marcus," she sniffs.

"Maybe, but I'll work damn fucking hard in piecing you back together."

Her lips curl briefly before sadness falls again. "My life is ruled by anxieties and therapy, Marcus."

"I know."

She lifts her chin up to meet my eyes as a single tear falls over her nose. Confusion and hope flashed her sorrowful blues as long wet lashes fluttered against her tear stricken cheeks. She truly was the most beautiful broken creature I'd seen.

"And that doesn't bother you?"

"I'm still here aren't I? And when you're ready, you can trust me in telling me everything." I place my lips on hers, showing her the truth behind my words.

"Thank you," she whispered.

"For what?"

"Being here and holding me. It means so much."

"I'm not going anywhere. Apart from the kitchen to grab the takeout I bought so I can feed this tummy of yours that's going all ass crazy and growling at me." She lets out a tearful giggle, wiping her face and sitting up. "I hope you like cold Chinese?"

"Sounds perfect."

I glance back at her curled up frame as I reach the door, I hated seeing her so distraught and vulnerable, she needs saving, taken care of and in this moment my need to have her in my life was far greater than I ever imagined.

Chapter Thirteen

Marcus

"So I find out about the Nadia Lenton Wedding via an Email! Nice Marcus, good job."

"I didn't know how to bring it up, I'm sorry." I sigh, pinching the bridge of my nose knowing there'd never be a right way in telling her.

"Your father may have fucked Lenton's wife and destroyed our family but I'm a grown woman. I'm not likely to need therapy sessions from some ass-wipe who can't keep it in his pants and a sour faced daddy's girl plastering the family name on the front cover of a celebrity magazine." The Lenton name was a bitter word in our house along with my father. After the discovery of dad's affair, Henry Lenton and Nadia slated my family like world trash and caused unnecessary heartache for mum on top of what she was already going through, and even with her hard ass attitude now, I know it's affecting her.

"Believe me I'm not happy about it either but we're too far in to pull out, besides Amelia has worked her ass off trying to please the woman. I'm keeping a close eye on them both and having regular meetings with Amelia, calling it off now isn't an option."

There's silence at the other end of the line and I'm waiting for that 'but what if', only I get the opposite. "Who is this Amelia you speak of and how long has she been in your bed?"

My deep laugh fills the room, "Amelia, is the Assistant Manager of The Grand and what makes you think she's in my bed?"

"I'm your mother Marcus; I recognised the change in your voice on the mention of her name. So spill. Are you fucking her?"

No! And god doesn't my cock know it. "We're taking it slow. Can we go back to the original topic, I'm finding discussing my sex life with you a little disturbing." Her laugh through the receiver was priceless; she always knew that sex talk made me feel like the fourteen year old virgin that's yet to be pussy whipped.

"It gets you every time dear boy," she sighs and become serious. "Does Nadia know of the connection with you to the Hotel?"

"I presume so. If not it's not hard to look it up on the web."

"Hum, just be careful, Marcus. People like the Lenton's don't spring up without having a hidden agenda."

I head into the Hotel after stopping of at Fitzford Hill to check on the developments, the team are almost at completion and the interior designers are drawing up the creations for the inside. Amelia's in deep conversation with one of the room staff as I head towards the lift. Her frame is confident and authoritative as she runs her pen down the paper that's connected to the clipboard, discussing whatever is on the sheet in front of them. I lean against the wall captivated by her in every way as my eyes roam her sexiness. Long legs stand in red painted heels and are pieced together in a pencil skirt and chiffon wrapped blouse that showed a hint of her bra line underneath. Perfection. I can't wait to worship every inch of her body when she's laid bare before me.

She knows I'm close. Her neck begins to dust pink as her cheeks glow by the second and as if on cue her eyes pops up and meet mine. We drink each other in as she bites her goddamn lip. Once the room attendant's gone I head towards her, wrapping my arms around her waist and stealing her breath with a kiss.

"Hmm and what can I do for you, Mr Matthews?"

"Go get your stuff, I'm taking you out."

"Uh, yeah my shift finishes in like four hours," she grins.

"Your shift finished as of two minutes ago. I want us to go have some playtime." Trepidation washed over her face as I felt her body retreat. I realised I'd said the wrong thing. Clearly she was thinking what I've wanted to do to her since day one but that right now was not what I had in mind. "Don't back up on me. It's not what you think. Do you trust me?"

"Yes."

"Then go get your things."

Today I want the smile to be etched on her face so her

cheeks hurt, she'd been better these last few days after the anniversary of her mum but there was still the drop of hurt from her father that struck her. I wanted her to forget about all of that, and after having fun on the Train at Primrose Lodge I knew of the perfect place to relive our youth.

I check over her clothes as she strides down from her bedroom, not missing the curves of her body as I cruise my eyes down her. "You're not wearing that, you need to change."

Her face drops and I'm almost certain panic flashes in her eyes. "What's wrong with it?" she questions, looking at her pale blue sundress and running her hands over it.

"Nothing, you look sexy as fuck. But where we're going is far too messy for decent clothes, sorry I should of said. Go find something old that can get dirty."

Amelia's nervous energy was on high alert whilst in the car. Constantly twitching, tapping and fidgeting with anything and everything as we head down the coastal roads. I could have eased her nerves by telling her where we were heading but I chose not to. I wanted her to be on edge, not because I was an ass and liked to see her suffer, but because I wanted her to feel completely comfortable with me and know that whatever her reaction to things it isn't going to change the way I am with her.

I switch off the ignition, focusing on the foreground in front of us as shouts and screams of laughter fill the air.

"Paint-balling?" her wide-eyes and agape mouth was humorous as I hold back a chuckle.

"You up for it?"

"Isn't it dangerous? People get hurt at these places and end up with bruises and shit," she turns in her seat to face me. "And if paint goes in your eyes you can go blind,

106

Marcus...*Blind*!"

My laugh erupts the space between us as she tries to sustain the disapproval look on her face. "I'm serious, this shit isn't safe." she chuckles as I unclip our belts before leaning forward.

"Babe, this is old school paint-balling. They don't use guns and even though the paint is non-toxic our eyes are protected."

Her eyes narrow. "So if there are no guns how does it work?"

"We just throw paint balloons and run round like mad fuckers. Trust me it's completely safe. Me and my sister came here all the time as kids."

Haystacks piled high with endless splats of colour decorate the area of the outside field; flags stand tall and vibrate in the wind above us as people sped around in their rainbow colour clothing. From the moment we stepped into the balling ground and started throwing paint balls, anxious Amelia instantly changed into a high-spirited chick with her none stop squeals of laughter, hot-footing it around like the roadrunner. Her laugh is infectious and her face lights up like the first ray of sunshine on a clear sky morning. I love seeing her like this, carefree and vibrant, this is how her life should be like and not forever carrying a dark cloud over her.

I quietly tiptoe around the stack of high hay blocks as I duck my body low trying to find her. I'm caught off guard and before I had chance to register her movements I'm hit from behind. Turning quickly, I take a balloon from my bag and launch it at her, splattering green paint across her back as she tries to run from me. "Take that, Weston."

She throws a balloon back but it hits the ground at my

feet. Another and it splats on the hay behind me. "You're really good at this aren't you?" I say sarcastically.

"Just you wait, I'll get your rainbow ass when you least expect it." I laugh at her choice of words and through another, hitting her on the stomach as she shrieks.

"Oops, pardon me."

She takes another shot, this time I'm hit full whack on the head, thick dollops of yellow drip over my hair and goggles as Amelia jumps up and down laughing hysterical. "Ha! Touché."

I smeared the paint from my goggles and began my plot of revenge, a mischievous chuckle leaves my throat as I slowly step towards her. "Now that was a wrong move, Weston. This. Means. War."

She darts with a shriek. Balloon upon balloon fly in her directing hitting her back, shoulders and ass before she reaches a dead end and becomes trapped against high haystacks. Covering her face with her hands I continue my attack, her body covered in a whirlpool of colours. The laughter and squeals blowing out into her hands is like music to my ears. She is loving every minute. Once my bag is empty I throw it aside along with my goggles. Striding towards her I pull off her own goggles, slam her back against the haystack and crash my mouth on hers, lifting her by the ass to wraps her legs around me. Her fingers lace my paint slick hair with a tug, causing me to groan. I can never get enough of kissing this woman. She's like a drug, each kiss is better than the last. It's hot, greedy and undoubtedly passionate as I work her mouth with mine. My cock was uncomfortably hard and pressed against her as I pull her bottom lip with my teeth. "Fuck, Amelia, you're killing me."

***

"Marcus can I ask you something?"

Picnic treats from our food hamper are spread amongst the straw bed as we lay resting under the scorching sun, fragments of paint dry in cracks on our skin as the rest of the thick clumps begins to fry under the heat. Hands entwined as we focus on the clear sky.

"Ask away."

"What was your last relationship like? How long were you together?" This was a conversation I didn't want to open up to, but I knew I needed to give something in return to build the trust.

"I thought it was a great one, we were together nearly four years. Then it went to shit when I walked in on them. Sadie was screwing my best friend right under my nose. Neither of them were who I thought they were."

"I was with someone that wasn't who I thought he was. People change when the door closes, yet still manage to fool those around them making out they're perfect."

"It was hard. Not only did I lose her, I lost my best friend. I lost control after that and went out and drank my way through the bars and fucked my way through half of London. I become a shadow of the person I was. Then one night a few home truths from my mum made me realise I was letting them win with the person I'd become."

"What happened?"

"I threw myself back into work as a distraction and gave my dick the biggest dry spell it's ever seen. I've not been near a woman in over a year. Then I found you. I thought Sadie was the one for me. I gave her everything. If she wanted something I'd buy it. If she asked for money, I'd give it. All the while she was laughing in my face and spreading her legs for another."

Amelia turns on her side propping her head up with her hand. "Materialistic things mean nothing. All a man should ever need to give a woman is his time, heart and protect her in all the rightful ways." Lifting a finger I watch as she paints an outline heart of blue on my bare chest. Flicking her eyes back at mine with contentment. "You are a good man, Marcus, don't let anyone make you think differently." Here was a beautiful angel in need for freedom yet she's consoling my insecurities and demons of my past whilst fighting her own.

"And you are breathtakingly special, and like no other woman I've come in contact with. I can't wait to make you mine." Her eyes flash with something, I'd like to believe its desire but as fast as I see it they're quickly flooded in fear. "But I only want that when you feel ready."

We lay silent under the sun holding each other's gaze with unspoken words; Amelia leans in to place her lips softly on mine before whispering, "Do you have paint on your fingers?"

"No why?" I say with questionable eyes, while desire now defiantly running strong in her pure blues.

"Make me cum."

My eyes-widen as she bites her lip with a naughty grin. "Here?" I look around. "Where anyone could walk by?"

"Please, Marcus." She lifts her hips to me and takes hold of my neck pulling my close, darting her tongue into my mouth to take control. Letting me know she's serious. I push her onto her back and beam at her naughty behaviour.

"You know for a woman living on her nerves, you sure

got some balls."

Her grin was a mile wide as she crinkles her nose up. "Well you see there's this guy and he's slowly bringing me back to life."

That was all I needed for my hand to invade her panties and my mouth to hit hers.

Chapter Fourteen

Amelia

Me: I'm super nervous; I've just fucked up the sauce for the third time. X

Megan: Stop freaking out and just breath, you will be fine. Love you x

It's been over a month since Marcus first walked into my life and knocked me on my ass, taking over my mind like a whirlwind and invading my personal space daily. Wanting and needing to progress our connection a little further, I decided to cook for him and I'd be lying if I said I was excited. I'm not. I'm totally freaking out. My nerves are off the chart for reasons beyond my control and my shaky hands are constantly dropping things.

My stomach somersaults at the sound of the door.

Just breathe, you can do this.

My breath caught once I opened the door; his white shirt heightens his tanned biceps while his dark jeans hug his hips as he stands with a look of awe, working his eyes down my body and causing a flutter in my belly. "Wow, Amelia, you look amazing." I've changed six times before he arrived and went back to the original bottle green dress I started with.

After pouring us both a drink I flurry around the kitchen, placing items in the oven and cleaning as I go along. Trying my hardest to keep myself busy from erupting into an anxiety attack. That was one thing I learnt over time when cooking for a man, I had to keep myself distracted from his disapproving gaze, only the eyes carving into me right now contain nothing but inquisitiveness.

"Can I help with anything?"

"No, no. I'm fine." My words show the panic behind them.

Marcus gently grips my wrist and draws me to him, taking my other hand in his he studies me. "But you're not fine. You're all over the place, Amelia. You've hardly spoke or looked at me since I got here. What's wrong?"

I look at our entwined hands and bite my lip, letting out a much needed deep breath. "I'm nervous." I whisper.

"About me being here?"

"About cooking for you. Whenever I cooked for Daniel he'd-" I didn't want our night to involve a conversation with his name any longer. This was our time and no other person needed to be a part of it. "-It just makes me nervous that's all."

"Don't be nervous babe, I want to be here. And

whatever is in that oven smells fucking incredible. Now, no arguments what can I do to help?"

"Well my glass is crying for a refill." I grin, his breath tickled my lips before they join mine, washing away the edge of my anxieties like he always had a way of doing.

Marcus set the table while I served us marinated duck in a five spice, cinnamon and soy sauce, along with roasted vegetables.

This was it.

Another one of my major steps in knowing what sort of man sat before me as I place his dinner in front of him and filled his glass with an unsteady hand, clocking his eyes on my shaky pouring. I held my breath and gripped the napkin under the table as I watched him take the first bite. His eyes briefly close and a deep hmm leaves his throat. "Holy shit, Amelia, this is amazing."

Relief left my lungs with a smile. "It was my mum's secret dish."

"Well thank you Mrs Weston for creating a remarkable woman who can continue with her recipes. Shit girl, I need more of your cooking in my life." He winks, and I fall into a relaxed state of mind and enjoy our meal together.

***

Leona Lewis plays softly into the low lit room as I cuddle up against Marcus, enjoying the powerful kisses he never failed to provide. My shoulders ache through a day of nervous energy, all the while I'm beginning to fight another round of anxiety to the one I faced earlier. I have no doubt Marcus will stay-he has on many occasions, but tonight there's been a shift between us and that worries me. It threatens everything we've done together over the last month. Because I know as quickly as he stormed into my world, he'll leave just as fast once he knows. Once he sees.

His hazel eyes burn like fire into mine as he lifts me chin. Chills cover my skin as his breath hits my lips, "Amelia, I've tried so hard to be patient because I knew it's what you needed, but I can't wait a second longer. I've wanted you from the first night I saw you in the club. I want to make you mine."

My insides tangle as panic threatens my chest. "I-I...Marcus, I-" I go to flee from the comfort of his arms but he grasps my elbow and stands from the sofa, pressing his front to my back. Deep breaths leave me as I try to control my nerves, hanging my head in shame of what lies beneath my dress. The evidence of what my history will show him.

My heart's racing, the intense heat from his body ignites within me. The light strokes of his fingertips down my arms cause my eyes to close, goosebumps to glaze my skin as he kisses the weak spot on my neck. I fail to hold back the whimper as his hand spans my stomach, pushing me against his erection. "Don't tell me you don't want me as much as I want you, because I know you do. I see it. I feel it. I taste it on you," he murmurs, his voice thick with lust. "Let me have you, Amelia. Let me make you mine."

I want him so much I can't breathe. But there's been no one since Daniel. I didn't want anyone close. I couldn't let anyone in.

"Take off your dress."

"Marcus, I ca-" Strong hands turn me, his hazel eyes darken and hold my gaze.

"Take it off, Amelia." His command was low, and there was something within his tone that made my guard slip and I find myself granting his request. My shaky hand takes to the zip and I let the green material slink to the floor. I stand before him trembling in my underwear with my eyes shut tight not wanting to see his reaction.

Exposed. Tainted. Vulnerable.

I gasp when his lips press to the silver scar on my chin, the ones on my collarbone, before dropping to his knees to kiss the burn marks that shimmer red over the left side of my waist. His kiss was like an angel's whisper. Loosening the heaviness in my heart in which I've carried all these years. Only Megan and Lucas have seen my body and the scars that tell a story. Scars from brutal hands and implements where I was once a victim in a cold case love.

"Turn around."

A hot tear rolls down my cheek, "Please don't make me do this."

"Turn around for me. I need to see you," he whispers, his eyes coated in both empathy and desire.

My chest is tight with emotion as I slowly turn my quivering body to reveal the scars that sicken me when I catch them in the mirror. The deep red marks and welts that lay like a crumpled road map on my back. The ones to this very day still remind me of the pain I faced.

The sound of his hitched breath makes my head fall into my hands and my heart hurt with shame. This was where he should have ran. Leave me and my vile body alone in the cold space of the room. But he never did. Sweeping my hair from my back and over my shoulder, Marcus gently trails his fingertips over my back before kissing every inch of my broken battered body.

I crumble above him.

Worshipping my body with his touch like no one has

before, healing me with his lips as he marks his ownership with them. This man has ways of making my greatest fear banish in seconds and make my hideous body feel anything but ugly. He stands to turn me, brushing away my tears with his thumbs, forcing me to look at him. "Is this why you've held back?"

"I didn't want you to see." I whisper.

He kisses my forehead, threading his fingers through my hair, "I don't see anything other than beauty. Your heart, the brightness of your soul, the richness of your eyes against your pure creamy skin. You're a beautiful angel, Amelia." His words were full of honesty and promise as his lips pressed to mine, and I felt as though the thick heavy smog that congealed my lungs had lifted and I could finally begin to breathe.

"Make me feel beautiful, Marcus. Make me yours."

His mouth hit mine with a kiss that was gentle yet hungry, exploring each other's taste as our tongues entwined. He swims an arm around my waist and I'm lifted like a doll to wrap my legs around him as he walks us to the bedroom. Placing me to stand, he pulls off his shirt, presenting me with hard muscle I've been desperate to touch as our mouths reconnect. I can't touch him, not yet.

My arms move to cover myself once my bra is unclasped. Marcus may have seen my scars but that doesn't stop the shame. "Don't." He orders, moving them away. I can't stop the trembles, I feel like I'm losing my virginity all over again, not knowing what to do or where to start as I stand here waiting to be taken. "Relax, baby," he whispers, kissing me again and guiding me to the mattress.

His tongue swirls my pebbled nipple, "Yes," I breathe, rising up into him as his thumb plays the other. My fingers thread his hair as he kisses a path down my stomach, caressing my body. The desire for him is too much, I ache for him, to feel him. When he stands and removes his jeans my heart rate quickens, I bite my lip. He was bigger than I'd ever had and incredibly beautiful. My hooded eyes took in every ounce of his muscular body as he stands grinning, enjoying my stare before coming back over me.

I can't help but cover my face when his thumbs hook my panties. "Don't hide from me, baby, let me see you." I watch as his eyes slowly run over the length of my body when removing my lace. "Jesus you're sexy, every goddamn inch of you." His voice lustful, the fire between my thighs throbs as my body succumbs to his touch. My hands fist the sheets, I desperately need to touch him, to feel his skin on mine, but he never said I could. In the past I had to ask permission and faced consequences if I didn't, my wrists were tied and that's where they stayed as he fucked me raw.

"Marcus, am I allowed to touch you?" He stops his trail of seduction, lifting his head with narrowed brows before realisation washed over him.

"Yes. Always."

My hands devoured the bareness of his shoulders, back and ass. Intoxicated and breathless with the feeling of his soft cotton skin, inhaling his divine scent that engulfs me. "You have no idea how good this feels just to let me touch you."

"You're so beautiful," he breathes into a kiss as his fingers play my soaked entrance before pushes two inside. Working me as he brought me to my climax, and increasing the pressure on my clit, letting the welcoming storm take over my body. My need for him is greater than I ever imagined, I want to feel every inch of him in and around me, like I've craved all this time.

Reaching to his abandoned jeans he removes a condom, "Marcus, wait. If neither of us have been with anyone in so long then..."

"Tell me what you want."

I remove my eyes from the packet and look at him, "I want to feel you. I'm on the pill."

His grin was sinful, tossing the condom aside before taking my mouth in hunger. The tip of his cock teased me as our gaze locked, soothing his hand over my hair and looking deep into my blues. "Don't run from me anymore, Amelia. Promise you'll never run."

"I promise." I whisper the words without hesitation as he slowly pushed inside, both escaping a groan with the invasion, I'm so tight around him but he feels phenomenal. He didn't move at first, just focused on me as I adjusted to him, and then once he did everything changed. My mind and body awoken to a million feelings that had been buried for so long. "Oh god, Marcus, you feel incredible." I wrap my legs around him, wanting to feel every inch of him on me as he revived me back to life with each thrust.

"Until I leave, you're forever with me."

I span the muscles of his back, I feel exhilarated, consumed with an ecstasy I don't want to end as he whispers words of beauty. My core burns with my orgasm that's building, sparks river up my thighs, pooling in my lower belly and intensifies by the second, "Oh, oh god!"

Fire runs my veins. I can't hold on much longer, and when he circles my clit I'm sent spiralling, stars form under my eyelids and I shatter around him, crying out with a voice I don't recognise as my own while unshed tears glass my eyes. I'm floating into a new world. A free world and one I never thought I'd never get the chance to be a part of again. All because of this man.

"Fuck, Amelia!" he groans, filling me with his own white heat. I kiss him, long and hard. I've had sex many a time in the past but not in the way I've just experienced. It was always rough, hard and painful as he took me anyway he wanted. But this, this was breathtaking. His head dips to the crook of my neck, hot breath hits my sticky summer skin as I hold him close while he's still inside.

"For years I've dreaded this day for many reasons. But you've made me feel anything but ugly, Marcus. That alone means more than you'll ever know. Thank you." His lips press to my neck, his arms tighten around me, telling me all the words he never needed to say as our bodies fall into one another.

I've come alive.

Chapter Fifteen

Marcus

I watch her while she sleeps.

I've discreetly tried over the past few weeks to gain more information from Amelia about her past. Getting her to trust me and open up. Letting her know I'm not like her last and that men aren't all ass-wipes with no feelings for others. I knew from her actions, words and hesitations, her past was dark clouds and shit storms. Talking about her parents was hard for her, but seeing her in such deep anguish was harder. You just had to witness the pain across her face to know. Riddled with grief and not being able to find a way out.

But even though her closed book was slowly starting to open and the pages be read aloud I wanted to jump right to the last chapter and know of her ex. Who he was. Where he was, and what he'd done to the beautiful creature that lies beside me, restless in her sleep as her face often showed signs of distress. The ones I've witnessed over the last few nights as I watched her sleep, while her red locks fan the pillow and her thin frame moulds into the mattress that was suffocated by her tightly pulled fucking bed clothes. Only now that I've seen the evidence that coats her body in demons, I'm unsure if I want to know at all. I don't wish to put her through the torture of repeated haunts and horror, and I don't wish to hear of what pain the fucker caused her. She doesn't have to tell me anything I don't already know. I see it in her eyes, I feel it in her trembles and I hate it when I see her slip into her world of the dark and dangerous past.

She wanted me, but was afraid in every way. It ran deep in those big cornflower eyes each and every time she looked at me. Even with her bright smile and brave face-I saw it. He's made her fearful of herself, people, life, even me. She had to ask permission to fucking touch me for Christ sake, that shit just ain't right.

Amelia's faced so much over time, yet today was mentally and emotionally challenging for her. Franticly flitting around me like a spinning top as insecurities oozed from her pores-the worst I've seen from her. I wanted to wrap her in the safety blanket of my arms and cradle her like a china doll to prevent her from breaking. Her body physically shuddering when removing her clothes, terrified of what my reaction would be. I knew she needed to break the pattern of barricading herself from me. Move forward. The closeness that I'd got to her was with my tongue in her mouth and my fingers in her pussy. I couldn't hold back any longer. My dick hurt like hell, my balls dragged like fuck with their deep ache. Even jerking off in the shower didn't help the craving. I needed to feel her, to touch her. To claim her.

It was hard for me to see her fearful, but there was no other way. She needed this. To overcome and to stop using her body as a fucking battleground.

She stole my breath when she took off her dress. My heart pounding against my chest. My dick fighting hard against the fly of my jeans. But as she stood baring all and shaking with her eyes closed, all I saw was the sexiest woman I've ever laid my eyes on. Her red mane covering her pale soft skin that's dusted over with light freckles, like the stars that coated the night sky. Her big blue eyes deep as the ocean, and the curves of her frame like a sculpted model of art. I knew there were stories of the scares I already saw, the hairline on her chin and the two pink identical marks on her collarbone, yet those stories seemed so small once she turned around.

My jaw clenched, my fists balled as the fury ripped through my chest like a hot bullet at the thought of someone doing that to her. Treating her like a fucking animal and not seeing the pureness of her true beauty. Instantly I wanted to take all the pain away, hold on and care for her like she deserves and cocoon her in a safety of what I know and can provide. All her anxieties come apparent the second my eyes latched onto those scars. The way her face drops and her eyes sadden when I say she's beautiful. The way she never takes a compliment like she should own it. Her shield that shelters her from another. It ticks all the boxes.

She has no idea what she's doing to me. I have no idea. Her eyes are my light on a dark night, her honeysuckle and vanilla scent is the air that I breathe and her wide white smile is my sunrise. I spoke truth when I said she had a beautiful body. Her flaws are a part of that beauty, her heart and mind are evidence on just how far she's come. She is like a rare diamond, quietly hidden away and waiting to be uncovered for all to see in its glory.

She shifts and turns herself on to her side, legs entwine with mine as she nuzzles her nose to my chest. Fingers tracing over my stomach sending goosebumps to pepper my skin as I sweep the hair from her face. "You ok?" I whisper.

She nods, still with her eyes closed. Milky skin dusted in freckles across her nose and long lashes that whisper against her cheeks. She really is oblivious to just how beautiful and sexy she is, and the only one that had no idea of the heads she turned when walking into a room. Every goddamn thing about her was perfection.

"Are you going to stay?"

"Of course I am, why would I not?"

"Because…because now you've seen all of me," she says barely above a whisper.

Annoyance glazed my body at the thought of her thinking of me this way. A quick cock fix with a nice-fucking-knowing-you ticket slapped on the side. But then I could understand why she would think this. It took her so long to show me her body, it's going to take time to realise it doesn't change a thing.

"Open your eyes." I ordered. Blinking them open I'm stuck by her blues. "So you think after seeing you and finally being with you after waiting all this time, I'd leave because of what lies on your body?" Her eyes dart away and I lift her chin making her look at me and like earlier they're filled with shame.

"I just…I just thought," she exhaled deeply. "You're a CEO, Marcus, a rich and popular man. You need a woman of faultlessness and class on your arm. One that says show girl and style not some closed off woman with a dark past and sca-" I steal her breath and kiss her hard. Holding her face and body tight against mine as I devour her taste. Making her moan into me, little moans of whisper like whimpers that drive me wild each and every time.

"Not all rich fuckers want show girls dripping in plastic perfection. Some actually like woman who don't need shit like that to stand out from a crowd. You're a sexy woman, Amelia and have a beautiful body. Don't ever hide it, not from me." She nods slowly as I run my thumb along her bottom lip as a wicked grin grows across my face. "Besides I'm letting you rest before I take you for round two."

"Oh really?" Her soft giggle bounced against my chest as her cheeks flush.

"You bet, can't get rid of me that easily, Miss Weston."

Content silence falls between us as Amelia runs her fingers along my abs, while I trace the outline of her tattoo. A small soft black and grey woman sat with her knees bent amongst flowers as her wings spread wide. Vibrant against Amelia's pale skin. "Why a Guardian Angel?"

"They say it's a spirit that's thought to watch over and protect you. I'm not a religious person but I believe my mother watches over me daily. I wanted her spirit as close as possible, so I got the tattoo."

A small smile ticks my lips as I place mine to hers for a soft kiss. "Well I can be your personal guardian angel now."

She shakes her head with a smirk. "Uh uh, I don't think you fit the bill to be an angel?"

"Is that so?" I grin, with raised brows.

"Yep."

She squeals as I roll her quickly onto her back and hover over her, pulling the sheets over our head to cocoons us in an ivory glow, making her body blend against the colour only for her eyes and hair to stand out. "Ok, how about Superman?"

"Nope."

"Captain America? Every woman in the world swoons over that fucker."

She shakes her head, holding back a smile. "You're more an Angel of the Greek Gods."

I tilt my head imagining the image in my mind. "Like Thor?"

"I don't think he's Greek babe, but we'll go with it."

My chuckle bounced between us. "You're amazing you know that." I kiss her soft pink lips, slipping my tongue in to greet hers. Tracing, gripping and moulding her hands all over my body like an addiction she can't get enough of.

"Hmm…the little guy down there is asking for attention," she breathes against my mouth, eyes closed and clueless to what she'd said.

"Little guy?!" I mock, a grin creeping its way out as Amelia's eyes spring open in alarm.

"N-no…I mean…what I meant was that…um…*shit!*" I look at her in amusement, the tips of her fingers over her lips as her cheeks turn cherry red and a giggle leaves her throat. "I'm sorry…you're not little. Fuck no you're not little."

"I should hope not. You can't tell a guy he's Thor one minute then crush him like that the next," I tease. "It does shit to the self-esteem."

Her giggle now erupts into a deep uncontrolled belly laugh. The laugh she hates is infectious causing me to follow suite and let the rumbles leave my chest. The more I laugh, the more she does and we laugh until tears fill her eyes and our muscles ache. Until we don't even remember why we're laughing so we laugh because of it. She's so fucking adorable. As we choke out the remainder of our hysteria Amelia suddenly becomes serious. Taking my face in her hands and smoothing her thumbs over my cheeks, looking deep into my eyes. "Thank you, Marcus," she whispers as tears glisten. Tears that I'm unsure are from her laughter or her gratitude.

"For what?"

"For bringing me back to life."

My ego soared. I felt like fucking King Kong had just been given the greatest gift and stomped around with excitement, letting the world know with his rumbles just how much that meant hearing her say that. I wanted her to feel, I wanted her to be free and I can't help but think a big part of that is because of me, if not all of it. She's overcome huge steps in breaking down her own walls, but I am a part of it regardless.

"Let's see what this *little* guy can do shall we? On your front." Her blue eyes darken and flash with heat as she turns. I run my hands down the length of her back and lift her up on all fours. My head dips to kiss the scars on her back, licking them to mark new ownership like a lion caring for its lioness, marks laced with cherishment and security and washing away any pain left on her. Her whispers of gratitude seep out from her lips just high enough for me to hear. I sweep my fingers along her wet pussy as she bucks against me, moaning my name with her head tipped back as I grip her hips and push deep inside her, feeling every inch of her tight pussy around my cock. My eyes drift close as I take her. Amelia is not like any other. I knew as soon as I was inside her the first time no other woman has or will even come close. The way she robs my breath. The way she feels, the way she consumes me. The way she cries my name when she cums, and fuck me the way my orgasm shoots like a firecracker chasing the night. It's all her. She felt amazing in every way. Like we belong as we moulded into each other. I thought she'd just be someone to have fun with. A summer romance. But as I bury myself balls deep inside her and drive her body with mine that slates slowly being wiped clean and a new one is beginning to unfold.

I fuck deep as I feel her beginning to tighten, my own climax roaring through my body like hot lava as the sweat from the humidity outside and the disorderly sheets coats our bodies in perspiration. "You feel so fucking good baby."

Her hands grip the headboard as I rock us, her sexy pants of my name leave her lips as she cries and combusts around my cock. I can't take my eyes from her as she turns her head to catch me gaze, her gorgeous flushed face sent my body and mind in a frenzy. My ass cheeks clench and the growl of my orgasm shoots into her over and over creating another climax from her as I tease her clit, riding the waves of each other before our bodies collapse to the bed.

This woman has taken me prisoner, gripped me from the insides and reeled me in. All I see is her. All I want is her. I'm slowly entering into a world in which I only see Amelia involved in and it confuses the shit out of me as I've never felt this way about anyone before. Not this early down the line. Maybe this myth about love at for sight shit was true, because right now all I know is I am falling for her.

Fast.

Chapter Sixteen

Amelia

My tummy growled with its need to be filled as my nose sensed the smell of bacon lingering its way through my house. There was no point searching the bed for Marcus as I could hear his hums from the kitchen as he listened to the radio.

I stretched my satisfied body and stifled a yawn before putting on Marcus's shirt and headed out the bedroom with a smile on my face, resting against the doorway of the kitchen and ogling the man that's working his magic over the stove in just his jeans while his mouth-watering back muscles flex as he moves.

"Morning gorgeous." He says without turning. How does this man know my every move?

I chuckle making my way over wrapping my arms

around him and resting my head on his back with a kiss and a content sigh. "You're cooking breakfast?"

"Indeed I am." His joyful tone made me smile as he and turns me in my arms. "My girl has to restore her energy. How did you sleep?"

"Better than I have in ages." I grinned. Which was true, my nights are often restless but I've slept better these last few weeks than I had in years. Providing me with a kiss and a coffee I sit and watch him work his way round my kitchen. Last night with him was way better than perfect. I faced my one true fear of uncovering the history of violent hands that scared my body and the one thing I feared more than anything was him running. He made me feel special and wanted. After all these weeks of telling me how beautiful I am he made me feel it. I didn't think I would ever have that again. My body to me was the devil.

"Where's your mind run away to?" he says, bringing me out of my thoughts as he rests his back against the counter across the room.

I search his face as endless questions hit the tip of my tongue. His eyes have always shown me kindness, faith and honesty. Never pity or disgust and the one looking back at me now are the same ones I've grown to enjoy watching me. I focus on my hands that play with my mug as my voice lowers. "Did you really mean everything you said? That I shouldn't hide myself from you?"

He sighs softly, turning off the stove before coming over and cupping my face, a gesture I've notice he does to calm me whenever I'm anxious. His hands are my bubble of safety and relaxation no matter where they land on my body. "Sweetheart, you need to stop doing this to yourself. I'm here because I want to be. I wanted you and still want you. It changes nothing." Tears glisten my eyes as I wrap my arms around him, the way he makes me feel is so foreign yet I don't think I want it to change. "Just promise me one thing. And that is when you're ready you will tell me everything. I need to know what happened, Amelia. I have to know." I knew I could never keep it from him. But the thought of reliving it caused a cold shiver to cascade.

"I promise I'll tell you when I'm ready."

"That's all I ask," his kiss was gentle, making butterflies to wake in my tummy. "So what are our plans today? Are we reliving the youth?" He questions, making his way back to the cooker.

"Ah, yes well here's the thing. I promised to spend it with Megan shopping. I've hardly seen her recently because some guy keeps pushing his way into my life."

His brows raise, "Is that the same guy who fucked you senseless last night and in the early hours?"

"Oh, you know about him?" I teased. "You don't mind do you? I just need some girl time."

"Not at all, I've got to head up to Fitzford Hill anyway so you girlies shop away. And while you're at it you need to take this-" he reaches to his back pocket and removes his wallet, taking out a credit card. "-to find yourself a ball gown."

I narrow my brows in confusion, clearly having no idea what he's talking about and more importantly why he's handing me his card. "Why do I need a ball gown?"

"Will you be my date at The Kingston Annual Summer Ball?"

My eyes-widened with excitement. The Kingston Ball was held for all local Hoteliers in and around the Coastlines to congregate with each other and awards to be collected.

I've always wanted to go but never got the chance. "You want me to go with you?" I squealed.

"Of course I do. Use my card and get what you need."

I shake my head and hand it back to him. "Uh uh, I can use my own card."

"No I insist. Use mine." Male generosity is something I wasn't use to. I was always waiting for there to be a catch, a gift that was later tainted. But there never was one with Marcus, every week I had flowers, each time we were out he would pay before I had chance and sometimes that was hard to comprehend.

"Marcus, I can't it's too much."

"Take the card, Amelia." I go to speak but he places his finger on my lips, putting the card in my hand again. "Take. The. Card. I'm serious. But for Christ sakes don't let Megan get hold of it. I'll be maxed out by the end of the day."

"I won't tell her you said that," I chuckle.

His arms snake up my shirt to caress the small of my back before lifting me off the breakfast stool and placing me on the counter. Kissing my neck as his hands descended between my legs to spread them wide.

"Hmm, what about breakfast?"

"You are breakfast," he growled, as he relished my body in every way he wanted.

***

Using the key she gave me I let myself into Megan's. The house is quiet and I knew she was still in bed. Creeping into her room, I curl my body beside hers and watch her in her peaceful slumber. Megan and I know each other well enough to not think this kind of behaviour is weird, after spending so much time together we feel comfortable in each other's presence, so the fact I'm laid on her bed with her naked under the sheets won't bother either of us.

I poke my finger on her button nose and chuckle softly when she bats it with her hand. I do it again, letting my giggle seep a little louder from my throat as my devilish mode takes over. Her eyes spring open and she freaks, flying her body up into sitting position. "Jesus fucking Christ, Amelia!" she holds her hand to her chest as she tries to catch her breath.

I'm still giggling as I speak, "Sorry babe, I didn't mean to scare you."

"No shit. What you doing here so early?" she says, rubbing her sleepy eyes.

"I have news."

"Well after that stunt it better be good."

"I fucked Marcus." If I had a camera right now I'd happily take a picture and post it on my fridge, her face said it all. Her jaw super wide, her eyes trying to match it as she focuses on me. I grin, nodding to confirm she's heard me correctly.

"O-Oh my fucking god, am I-" she looks around running her hand through her hair, "I am still dreaming?"

"Nope it's all real." I giggle.

"Wowzers check you out, rebelling and screwing a hot hunk. Told you, you had nothing to worry about," she sighs in defeat "Jesus that's one guy you beat me too."

I chuckle and turn on my tummy holding my head in my hand as she pulls herself back to rest against the headboard.

"Sooo-" she grins, leaning her head to the side. "Tell

me all the details… and I mean ALL the details." I told her everything and how alive he's made me feel. Not forgetting the important news of the summer ball. I thought that would be enough to keep her going, until she cocked a brow and asked how big his dick was. I knew I'd never live it down if I kept my mouth shut so I told her every detail of his body.

"Shit babe I'm so proud of you, I could easily fuck you myself right now." We giggle as I make my way off the bed, grabbing the corner of the covers and pulling them off her as I leave the room.

"Get your pretty ass out of bed, we have shopping to do."

***

"Where the fuck do you find a ball gown at the coast? It's all board shorts and wetsuits." I huff, pinching a crisp from Megan's packet and popping it into my mouth.

"Tabitha's Trinkets."

"Where?"

She rolled her eyes. "Jesus, for a woman you really don't know shit when it comes to shopping. Tabitha's Trinkets is one of the biggest known dressmakers in the area, with a range of fabulously stunning dresses all lined with lace and pearls that has regular dealings with celebrities. *That's* where you'll find your dress and *that's* where we're going."

I'd been inside the shop for ten minutes and I'm yet to take a breath. This place was unbelievably stunning. Spot lights, larges mirrors, velvet chairs and rows upon rows of dresses. All shapes and sizes that twinkles against the light. I wasn't at the coast nor was I in Hollywood; I was in a dressing room of Disneyland waiting to find a dress for my prince. How in god's name did I not know of this place?

"Good morning, Miss Weston. I received a call from Mr Matthews to say you were heading here with Miss Simmons. I'm Emily and will be your assistant in finding the right dress for you today."

How the hell did Marcus know I was coming here?

"Amelia, it's the only place around that makes dresses like this. Take the puzzled look off your face." Megan said, collecting a fashion magazine and flipping through the pages. Am I really that easy to read?

"Thank you, Emily, please call me Amelia. This place is stunning by the way."

"Thank you, shall we get to work?"

I'm overwhelmed and completely suffocated with dresses and shoes. My mind is on overload and the flusters have begun on which dress to choose. They were either clashing with my hair, too short, too much dazzle or too low for my back, and I swear I've irritated Emily on refusing her help and wanting Megan when getting changed. Wondering eyes on my body will leave pitied faces and judgmental minds in which I can't be dealing with.

I look over myself in the mirror as I try to imagine myself in different dresses and which one Marcus is likely to like me in. Then it hits me.

"He likes my eyes." The girls twirl their heads in confusion as I look back at them through the mirror. "Marcus. He often passes comment on my eyes. I need something that reflects my eyes."

My breath hitches as I run my hands softly over the dress that screams, beauty, class and sexy. The floor-length royal blue mermaid style dress had a wide train with cap sleeves and a touch of lace around the high neck, giving it a look of elegance as the odd leaf of the lace sparkled. I loved it and felt incredibly special whilst stood in it.

"Can you see my scars?" I whisper to Megan.

"No babe there all covered. Although as beautiful as it is, it'sa rather expensive dress."

"Don't worry it's fine."

It was expensive and I did feel a little guilty, but it was perfect and I knew Marcus would love it. Megan sweeps my hair aside and rests her chin on my shoulder, wrapping her arms around my waist as she locks onto my gazes, "He's making you flourish into the woman that was desperate to be set free. You look absolutely stunning babe."

I smile at her honesty, I couldn't agree with her more. Just a few months ago I was trapped in a world I couldn't find a way out of, now since Marcus has stormed into my life I don't wake up dreading my day that lays ahead of me.

"Thank you so much, Emily, the dress is perfect." I smile handing her the credit card. Emily runs up the total of the dress and shoes and breaks the news, leaving Megan wide-eyed and open mouthed.

"Amelia, it's like half your monthly wage!" She whispers high pitched as I head for the door.

"It's fine, Marcus gave me his credit card."

"What! And you're just telling me this now?... When are they closing?!"

I giggle heading out the store leaving an astonished Megan inside and a blissful feeling in my belly.

Chapter Seventeen

Marcus

"Are you going to be much longer? Andrew will leave before we get there." I shout from my living room. I heard her feet pad down the wooden floor of the hall and appear at the doorway looking surprised.

"Andrew is coming?" she asks, in a different outfit to the one she had on half hour ago.

"Yeah I know right. Can you believe he's taking an afternoon off?" I chuckle.

"Wow. You obviously have an effect on him that brings him out of his shell."

"I have that effect on most people," I grin cocking a brow. "Now go get ready I don't want to be late."

"Come help me pick out a dress. I want to look good on your big day."

I had confirmation earlier in the week that the new builds on Fitzford Hill were complete. This afternoon I've invited a small group for drinks and a chance to look around before heading to Rubies for the evening.

"Wear this one." I hold up a smoky grey dress from the small collecting of clothes Amelia keeps in my wardrobe for when she stays. Our nights now are never spent apart; we're either here or at hers.

She glances at me through the reflection of the mirror-applying her mascara and stood in her black lace underwear looking sexy as fuck. It took a few times reassuring her she doesn't have to hide her body from me, but now I love the fact she's finally at ease in parading around the house without a care in the world.

"I was thinking of wearing that one," she smirks.

"You were not. Now hurry up and get dressed, if you stand around half naked any longer we won't make it out this damn house." I tap her ass making her jump with a squeal as I head out the room.

"Do I wear my hair up or down?" she shouts as I head to the kitchen, collecting my phone that just signalled a message.

"Your choice, but it's hot out."

Andrew: I'm at Fitzford Hill. Where the fuck are you!! Hurry up.

Me: At home. What's with the urgency?

Andrew: I'm with the reception girl from work.

I chuckle at his lack of knowledge when it comes to the

staff he works with.

Me: Her name is Megan, talk to her you might actually like her.

"What's funny?" Amelia questions, entering the kitchen in the dress I chose and her hair up.

"Just Andrew being a prick. You look amazing babe." I kiss her cheek as they blush. "Let's go."

I felt like I was about to burst with pride. Stood before us was a block of eight semi-detached homes along with three detached high quality apartments all lined with balconies, high glass windows and a picturesque view of the coast. Derek and the team have worked their asses off in completing the builds within the time frame and now the friends that stand before me get a glimpse of what lays behind the doors.

"Marcus, they look incredible." Amelia gasps as I open the car door and take her hand.

"I know right."

"So apart from owning places and hiding away from them for months on end, you design and develop buildings like these?" she says, eyes scanning everywhere.

"Yeah, pretty much."

Derek heads towards us dressed in a grey suit, it's a good look compared to his regular dirty jeans and hard hat. "Marcus, pleasure to see you again. What do you think of these beauties?"

"I'm impressed. I've no doubt the insides are just as impressive."

"Now talking of beauties, who may this young lady be?" he nods at Amelia, taking her free hand as she smiles.

"Forgive me. Amelia, this is Derek the man behind the bricks and mortar, Derek this is Amelia, part of The Grand management."

"Pleasure to meet you Derek. If you'll excuse me, I need to see, Megan." She hurries over, collecting a glass of champagne off the drinks stand and heads toward Megan and Andrew while I finish my greetings before making our way inside.

I was like a kid at Christmas, wanting to view each room at the same time before running back to start all over again. The rooms where vibrant, crisp and airy. Marble counters, large dining tables, en-suites and king-size beds. Andrew and I looked around together discussing the layout of the rooms as the girls chatted in excitement where they would put things if they lived here. Squealing and giggling when entering each room and testing out the furniture of the apartments that were already furnished.

"Oh now this is what I call a bed. Say Andrew, why don't you uh, come lay down check out the mattress with me?" Megan grins, laid on her side patting the covers and winking at Andrew. He cuts her a look, shakes his head and mutters under his breath as he heads out the room, leaving the three of us laughing.

"Megan, you're crazy."

"Just you wait, Marcus, I'll get him hard one of these days."

"Well good luck with that, reckon the poor bastard's forgot what a hard on feels like it's been that long."

"I'm just waiting for the right moment." She stretches herself on the bed before standing. "Talking of the right moment, I do believe it's almost six and you know what that means ginger?"

"Tequila time!" They both say in unison leaving me grinning.

"Come on let's go."

My cheek hurts through smiling as Megan does her all-important barefoot dancing on the table at Rubies, glass in her hand as she sings full pelt from the top of her lungs. She really is a joy to be around and she oozed attention in a none needful way. Frantic fun and laughter was all her and whichever man held onto her at the end of the night was a lucky bastard. She is without doubt a sexy woman and just as clueless as the red beauty sat across from me.

"Is she always this lively and full on?" Andrew inquires, tipping his head toward Amelia as he watches Megan through disapproval eyes.

"She's a firecracker. You see how good it is to see other people's personalities as oppose to just your own, Andrew." She grins, pinching the dark scruff of his jaw.

"Told you dickwad." I chuckle.

"God bless her parents for creating such a remarkable rebel," Amelia giggles. "I love that girl."

"She seems a handful that's all." He shot back.

"Why don't you take her on, you know you like a challenge." I cock a brow raising my beer towards him with an amused grin.

"Fuck that, she seems too much like hard work. I like graft not a death wish."

Amelia gasps at him, throwing back her Tequila and stands. "You know, Megan is right. You really can be an asshole at times."

I laugh as Amelia joins Megan on the dance floor, bring her down from the table to grind against each other like two tequila dolls as the music blasted out the speakers.

Throwing back their heads in hysteria as they twirl around in a dizzy spell.

The best thing about owning a club but not running it was that you could slip behind the bar and help yourself without anyone questioning your invasion. Only on nights out with others I stayed their side of the counter and waited for Jack to serve as singling myself from them was never an option. I was one of them regardless of my wealth.

"She's a lucky bitch you know. Having someone to snuggle up to on a night and worships the ground she walks on. I wish I had that." Megan says approaching the bar. Her eyes seem a little hurt and empty. This was a side to Megan I'd not seen before. She was always the life of the party but as she props herself on the stool a small vulnerable girl is staring back at me though Tequila filled eyes. I wrap my arm around her, placing a kiss on the top of her head.

"You'll find someone when you least expect it and he'll treat you like a princess and love you unconditionally."

"Jeez, since when did you become soft in the head?"

"A few weeks ago." I grin.

"Well if it's true he needs to hurry the fuck up as I'm getting tired of waiting."

"Megan, are you ok?" Amelia questions joining us.

"Yeah, I'm just trying to hit on your man here but he's having none of it. Seems someone beat me to it. Rude of her don't you think?"

"Very," she grins. "Come on my feet don't hurt yet which means I'm not finished dancing."

The club was packet with bodies and women in little clothing. The buzz swelled in my chest at just how popular this place had become in the last few years. This was what I wanted, and loved that I'd finally achieved it.

Returning to replenish their thirst the girls sat as me and Andrew continued our debate over the Lenton wedding, a conversation I didn't want to discuss to begin with but he never dropped.

"I'm visiting Gran that weekend so I won't see this fabulous dress of hers." Megan says taking her drink.

"Oh I'm sure it will be better than royalty, with the amount she's paying out."

"Marcus, was just saying he's looking forward to the shit ass pay-check he's going to get, so he can buy a new mansion." Andrew said to the girls. I shot him a look knowing full well that is not what I'm wanting from her at all. She can use some other hotel facility for all I care. I can't stand the woman.

"I'm hoping someone attends the wedding and will finally remove that stick from your ass." I joke as the girls giggle.

"Fuck you. I can't wait to get some peace once you fuck off back to London in a few weeks." He blurts, instantly killing my mood. My eyes flicked on Amelia as the table fell silent, her eyes were hidden as she plays with the hem of her dress. She heard him loud and clear, the anger beginning to rise in my chest.

"I-I'm just popping to the ladies," she mutters getting up in a hurry, followed by Megan.

"Nice one ass-wipe!" I shot at him.

"What did I say? You always go back after the summer."

"I know."

"So what's the problem?" he jabs.

"The problem is a redhead I don't want to leave!" I scrape my chair back and head to the bar. Rubbing my face in frustration I order another drink trying to figure out what the fuck is going on with my insides, and work out what the hell I'm going to do. Truth is I don't know what will happen. Any other year I'd be here for the summer then head back to the city for the winter. But this isn't like any other summer for me. And she's not like any other woman. I just need to time work things out.

She was quiet the rest of the night and I've been dying to talk to her. But as I strip my clothes and join her in the shower all sense of talking is washed down the drain as I'm engulfed by her sexiness. I wrap my arms around her waist, kissing her neck as she falls into me, my dick hard against her ass as I rub my thumb over her perked nipples. "You're so fucking sexy, Amelia." I murmur. "I'll never get enough of you."

"Marcus, I need to ask you something about earlier."

"Shh, not now baby."

She moans as my hand moves lower, her body slowly melting by the second. "Marcus, please?"

"Shh."

I spin her round, taking the pin from her hair so the water pastes her red locks down her back, slipping my tongue into her mouth to connect with her softness as I explore her taste. Her hands wrap around my hard length. I groan into her mouth as she squeezes, running her hands along my shaft, stroking and pumping, bringing me to the point of near on explosion. I don't want to cum this way, I want to be inside her. Moving her hands to my neck, I lift her, turning her back to the shower wall and I sliding deep inside. "Thank you for supporting me at the new builds today, we make a good team me and you."

"Best make the most of it then before you go." She

breathes.

A twist of something I don't recognise hit my gut. I'm unable to read her eyes. They look lost, sad, maybe even angry, or that could just be me seeing my own reflection in her cornflower blues.

"Let's not think about right now, baby."

I take her mouth in a long controlled kiss, giving her everything I had. I'm yet to fuck her but just being inside her and feeling her around me is enough to nearly come. The words I said to Megan earlier come flooding back. Maybe Amelia is *my* unexpected. Maybe I was meant to have last summer off for a bigger reason than what I thought it was for, and maybe she is the one I needed to be found by.

Chapter Eighteen

Marcus

The hotel this week was swarmed with people and today was no different. Holiday makers, staff and large business meetings in the conference rooms took over the grounds along with the humidity of the summer heat that drained your body with every hour. Amelia herself was bogged down with preparations for this weekend's big birthday party in the function room and I've hardly had chance to see her all day. We've not spoke of my return to the city since the other night at Rubies and I can't work out if it's bothering me that we haven't discussed it, or if it's bothering me more that she not asked any more of it.

"Fuck that was insane, same time tomorrow?" I exhale with a chuckle. Amelia lifts herself to stand as I zip up my fly. As soon as she entered my office I didn't hesitate in taking full advantage of her body, pushing up her dress and getting her to ride me.

"You know a few months ago I wasn't even thinking of sex let alone having it in your office… with you. You're a bad influence Mr Matthews."

"Well, if you think this kind of behaviour needs addressing Miss Weston, there's always the staff complaints form to fill out." I tease.

"Oh I'm not complaining. I like this naughty school girl thing of waiting to be caught by the head teacher." she giggles correcting her dress and coming to sit on my lap. Sex with her was the best I'd had with any woman; her confidence soared each and every time.

"Isn't that part of the fun?" I kiss her hair.

"Well yeah, but can you imagine if someone ha-"

"Hey, man do you fancy a-" Andrew enters my office and halts. "Oh sorry."

"Andrew. Door. Knock. Wait." Amelia says sarcastically with a chuckle. I can't help but grin, if he'd of been any earlier a live porn movie would be playing.

"I'm sorry sweet pea; I just wanted to ask Marcus, if he wanted to go for a late surf?"

Amelia sits up on my lap. "Wait a minute, two nights out in a week? Shit, Marcus, I've come over all faint." My laugh vibrates through me as she holds the back of her hand to her forehead lying against me mocking him.

"Can I please have the old Weston back, she was a lot quieter and less sarcastic. Do you want a surf or not?"

I didn't have chance to answer before Amelia jumped in an arranged my night with a guy that choose to speak when he wanted and doesn't even know the meaning of a good time if it smacked him in the face. "Yes, Marcus would love to hit the waves with you, Andrew."

I raise my brow as an amused look hits Andrews face. "Doesn't look like you have a choice man. Meet you in a bit," he heads to the door. "And open some windows, it smells like sweaty sex in here."

Amelia cheeks flush with a grin, when she glances back at me her grin disappears as my look to her is straight. "Don't look at me like that; Marcus the guy needs to get out more. Besides I want nothing more than a long soak and an early night. Go find him a woman."

"Yeah right, finding him a woman won't be a problem, getting her to stay with his moody ass is the issue. I'd rather have more playtime with this beautiful body of yours and all the naughty things I want to do to it." I kiss the sensitive spot just behind her ear, but her voice doesn't falter and she hops off my lap.

"You can do that after you've had some male bonding. Now I'm going to your place to get all wet and naked with a bath of bubbles." She wiggles her ass and swiftly moves before I can get her. "Have fun with Mr Dark and Mysterious."

***

Rixtons bay was the longest beach in Spring Rose, carpeted in golden soft sand and had a reputation for top quality waves. Rolling in around 15ft most days. Andrew and I paddled out to take our spot on the water as adrenaline rushed through my body. This was one of the things I loved about being home. Wasting time but in the best way possible. The rips and curls of a controlled board felt like you were gliding the air as you rode the wave, skimming along like a king before it got the better of you and took a nosedive.

After cruising many waves we head up the beach, taking five minutes out as the evening sun glows straight ahead. "So things are good with you and Amelia? I've noticed a change in her recently. It'srefreshing to see her so happy." He states dropping down to the sand.

"I know, and we're good. Has she ever mentioned her reasons for moving to the coast?" I knew if anyone other than Megan would know it would be Andrew with working so closely together.

"I probably know as much as you. When she first came here it was evident she was a broken woman. I often heard her crying in her office but I never asked and she never told. She threw herself into work and eventually settled." He had this look of concealment in his eyes, I've none Andrew long enough to know when he's hiding something, but there was obviously good reason. I knew he wouldn't divulge something that wasn't for him to say.

He's many things but underneath his hard ass attitude there was a soft side to him, only you have to look real close to see. I, on the other hand, wore my heart on my fucking sleeve which often resulted in getting me into some form of trouble when it came to woman.

"She's blown my mind Andrew. Like no other has. I hate when I'm not near her and when I am I can't get enough. I've got no idea what to do."

A deep chuckle rumbles from him and I can't help but smirk, it's not often you hear Andrew laugh. "You've been pussy whipped by a mane of red. She a rare one, look after her."

"I'll do my best. Anyway enough of my shit how's

things with you, and I don't mean work."

He sighs, looking towards the water. "I'm ok. Each day gets better but it is what it is, I can't do shit about it." We've both been thrown some shit over the years where women are concerned, him coming off worse than my crap with Sadie. People think he's an ass and has no concept of fun. It's not like that at all; it's just his way of getting through his own wars of his past and keeping them from others to deal with them better.

Ending the conversation I knew wouldn't go any further he stands. "Ready to go again?"

"Shit me, another round? You feeling alright?"

"Fuck off ya little prick." he chuckles, jogging back out to the water.

***

Cheese burgers and a beer finished our male bonding, and eventually I drag Andrew's ass off the beach just after sunset. All I wanted to do was curl up into the arms of an angel that's filling the air with her vanilla and honeysuckle presences.

She's sleeping when I get home, the bed covers drape over her lower body as she lays wearing one of my t-shirts I loved to see her in. Placing a kiss on her head I go and take a shower washing off the ocean and glittering sand before heading to bed.

"NO!" I was halfway through drying when I heard her bloodcurdling cry. Never in my life have I ever been so horrified of the sight before me. In the depths of sleep Amelia's head shock against the pillow, body rigid as her chest heaved harshly, yelling out cry's to stop.

"Amelia, wake up."

My call did nothing to stop her thrashing. She digs her nails at her neck, gasping for breath. Legs kick out, moving her body up the mattress in distress and showing no signs of coming out the nightmare she's in. She lunges, slapping and punching hard at my chest, screaming through haunted cries. "LET ME GO!"

"Amelia, stop!"

Shouting her name over and over I shake her shoulders firmly, fighting against her blows. Her bloodshot eyes pop open standing out against her ghostly sweaty skin. "Sweetheart?" I murmur, my own body riddled with fear as I stroke her hair. Heavy eyes blink a few times, the sweat trickles down her neck and her chest swells with each hoarse breath she takes. "Baby, it's me."

"Marcus?" Her fearsome voice cracks as her eyes scan the surroundings of the bedroom.

"Shh it'sok, I got you." Cradling her in my arms, I rock her trembling body as she sobs uncontrollably in the crook of my neck.

"I'm safe." She cries.

"Yes baby, you're safe. It'sjust us." Holding her tight as I stroke her hair. I feel sick to the stomach. I never fucking want me or her to go through this gut wrenching ordeal again. "I've got you, baby."

Unsure how to console her I run us both a bath while she laid staring into space, the life that sparkled in her eyes just hours earlier had died. Carrying her to the bathroom I remove the shirt from her sweaty body. Never once did she look or speak, just drifted into the world of darkness. I wash her hair in silence as she sat hugging her knees. I hated this, I felt completely lost and vulnerable myself. I had no idea what to say. My own mind was racing. People have nightmares, but that was something from the underworld.

Placing a kiss on her shoulder I guided her back to rest against me, entwining our hands and wrapping my arms around her. I can't recall how long we stayed silent before she softly spoke.

"They come from nowhere. My nightmares that replay what he did as if it were still real. As if it's happening all over again and I'm not asleep. I hear his words, I smell his scent and I feel every hit, every cut and every scream that left my throat when I begged him to stop." I close my eye as she takes my hand, holding my fingers to the scar on her chin.

"This was the first one Daniel gave me. He hit me and I fell against the coffee table. He was so apologetic and took care of me for days after. He was all I had and I stupidly forgave him because I needed him." She moves my hand to her collarbone. "This was his razor. I didn't iron his work shirt correctly so I faced the consequences."

My chest burned as anger rippled through me. I wanted her to stop. I needed her to stop, but I knew I had to listen.

We moved to her ribs. "This was boiling water. The blisters lasted weeks. By that point he didn't need an excuse. I just had to look at him wrong and he'd hit me, threaten me, do anything to see me suffer, he thrived on seeing me in pain." Silence fell between us as I tried to comprehend everything that was running in my head. Nobody deserves to go through such torture from the hands of a vile unlivable piece of fucking filth. I'd kill him with my own bare hands.

But there was one set of scars she never spoke of and they were the ones I needed to know. "And the ones on you back?" I asked just above a whisper with a clenched jaw.

"We were having dinner and he was fed up of my saddened mood and lack of communication. In his rage he swiped everything from the table, glasses and porcelain smashed everywhere as I sat trembling and waiting to be punished." Her voice broke into a shaky cry. "He grabbed me by the hair and kicked me to the floor. I screamed through the sheer pain of the broken glass and crockery that scored my body as he fucked me in anger. My back was on fire, while my body become a disgusting shade of colours. With each scream he hit harder.

"I couldn't find a way out. I never spoke of it to anyone as I was too scared to. Megan found me. Daniel had stormed out after, no doubt to drink the profits of bars. Disappearing off the radar the police eventually closed the case. I spent two weeks in hospital and I cried like a baby when I stood before Lucas in my underwear. I was so afraid, Marcus, nobody knows what it's like."

I swallow back my emotion and cup Amelia's jaw, tilting her head to look at me. Sadness and pain coating her face. "I wish I could take all that pain that consumes you. Wash away all the darkness of your past and set you free. You're incredibly brave and unbelievably strong. I will never do anything to hurt you, Amelia. Don't ever think you have to hide yourself when around me. That you can't say what you feel, because you can. I need and want you to feel safe with me."

"I do feel safe with you, Marcus, and it's that that scares me. I've never had any of what you have provided for me. I never had anything with him like I have with you, and whatever this is between us I don't want to screw it up."

I was already beginning to realise what it was between us. What I want it to be. She's still incredibly fragile and we both have more mountains to climb, but finally she's opened up, this means more than anything right now. This girl is by far more stronger than what she gives herself credit for, she just has to believe. I place a soft kiss on her lips as I stroke her cheek. The lukewarm water causes her skin to shiver as she looks up with teary eyes. "For years I lived in hell. With you, every day is heaven. Thank you for making me feel safe."

Chapter Nineteen

Amelia

"So you said you suffered a nightmare, tell me what happened." Dr Thomas says softly over her black framed glasses. After the other night-and the new feelings that's been running my head since Marcus come on the scene-I thought it best to talk to her before it magnified out of control. I've hardly spoke to anyone since it happened. Just floated around in my own little fuckup zone as the feeling of drowning in unsheltered water hadn't left me since the carnage of the nightmare. I've not had one that bad in over a year and it scares the hell out of me as to why I'm having them now.

"He held me down by the throat like he always did when he wanted sex. My hands weren't tied but I couldn't move them. I couldn't see. Everything was dark. Then he started taunting me and hitting me, screaming right up in my face. I can still hear my bones snapping like twigs with each blow." My voice is thick in my throat. The waterfall of tears flow from reliving the night terror out aloud. "Then I could see him. I could smell him and hear him shouting at me as he hit me over and over. But it wasn't him. It was Marcus. All I saw was Marcus. Then I woke."

Dr Thomas did her usual jotting of notes as she hands me a tissue. Her work with me since arriving at the coast has been phenomenal. After intense therapy sessions in London with Dr Ahern, she has provided me with the help and support in order to continue moving forward.

"And when you woke, what happened then?"

"I realised it wasn't real. Marcus held me close, told me I was safe. He looked terrified." I can only imagine what went through his head. In the past I've scared the shit out of Megan and Lucas but they knew of my history and was aware things like this happened. With Marcus he knew very little. My body was heavy with sweat and from the marks on his chest I knew I lashed out. I never meant to hurt him.

"Did you feel safe?"

"Yes. I always feel safe with Marcus. That's what I can't get my head round. His ability to make me trust him is something I've never experienced before and that scares me because I'm not afraid of him. But I'm terrified of falling into a world where it will all come crashing down around me and because I trust him I won't see the signs."

"Have you spoken to Marcus about your history and how you feel?" I nod as I soak more tears into the tissue. How could I not tell him, I said I would tell him everything when I was ready, I knew then I had to bare all and let him in regardless if I was ready or not. But as for telling him how I feel in the present isn't an option. Because I don't know how I feel. My feelings for him grow more each time we're together and that is something I can't even begin to process.

"He's been so patient with me. I just hope that this time things can be different."

Dr Thomas removes her glasses and moves forward in her high back leather chair. A sure sign I knew the straight talking was on the cards and no medical crap I didn't understand. "Your nightmares indicate a separation between your heart and mind. It's a literal disconnection of how you feel and what you think. A feeling of confliction. Fighting a war to stay in control and not let the fear of what happened take over. But what you have to try and remember Amelia, is that no two men stood side by side are the same. I think you know this deep down because of your ability in trusting him. You just have to learn to believe it. Believe in yourself and you're halfway there."

The roar of the waves crash against the rocks, the breeze cleansing my pores as the summer sun soaks into my muscles, healing my soul from all around me. Dr. Thomas helped put my mind at ease and provide positivity of present day, and there was only one person that was overflowing my thoughts with the present. Life has changed in a way I never imagined. I never saw myself ever being able to fit into this position again. That night was a mixture of dark, dangerous and devotion. After the onslaught of reliving my past through terrifying actions and painful words, Marcus caressed, cherished and worshipped my body with delicate hands and kisses as he drove me into a world of unconditional tenderness. Holding me close and protecting me throughout the night. There was nothing more I had left to give him; I laid out my history on a platter and every ounce of life as I knew it, was firmly in his hands.

He makes me feel like I'm flying. His arms are my safety mechanism and each day that I'm with him another piece of the broken girl is fixed back together. However, there was one thing that sat at the back of my mind and was the one thing I tried my hardest not the think about, because I knew it would crush me. But each day that past I thought of it more and I knew I'd have to voice my concerns, however this was the one question I was afraid of asking. In just a matter of a few weeks this year's season would be over, and the man that leaves me breathless and protected me like a falling angel would be leaving the coast and heading back to the city.

"I was wondering where you got to. I got worried when Megan said you needed some time out." He comes to sit behind me, enveloping my body with his as he wrapped his arms around me.

"I needed to think."

He said nothing, just rested his chin on my head, knowing that he was giving me the time I needed in order to talk when I was ready. His patience with me always blew my mind, never once did he pressurise me to talk; he just provided the reassurance I needed and listened when I was ready.

"I hate it. I hate after all this time he still has control over me. My moods. My thoughts. My sleep." He lifts my chin so I can see his warm hazels. The features of his beautiful face never fail to take my breath.

"But he doesn't. You have control. You've moved on, took huge steps and built a new life. You control that babe not him. It's just unfortunate we can't control our bad dreams."

Finally telling Marcus everything had lifted a heavy weight I didn't know I was still carrying. It's like the feeling you get in water where you're dragged down to the bottom fighting before being released to slowly float back to the surface. Back to the light.

"I saw Dr Thomas this morning. We talked about the last few weeks and I told her about my nightmare. She helped put some things into perspective. I'm sorry if I freaked you out."

"You did. But I'm just glad you told me. You can always talk to me Amelia, you know that right?"

Marcus has transformed my life over the weeks, he's managed to knock down walls I built and lived behind for years. Brushed away the thick dust from my heart so I've been able to open up to him. I've never felt so at ease and fearless with laying my heart, soul and history in someone else's hands. Revealing my demons and baring my body. "I know." I whisper, turning back to look at the shore as we sit in each other's embrace.

"Although I am a little disappointed in you," he says shortly after. An unpleasant feeling curls in my belly as I tilt my head back narrowing my brows. "Why didn't you tell me it's your birthday on Saturday?"

"You mean you've invaded my space all these weeks and you didn't know? Some stalker you are." I tease, but his expression was serious. "Ugh, I'm not a lover of birthdays anymore so the less people know about it the better. How'd you find out anyway?"

He gave me a knowing looking and Megan's face appeared in my mind causing me to roll my eyes. "She told me earlier when I ask where you were."

"I just want a few drinks like we normally do, nothing special. Besides the Kingston balls the night before so that is my treat." I never really had a birthday since my mum died. Dad never remembered afterward and Daniel never gave a shit. Then I was never in the right frame of mind to even think about celebrating so movie nights and drinks where what each year was spent like with Megan and Lucas curled up on the sofa eating pretzels and drinking tequila.

"You up for a day trip?"

I smile at his childlike ways. He must be the only owner of a seven star hotel that lets one of his staff take day trips during their working week and still get a full wage. I gave up arguing about it with him after we went to Primrose Lodge as I was near on fireman lifted out the building. "Does Andrew know we skulk off on day's trips like we do when I should be working?"

"Fuck no; he thinks you're helping me on interior work on a new project back home." My head tipped back with a giggle as Marcus pulls me up.

"So this day trip, what part of our youth are we reliving this time?" I ask taking his hand.

"Where not. I'm taking you somewhere special."

***

My ability to breathe had been stolen. I've been at the coast over eighteen months and seen most of the bays but this one was nothing like I ever imagined being here. Closed off from the world Marbles Cove was a small bay of pure white soft sand and turquoise blue sea rolling in onto a thick band of colourful shells. It was like undiscovered territory and only we would ever know it existed.

"We've been here nearly two hours and no one has stepped foot on the beach. Just how private is it?" I ask, backing into the water and rubbing the rest of my sun lotion in while Marcus annoyingly takes pictures of me with his camera phone. The sun scorches down on his shirtless body causing small beads of perspiration on his abs that looked ever so inviting to the tongue.

"Very private. So you can take off your dress now, I want to see that bikini of yours." I shake my head biting my lip and continue heading back into the water. My Maxi-dress now clinging to my thighs like a second skin.

"Very private as in?"

"As in I can guarantee that no one other than us will ever be on this beach." He said with a wicked grin.

Reality slaps me in the face. "Holy shit! Are you telling me you own this beach?"

"Sorry, forgot to mention that when you grilled me in your office a while back," he chuckles. "Now take off that damn dress it's forbidden to the public so you don't need to worry."

"Fuck me are you god or something? Next you'll be saying you own a boat and sail around topless."

"Now there's an idea. Take. Of. The. Dress."

"Nope, sorry not today." I say on a sigh.

"Right that's it." He throws his phone down on the towel and strides into the water. I screech trying my best to fight the tide in escape but I get lifted in seconds and thrown deep under the water as waves crash over my head.

"You asshole!" I gasp on a chuckle; Marcus curled over in fits of laughter at my drenched state. I splash water at him only for him to return it and start a full blown water war. Of course my small hands compared to his large shovels were not in any form going to help my victory of winning. He'd already won by dunking me to start with. I make my way back toward the shore as the sand below began to get unpredictable for my footing.

"Giving in already?" he shouts.

"Nope. You may see me struggle, but you'll never see me quit." To my own revelation I lift my wet dress over my head and throw it back toward the rest of our clothes, along with my bikini top. Looking back at Marcus with my arms out wide showing him with action that my body was on full show and only for him. "Ta-Da."

His expression went from a wide smile to serious in a matter of seconds and a feeling of dread ran over my body. I stood as firmly as I could on the wet sand that swallowed my toes as he waded through the water, never taking our eyes from each other. My uncomfortable feeling instantly turning to heat the nearer he got. The lust in his eyes turned them to liquid which exploded fireworks inside me and soared once his mouth crashed to mine. Taking the back of my head in his hand to keep me in place as our tongues run wild, making my knees weaken the more he stole my breath.

Guiding me down, our bodies lay on the shore, waves crashing just below our feet and rolling in around us. Long, deep but evenly slow strokes of his tongue played with mine, drinking in the taste of each other and the salted ocean. He was hard against me and I incredibly turned on, but neither of us needed more than what we had right here, right now. It was a kiss of connection. A kiss of acceptance. A kiss that confirmed and ignited a feeling that had been smouldering inside me for some time.

Chapter Twenty

Marcus

"Tell me something true?" Amelia coos, slouched on the balcony chair as we have breakfast. Her hair is up in a messy bun, face make-up free as my shirt she wears drapes off her shoulder. Even with her laziness she's sexy.

"I'm buying a boat tomorrow."

"Is that so?" she chuckles.

"Yep, you can help pick which one you want to see me shirtless on while we sail around the coast. Your turn." I pour us coffee as Amelia continues to pick at her bagel rather than eat it, a sign that something is bothering her.

"I'm hitting the beach after work with Megan to watch the sunset; you can come if you like?"

"Sounds great. Now tell me what's on your mind, you're not eating." She flashes her eyes at me before rolling them with a heavy sigh and pushing, plate away.

"I'm stressing."

"About what?"

"I'm stressing about stressing, then I'm stressing because I'm stressing." Getting up from her seat she starts pacing. My shirt just covering the cheeks of her ass as her pink panties peep once and again with the breeze. "These next two weeks are a big deal, Marcus. And when you're easily anxious like I am the stress doubles. It's the Ball on Friday and I'm nervous, I don't even know how to dance ballroom style, my birthday's on Saturday not that that's of any importance. Then at some point next week your mother is coming, what if she hates me or thinks I'm some gold-digger. And I've got so much to do for the following week with this fucking wedding, Nadia has me constantly on speed dial and I feel like my head is on overdrive, I. Am. Stressing."

She's adorable when she's flustered but ever since her nightmare she's been more unsettled. I leave the table and got to her, massaging her tense shoulders as we look over the bay.

"We just dance at the ball, no fancy shit. Your birthday is important. My mother will not think you're after my money purely because you hate it when I buy you things and as for the Lenton wedding there are enough people to help out-"

"And if it doesn't go to plan? There's a lot riding on this."

"It will. Just have faith babe."

She sighs and leans into me. "You have this excellent way of keeping me grounded, Mr Matthews. You're like my personal relaxation tape."

"I'll take that as a compliment?"

"And so you should," she turns in my arms. "When it stops I stress until it plays again."

She plants a quick kiss on my lips and moves from my arms looking less hassled then she did five minutes ago. "I'm going for a run, I need to try and clear my head. See you at work, I'm not in till ten."

"Oi Weston." I grab an uncut bagel from the table and toss it towards her for her to catch. "Eat. Then run."

"Yeah. Yeah." Waving me off.

"I mean it, Amelia, you need to eat."

"Ooo so demanding." She blows me a kiss before taking a bite. "Laters big guy."

***

I was scrolling the internet looking at possible options for Amelia's birthday present when my ears perked up at the sound coming from the hall. It's not Amelia as she's currently singing from the top of her lungs in the shower. Closing down the web and head to the disturbance when brown eyes catch sight of mine.

"Mum! You're early." Wrapping my arms around her.

"You expect me to stay in London with dirty air and traffic when I can have sun and sand on the holiday weekend? I don't think so." She snorts wheeling her case into the kitchen and removing her heels. "Besides I wanted to see these apartments of yours while they're still empty. I might take one up as a holiday home," she turns quickly. "They are still empty aren't they?"

"They are yes." I round the island to make us coffee, still surprised of her arrival. "I have a few viewings in the week but other than that they are free to view."

"Good. So what have I missed? How's Andrew, I've not spoke with him recently, is there a lady in his life?"

"No. He's still in a relationship with his office. But he's doing well."

"Hmm he's been through a lot. Relationship aren't always rosy." She sips her coffee, swallowing it down with a hum like most people do with their first drink after a journey to a destination. "Talking of relationships, how's things with Amelia? I can't wait to meet her."

"We're good, she just finished getting changed." I said as I hear her pad down the hall. Mum turns to look in the same direction.

"Marcus, have you seen my-" stood in a crimson bra and black hot pants Amelia halts in the doorway at the sight of my mother. Her cheek matching the colour of her bra as she quickly covers tits and waist with her arms. "I-I'm sorry I didn't know you had company. I'll just go grab so clothes."

"Oh nonsense dear don't worry about that, I take it you're the lovely Amelia?" Mum beams.

"Baby I'd like you to meet my mum. She's early."

Mum makes her way over taking her in her arms for a hug; Amelia clearly unsure what to do as her cheeks flush even more as she bites that god damn lip.

"Don't be embarrassed sweetie, a little red lace on our first meeting doesn't bother me at all. I'm a woman of the world."

"Nice to meet you, Mrs Matthews," she says softly.

"Rosa, please. I haven't been a Mrs, since my prick of a husband got his end away with a woman full of Botox. But never mind that, you are absolutely beautiful. Those eyes are stunning." Amelia flicks her eyes to me and I wink, before her face suddenly clouds with panic.

"Mum wait!" It's too late, she's already seen Amelia's scars as she walks full circle round to check her out. Like she did with most of the woman I'd take home. I told mum of Amelia insecurities but I never mentioned what, and stupidly I was so wrapped up in looking at Amelia to even register she was uncovered. Her scars don't bother me at all. Only I forget they do her. Mum's eyes flash to mine as Amelia's stood trembling, face drained in colour. Striding over I wrap my arm around her and gave mum a look that stated not to ask.

"You're a gorgeous woman, Amelia. I see now why my boy won't stop talking of you." Mum says with honesty placing a kiss on her cheek. Amelia smiles, fisting the back of my shirt trying to gain control of her emotions. "Now, Marcus, forget the coffee and get the wine. Us ladies need to get to know each other and talk about you as a young boy. Thank god I left the family album back home." She chuckles, walking back into the kitchen and raiding the cupboards for glasses. Five minutes of being here her tired eyes have come to life and the stress of the city has vanished as she's make herself at home.

Amelia moves from my hold but I pull her back. "I'm sorry babe I didn't think."

"It's ok, least I don't have to worry about covering up. All I need to do now is show her my panty collection and we're all good," she smiles placing a kiss on my lips. "I'll just go get dressed."

You know that feeling of dread that runs through you when you first take your girlfriend to meet your parents, and you're unsure if they'd like each other? I have no worries.

Mum and Amelia have done nothing but talk and giggle at stupid woman stuff since the wine was opened. It's as if they've known each other for years and just catching up on a reunion. It was never like this when she first met Sadie, they hardly spoke and if they did it left an awkward atmosphere. But as I watch these two from across the living room I can't help the smile that's currently taken over my face.

"So, Amelia, Marcus said you're going to the Kingston Ball on Friday? Not that I'm jealous or anything. Have you got a dress yet?"

"I got it a few weeks back. I'm super nervous though. Keep having visions of falling down the stairs because I can't see my feet."

"You'll be fine. I love that they've still kept the tradition of entry, so magical. Would you let me do your hair? I use to love doing my daughters hair."

Amelia's eye glisten and I know exactly who she's thinking about at this moment. Every girl want's their mum to be around when parading around in a big posh dress with hair pieces and jewellery, regardless of the occasion. It'sa female thing. "I'd like that, Rosa, thank you."

"Babe, if we're meeting Megan we need to get going. She's text me twice asking if you've fallen off the earth."

Amelia looks at the phone, "Shit it's on silent. Rosa, do you want to come to the beach with us?"

"I'd love too."

One of the best scenes in Spring Rose was the view of the sunset down on Briston beach. Setting in the west of the coast the scorching summer sun never failed to provide a spectacular picture postcard of vivid colours as the silhouette of Briston pier ran along the skyline. The view from Amelia's front porch was good but nothing compared to down on the beach. Most evenings were spent walking along the sands with Amelia, eating chips from paper cones and talking about our plans. This evening was no different other than the company of Megan and Mum.

"Oh look, Marcus...there's a seagull. Shall I feed him some chips?" Amelia teased as she sat between my legs knowing of my phobia.

"Don't even think about it. You know I don't li-"

She did. I immediately felt my body tense. "Amelia, what the fuck?"

"Hang on a minute, you spend nearly half the year at the coast and you have a fear of seabirds?" Megan questions, lifting her shades up to look at me with the naked eye. The gull scuttled its way towards where Amelia had thrown her chip, the cold sweat begin to run through my veins and I swear it's eyes were only focused on me.

"He use to run from them screaming as a kid. A few times he wet his pants."

"Mum!" The three women around me fell into fits of laughter and I suddenly felt outnumbered by their torment. Where the fucks Andrew when I need him?

"Ah babe I'm sorry, but you do look kinda cute when you're scared." Amelia smiles, running her finger down my cheek before getting up to dust off her ass. Pulling her hair back into a sexy messy bun she taps Megan on the ass with her foot. "Come on I want to go down to the water. Sunset isn't for another hour so these two beauties can catch up."

They race each other to the water squealing and shrieking as they go causing heads to turn and a smile to plaster my face. I love seeing her like this.

"You were right when you said she was pretty. I like

her." Mum says knowing her mind is running with questions. "Marcus, what happened to her?"

"She was in a violent relationship," I sigh, thinking back to the night of her admission. "She's restless at times, anxious and often has nightmares that scare me shitless. She looked so lost when I found her. I had this instant feeling come over me that I knew she was different, special. I just wanted to protect her."

"What about her parents are they around?" she takes her eye from Amelia and Megan and looks back at me.

"Her mum died years ago and her dad couldn't cope with their similarities so shut her off. That's when she found the fucker that done that to her."

"Grieving and looking to be loved. She must have been so alone."

I rest my arms on my knees as I watch Amelia and Megan doing cartwheel along the shore, both in fits of laughter as the waves catch Megan unexpectedly. My hearts smiling at the pair of them together and the happiness that radiates around Amelia, wondering if she will still be this content if I left her behind. My gut twists at the thought. "I never expected this. I come back here for two things, little work and a lot of surf. Amelia's stole that from me but in the best way. I've done more work than I've surfed because I spend work days with her. I'm at the beach with her. And I know if I go back my ability to focus on the job won't be to the standard I'd like because there'll be something missing."

"So what are you saying?"

"I can't leave her mum, not now that I've found her. I've not felt like this before, not even with Sadie. I can't stand not being around her and I can never get her out my mind. I'm too far in to let her go."

She places her hand on my arm, a soft smile graces her lips. "Then you know what you need to do. Only you can make that decision, Marcus, and whatever you decided I'll be with you every step of the way." I knew mum would be with me on whatever I decide. However Amelia only gives away so much and I'm still breaking down her walls. It's a risk but my only hope is that the red headed beauty that's stole my heart would consider handing me hers.

Chapter Twenty-One

Amelia

"No, Marcus, we can't." I whisper high-pitched as I slap his hand.

"Why not?"

"Because your mother is in the next room."

"But I'm hard."

"Well go have a shower and rub down or something." His low laugh tickles my skin as he kissed his way further down my body, trying to make me give into my weakness for his firm body so his morning glory could be petted.

"You look incredibly sexy this morning, Amelia, did I tell you that?" he questions with a kiss.

"You did."

"And did I tell you do crazy things to me when you're within my presents and I think about fucking you every minute."

"You did." I say on a sigh as he reaches my navel. My pussy is aching for him right now but I'm not giving in. I place my hands around his biceps to pull him back so I can see his eyes, taking his cheeks in one hand so his mouth is squashed. "And did I tell you that your mother is next door and sex is off limits till we're back at mine?"

"Not even just a little bit?" he said through his crushed cheeks, a disappointed look on his face.

"Nope, not even a little bit."

"Ugh." He collapsed on the other side of the bed giving me the opportunity to escape from the covers. Today was the day of the ball and I was super excited as well as having the odd wave of nervous grant my belly, it would be the first big event were Megan wouldn't be at arm's reach if I needed her.

"Morning sweetie, can you believe people go to the extreme of making themselves look younger but end up like this?" Rosa was sat at the breakfast bar looking over the morning paper, turning it she shows a person that appears to be a woman with her lips fuller than a rugby player with a gum shield.

"Eww nasty. You want coffee?"

"I'm good thanks honey." I make my drink and sit on the bar stools beside her. "So what are we doing with these pretty locks today?" she says, running her hand through my hair. It's surreal how well we're getting on when she's only been here two days. It's like I've known her a lifetime.

"Well I was thinking of having it up, I bought a silver pin with beads and pearls to hold it with."

"Sounds lovely, when shall we get started?"

"Well I'm of for a run shortly so once I'm back. And

as soon as Marcus gets up."

"Great, I'll just go get sorted. We'll do your nails too." She finishes her coffee and places her cup in the sink. As she goes down the hall towards the bedrooms I hear her shout. "Marcus, you're no longer a teenager, get your lazy ass out of bed. I need to get preparation under way to make your girl look glamorous." Leaving me chuckling to myself in the kitchen.

Marcus hit the gym before heading to The Grand for a few hours and left us ladies in making me look the part for the activities ahead. Megan's painting my nails a soft pink as Rosa curls my hair before placing it up in the hairpiece. All I need now is for someone to give me a foot massage and do my make-up and I'll feel like a celebrity.

"I wish I could go with you. Why is it always management that goes to these things? A receptionist is just as important."

"I'm sure Marcus would happily let you come with us babe but sadly you can't dance on their tables." I tease.

"I danced on tables once in my younger days. That was the first and last time." Rosa chuckled.

"What happened?"

"I was trying to gain attention off this guy with my provocative dances moves when I misplaced my footing falling into a group below, not only was that bad enough, as I got up I stumbled forward and grabbed the legs of another guy to stop myself," she paused and reached for a hair pin. "I fell so hard I pulled his trousers down and we both stumbled to the ground, I fell face down onto his cock…He was commando underneath." Our giggles play out in the room as she relived the memory. "I was mortified and hide myself away for weeks."

"Well I've never managed to do that when out, even with half of Rubies bar inside me." Megan chuckled.

"Oh there's time yet, Megan." Rosa chuckled.

***

Kingston Hotel was like the inside of a history theatre. The height of each room was endless as thick archways held the carved cream and gold ceiling, flowing down to the wide marble staircase. The tradition of these events usually meant the women followed the men separately after their arrival and then reunited with each other at the top of the stairs before the evening started to take place. I couldn't do that and I knew that Marcus knew I couldn't do that as I'm freaking out already. He booked a double room with two en suites so we could dress separately without seeing each other but I'd know he was close.

"Just breathe and relax. I'll see you soon." He cupped my cheeks and kissed me before disappearing to the far end of the suite to change and leave ahead of me.

I applied my light grey eye shadow to each eye and blended it together with a silver shimmer, black eyeliner along the upper lids and a couple sweeps of mascara over my lashes. Finishing it off with a touch of blusher and a smack of the lips once applying my soft pink lip-gloss. Slipping into my lingerie I leave the bathroom chanting to myself I could do this, while my belly churned. Once I entered the bedroom my eyes caught sight a gorgeous wrist corsage of red roses and pearls laid on the table with a note.

To a beautiful woman with beautiful eyes. M Xx

The same words he used when I received the first bouquet of flowers from him all those weeks ago. A smile hit my lips at his affection. Putting on my long ball gown, I slip into my heels and finish off my evening wear with the corsage. Taking a deep breath and one final look in the mirror I leave to meet my prince.

I stand behind the red curtains waiting for our names to be called. Anything about tonight was classic, crisp and sophisticated. I felt like royalty waiting on the announcement of my entry to the central staircase of the ball floor. Nervous swamped my body as my ring twisted my finger. I was desperate to see Marcus and the fact he stood on the other side of the hall waiting behind his own curtain was torturous.

"Ladies and Gentleman, from the seven star of The Grand Hotel, Mr Marcus Matthews and Miss Amelia Weston."

This was it; I had no time to back out as our curtains pulled back in unison. My breath hitched as a man in a cream tux appeared before me. I saw his own breathing halt as desire hitting me like a rocket. With locked eyes we take our steps towards each other, stopping at the centre of the high staircase as the front of my body brushed against his. Neither of us spoke. We didn't need to, our eyes said it all.

Taking my hand with a gentle squeeze and a deep breath we face the glistening crowd and head down the stairs, applauds welcomed our arrival. This was way too surreal. Pearls, sequins and tuxedos lined the marbled floor, eyes follow our every pace and my cheeks hurt with the smile I couldn't hold back. Once at our table Marcus's arm rose creating a bridge for me to twirl under before I come to stand in front of him.

"Hi," he whispers against my lips, hazel eye full of awe and heat. "You look breathtakingly beautiful. Have we met before?"

"Hmm I'm not sure, you do seem familiar," I place a kiss on his lips and whisper. "Do you like my dress?"

"It matches your eyes."

"I thought you might say that." My floor length mermaid style dress made me feel sexier now that I was stood before him than it did in Tabitha's Trinkets. I close my eyes, breathing in the heavenly scent of him and the surroundings that engulf us, my belly now fluttering with excitement. "I feel like a princess."

"You look like a queen."

Once the introductions of business associates and CEO's were done the evening was followed by an Award ceremony, drinks and a dance. The Awards were in full swing and my ass was numb with too much sitting. One of The Grand's rivals from the next coast had just swooped two awards for the interior design of their new Restaurant and Bar Room. Not that Marcus was at all bothered; apparently even with their new interior it was still out dated to what it should be.

"And finally the Award for best overall Achievement and Accommodation goes to... The Grand Hotel of Spring Rose Bay."

"Oh my god, Marcus!" I clasp my hands together with excitement as applause fills the room. His eyes look like they're about to pop as the wideness of his smile brought tears to my eyes. Leaning forward and plant a kiss on his cheek. "You did it!" This was what he worked for and he's proven all his work has paid off.

Making his way to the stage he chucks with shock.

Shaking hands with the presenters he takes the deserved award and clears his throat as the room falls silent. "Thank you so much. I'd just like to say that I couldn't have done this without my team that work within The Grand, they deserve this more than I do." He paused to look at the glass award in his hand before flashing his eyes to find mine. I was overwhelmed with pride for him and my smile said it all. Marcus holds out his hand for me to go to him, nerves hit my belly at the thought of being in front of the crowed but I knew with him beside me I'd be ok. Lifting my dress I take the stairs and feel instant calm wash over me when I take his hand, before he continues.

"Spring Rose Bay, holds a special place in my heart, it's not just the surroundings, or the environment, but mostly the people. I've meet a lot over my time here but there's only a few that captured me from the moment I met them. I have every confidence that The Grand provides that same feeling when entering the building and a big part of that is to the team and this beautiful woman beside me. Without them, this wouldn't have been possible. Thank you." Applauses, cheers and camera flashes go off and I turn to the man that made all this possible.

"Congratulations, Mr Matthews."

"Thank you, Miss Weston." I kiss him on the lips as he pulls me closer. "I hated every part of that until you stood with me."

"I never had you down as the nervous type. And here I was thinking you were all strong muscle, possession and self-assurance." I tease.

"Yeah but-"

"Excuse me for interrupting, Mr Matthews. Peter Bradway, U.K's Hotel and Accommodation journalist, would it be possible for a photograph and a short interview?"

"Of course, ask away."

After the awards champagne and canapés were served and gave the opportunity for the guests to associate. Marcus proudly took his new trophy back to our room before the proceedings took place for the evening dance. Everything about this part was like Cinderella at the castle, ladies in stunning dresses swung their wide train round the floor as they rotate in circles whilst the men guided them by their hips and hand. I moulded into the closeness of Marcus as we danced, soaking up the magical atmosphere.

"Look around you Amelia, what do you see?" he murmurs.

"People enjoying themselves, I know I am."

He shakes his head. "Look again."

My eyes scan the large room where people sat at tables overlooking the dance floor. It wasn't until Marcus spun me around that I realised we were the only ones in the centre of the floor. My breath caught as eyes followed. "There watching us." I whisper.

"No, they're watching you. Don't you see what you do? You light up any room; you captivate every eye with your smile, eyes, and presents. You're a remarkable woman, Amelia Weston and all these people know it. I know it. You just have to believe it and learn to love yourself for who you are. You need to see what we all see."

His words brought a lump to my throat. I've never thought of myself in any other way other than an outsider, a broken girl who took the wrong path and hid away once things got tough. I've never saw what they saw, but with Marcus he makes everything different. New. Fresh. He's helped me realise that I don't have to hide away anymore. I wouldn't have done that if it wasn't for him.

"How did you find me when I never wanted to be found?" I murmur.

"They say that one day someone will walk into your life and make you realise why it never worked with anyone else. You will always hold a special place in my heart Amelia, I'll take that with me forever."

My stomach dropped with that one word 'take', I couldn't bring myself to think of what will happen when he leaves. Will I cope? Was this just a crash course to show me that no two men are the same or could there be more? Did I want more?

No. It can't be any more than what we have now, whatever feelings I may have for Marcus had to be buried as that is better for the both of us. I swallowed back the thick ball in my throat and said the words I'd been wanting to say for weeks, because if it wasn't for Marcus, I wouldn't be the Amelia I am today.

"I'm glad I was found by you."

Chapter Twenty-Two

Amelia

"I still can't believe you won." I smile as we enter our hotel room, placing my corsage on the table. The magical events of the evening were finished and the Summer Ball was over for another year with Directors and Business Partners ecstatic with their prizes.

"We won baby, you worked hard for this too." Marcus replies taking off his jacket and bow tie followed by his shoes-before heading to the mini bar. This was true, I do work my ass off at that place and more often than not take on things that aren't even in my job description, but I do it as it keeps me focused.

"It seem as though I've hardly work at all these last couple of months. Not since I was swept off my feet by some guy that drives me crazy." Shit, my champagne slip of the tongue was not what I should have said and not what he needed to hear. I escape his watchful eye to take off my heels and jewellery, trying to ignore the feeling that's burning a cavity inside me. I turn when I still feel his smouldering gaze, enjoying the fact his stare was full of yearning and nothing unpredictable. "What are you looking at?" I murmur.

"You." His voice lustful and raspy. "Does it make you uncomfortable?"

"Only in the best way." I focus on his panty-melting stare that's sending my body spiralling. Even in the dim-lit room I saw his eyes darken as they run full length of my body. The butterflies took flight in my belly with the way he was making me feel, the ache between my legs escalated and my heart was falling heavier for him. "Is this the part where we rip each other's clothes off and you fuck me hard?" I say, biting my lip with anticipation. He didn't answer at first, just focused on me with his inevitable gaze.

"No," he murmured, placing his glass down and slowly moving towards me. My breathing shallowed. Heart thumping harder in my chest with his proximity as he whispered a breath apart from my lips. "This is the part where I take off your dress very, very slow and I make love to you."

My breath caught. He can't use that word, this is not what this is between us, yet I couldn't stop the whimper that left my lips when his angel whispered kiss touched the side of my mouth. Closing my eyes as once again the powers of this man have engulfed my body paralysing me in a mind blowing way to only his touch.

"Will you let me Amelia?" he whispered. "Will you let me make love to you?" The thoughts in my head and my feelings I have for him where fighting a losing battle. The need to have him now was far greater at this moment than it had ever been in all the times we'd shared together, and I knew that whatever happens between us he would break me one way or another and my heart would yet again face its wreckage.

"Yes," I breathed.

This was all he needed to take hold of me in every way. His lips massaged mine as the tip of his tongue coaxed into my mouth with grace, making my insides somersault with yearning as his fingertips brush my jaw. The hairs on my neck stood tall when his other hand swept over my behind, pushing me closer into him so I could feel what my body does to him. His kiss made me weak, I wrap my arms around his neck to keep me from falling, lacing my fingers through his hair. Gliding his finger over my forehead he tuck the strands of hair behind my ear, trailing it down my neck and around my back until he finds the zip of my dress. Hazel eyes hold mine as he unfastens the chiffon material, it's unbearably slow and with each section of my back that's exposed to the air, my body burned like wildfire.

I stood powerless before him. He slides the fabric down my front, freeing my arms and letting it fall to the floor in a deep pool of blue. My heart is thumping, raising my chest into him as he circles his thumbs over my nipples through the thin layer of the gunmetal lace. My lips part and a moan escape as he played me.

"You're so beautiful, Amelia, you forever take my breath."

I don't answer as he removes my bra whilst kissing the weak spot on my neck, I'm afraid of what I'd say if I open my mouth. The need to feel his skin is too much to handle and just like my dress I repeat the tortured movements with my own fingers and take to the buttons of his shirt. Slipping it over his shoulders for the warmth of his body to hit mine. I kiss along his collarbone, down his chest as my hands span the width of his back before pressing my chest to his so I could feel him on me. His skin makes me breathe, makes me feel alive. I want to carve out a piece from him so I can hold it forever when he leaves.

Without words he lifts me and walks us to the bed, buried in the crook of his neck I breathe him in as his own heart beats rapidly between us. Once on the bed he gets the sleep mask that hangs over the bedpost. Anxiety floods through me. "Marcus."

"Shh, it's ok; I'm not going to hurt you. I want you to wear this so all you can focus on is our connection, what you feel when you're with me. What it feels like to be completely free from fear."

I glance up to meet his eyes and the trust is there shining back at me. I nod and take a breath as he places the mask over my eyes, shutting me off from his beauty body. The sweetest kiss brushed my lips, calming the wave of nerves that run my body. "Do you trust me?" he whispered.

"Yes,"

"I just want you to feel, baby."

Guiding me back he peppers my skin with kisses, my heart rate pick up as he descends. Every inch of my skin tingles with his touch, a tingle that marked me in the most dreamlike way, and when he shoves a pillow under my ass electricity shoots through my body, knowing exactly what's coming when he slides my panties down my legs. His lips press along the soft skin of my inner thigh, my whimpers get higher, breathing gets faster as I feel him so close to my sex.

"Oh, god!" He sweeps his tongue in one long stroke bottom to top, my fingers tug at his hair from his heavenly abuse, running his tongue in even strokes over and over as I cry out with the drug-craving sensation. My hips jolt, forcing him to place his palm on my lower belly to hold me down. I want to see him, I want to watch what he's doing to me but my blindness to him makes it feel even more erotic.

"Fuck, Marcus!" My core burns with the repetitive movements of his relentless tongue, working me to explosion as it begins to rip through me. Adding more pressure as my cries increases and when he sucks on my clit I'm gone. Sent on a toe curling ride of ecstasy as I come undone around him, ripples of fire shoot through my veins and my rapid breath beats hard in my chest. I don't have chance to recover before he's taking my mouth and the taste of my climax salts my tongue.

"You taste so good, baby."

"That was insane." I pant, with my eyes still covered.

"Turn over." I'm flipped onto my front and the bed rises as he leaves. My head shoots in the direction to the sound of his belt. "I'm just removing my trousers," it's insane how this man can read my thoughts, I don't think I'll ever get use to that.

Angel whispered kisses continue to mark my skin, paying more attention on my scars as his cock pressed hard against me, my pussy screaming with the need of him to be inside me. "Marcus, please." I pled, not being able to take any more as he teases my body with his powers. "I need you to fuck me."

He kissed the rapid pulse in my neck, "But I'm not going to fuck you, Amelia. Not in the way you want. I want you to feel and remember every second of tonight. I want you to feel what I do to you. Say it, tell me what you want?"

It's like he knows me inside and out, reads my mind, hears my heart and sees into my soul. Knows that I'm tangled with the meaning of that word he's waiting to hear but will get me to speak it one way or another, torture my sex craved body in order for it to leave my lips. I can't say it, it means more than what this is, what it can't ever be.

"You're driving me insane, please, Marcus." I beg.

"Say it, Amelia. Let me hear you say it."

"I want… I want you to make love to me."

He's won. My fragile state of mind and my longing for him took over and the words left me before I could stop them. He slides deep inside, filling me with everything he had, entwining our fingers as he begins to rock us. He was right when he said no hard fucking would take place, he's passionate, deep, beautifully intense and fuck me it feels incredible.

"Oh god, don't stop."

I close my eyes under the mask and focus on the feel of him inside me. I feel beautiful, sexy and overwhelmed with lust as I give my body and soul to him. Drinking him in in every way as our bodies become one. The heat of his heavy pants hit my face; the movement of our body rubs my clit against the mattress making my insides rage with unbearably pleasure. The tingles race up my legs, the blaze in my core increases with each drive of his cock and I clench our fingers together as the sensation takes over my body.

"Marcus," I cry.

"Wait, Amelia."

I can't hold on much longer as Marcus chases his own climax, hitting me deeper every time. Coloured stars build behind my covered eyes and I'm losing control of my emotions and what this beautiful beast of a man is doing to my heart.

"Marcus, I ca-"

"Cum for me."

I crash violently like the waves that slam the rocks as we hit our orgasms in unison, the friction of my clit against the mattress creates another to ripple through me when he doesn't stop his thrusts. My limbs lax and hum in tranquillity, my pulse beating like a drum as he rests against me. "You blow my mind, Amelia. Every fucking time."

Marcus removes the sleep mask and I lay immobile, gaining control of my breathing as he kisses my shoulders and neck whilst still inside me. Gravity hits my heart as I come back to reality, and I can't stop the silent tear that soaks the pillow. Closing my eyes to take in the surrounding of him, us. His skin, his heartbeat, his touch. I couldn't ever get enough of having him close; even though he found me I was forever lost in him. He may take the memory of me with him but what will I have? Nothing.

I told myself countless times it's just for summer but the more time we've shared together the more I've realised he's different. The more he's made me come alive. But from my own experience the more time people spend together in a sexual connection like we have, the higher the feelings can grow and I can't put myself or my heart in that position again. I can't let my guard down and leave myself wide open. I've been down that road once before, I can't go there again.

***

As I stir in my sleep a satisfying feeling oozes through my body of having attentive eyes on me. I bite the inside of my cheek to stop the smile so I can relish the feeling a little longer. Yesterday was perfect in every way and that along with every other day spent with Marcus will be with me indefinitely.

"I know you're awake."

My smile stretches across my face but I don't open my eyes, I knew if I did, that unfamiliar feeling that continues to build inside will no doubt hit me again full force. "Rumbled." I smiled.

His low laugh brushed against my forehead as he swept the hair from my face to place a kiss on my lips. "Happy 27th, beautiful."

I forgot it was my birthday with all the hype from the ball and the busy week at work, or maybe I just didn't want to acknowledge it as it's another year without my parents. No matter how much you try to push it to the back of your mind there's still that little pocket of solitude waving at you as it sits on your shoulder.

"Have you been awake long?" I ask, blinking my arm open with a stretch.

"Long enough to watch you sleep."

"Still doing you stalker routine I see." I teased

"Always. I've ordered breakfast it will be here soon. Would you like you present?"

"You got me something?" My eyes widened with surprise, I didn't expect anything from him. He reached over the side of the bed to the draw and brought back a long black jewellery box tied with red ribbon. My stomach churned with an unpleasant state of excitement as I sat further up against the headrest.

My eyes flashed to him with hesitation when he placed the box on my lap. "Open it."

Undoing the ribbon, I opened the box and my breath was stolen on my discovery. Placed amongst the black velvet was a gorgeous white gold diamond bracelet twinkling against the light of the window. It was absolutely stunning and like nothing I ever had.

"Oh my god, Marcus," I whisper. I'm still trying to get my head around this man's generosity and how much he looks after those close to him. It's breathtaking and with that and the way he's making me feel it caused the tears to fall. I'm more confused now than I have ever been in my life and I can't do shit about it.

"Do you not like it?" he asks, concern and a little disappointed. "We can change it."

"No, no I love it. It's beautiful."

"But you're crying."

Wiping my tears I run my finger along the twinkling rocks still at a loss for words as I take every inch of it in. Placing it on the bed I look at Marcus, his beautiful face still washed with concern. "I'm crying because I love it. It's beautiful and unexpected. You have always been so good to me, Marcus. So kind and caring and I will be forever thankful for that." I move forward wrapping my arms around his neck as his arms come round me in a tight embrace.

"I've told you before; you deserve all the kindness and affection in the world. Happy Birthday beautiful, let's make today special."

Chapter Twenty-Three

Amelia

When we returned home from Kingston Hotel later in the morning I was hit with the heavenly scent of flowers that flooded my house. Dozens of bouquets filled every available space bringing rainbows of colour into the room. Megan text to say she would see me after work and Rosa and I went for lunch at Rock Waves for a birthday treat, whilst Marcus stopped off at The Grand to check on a few things. I can't remember the last time I spent my birthday with so many people and actually enjoyed it.

"Now we can't start the celebrations off without this little beauty." Megan beams as she strides into my room with Tequila and glasses. I decided earlier in the week I didn't want a fuss and a few drinks at Rubies would be fine but Megan insisted as there was more of us a few drinking games were needed before hitting the dance floor later.

Throwing back my drink I continue to finish my make-up whilst Rosa, Marcus and Andrew talked in the living room about a new club that's looking to be Rubies latest rival if it should go ahead and open in Spring Rose.

"Have you heard from Lucas today?" Megan asks, flopping herself on the bed in her sexy red dress.

"No, I tried to call earlier but I've heard nothing from him."

"I seem to remember him saying his internet was down so he couldn't Skype us."

"Maybe."

I switch to the other eye with my mascara wand as laughter from the other room seeps in through the door. Chucking my mascara in my bag I join Megan on the bed as that unfamiliar feeling grips my belly. "I'm scared." I whispered. Her eyes flashed up from her phone before quickly turning onto her front with her leg bent up and crossed at the ankles.

"About what?"

"About what will happen when he leaves, I've not felt like this in years and I like having him around."

Her ice blue eyes shot wide as a gasp takes over. "Oh my god, do you…do you-"

"No I don't!" I knew exactly what she was implying. "I'm just saying I don't think I'll be the same once he goes. But if he stays, not that he can, I'm not sure what that means for us either."

"Why?"

Because history has a way of repeating itself. Because bad luck comes in three's yet mine so far is my whole adulthood. "Because I'm damaged goods and he doesn't need that complication."

"Right stop with the bullshit! First of all you are not damaged goods and second I think you should to talk to him. Distance relationships can work if that's what you want and whatever happens I'll be here to help you drown your sorrows with Tequila." She jumps up from the bed and takes the bottle with a wink, doing her let's change the mood vibe. "And third this baby here needs some attention. Let's go get shit-faced and wind up Andrew. I'm yet to see him smile."

"Do you have a plan?" I chuckle straightening my dress once I get up.

"Nope, but I'll think of something."

***

The drinks are in full swing, music plays in the background as Megan's game of Truth or Dare continues. Marcus just had to swallow three large spoonfuls of extra hot chilli sauce, his eyes are still streaming and throat still recovering from the gallons of milk he downed straight after. My choice was truth and I had to confess to my internet crush on Johnny Depp and that I once had a scrapbook that was full of him.

"I loved him as well, Amelia, it's the eyes that draw you in." Rosa chuckles.

"What is it with girls and that dude?" Marcus shouts from the kitchen.

"You're a guy darling you wouldn't understand. Me and Amelia though, we totally get it."

"We sure do." I chuckle leaning forward to get my glass off the table. "Whose turn is it?"

"Mine."

"Ok, Megan, truth or dare?" Marcus asks, returning from the kitchen. I don't even know why he asked her, this is Megan we're talking about.

"Ugh, dare obviously."

Marcus thinks for a moment tapping his fingers to his beer bottle before a grin hits his lips. "Ok, I dare you to seduce Andrew."

I gasp as Andrews face drains with a shake of his head. "Come on man your mothers in the room," he says, shifting himself in his seat looking uncomfortable.

"Andrew, darling it's nothing I've not done myself over time. Megan, sweetheart you carry on, make him squirm." She winks at her as Andrew cut her a look.

Both Marcus and I knew that Megan wouldn't back out and the look on her face suggests she's up for the dare. She stands with an enthusiastic smile and throws me a knowing look as our earlier conversation flashed in my mind. Brushing her dress down she makes her way over to where Andrew sits on the high back kitchen chair looking absolutely petrified. "Megan, you don't have to do this." I'm almost positive there was an edge of panic in his tone.

"What's wrong, Andrew, you seem a little…uptight. I'm not one for backing out on a dare." This was true, Megan loved to have fun, it ran through her veins. Andrew straightens himself in his seat as Megan seductively strides towards him, swinging her hips like a model walking a catwalk.

"This is going to be interesting." Rosa whispers with excitement in her eyes.

Megan circles his seat, running her palm flat around his upper body. Lifting his chin she connects with his eyes, all focus is on her and what seemed to be a man protesting is now slowing falling into her trap of seduction. She moves behind him a second time and whispers unheard words before running her tongue along the rim of his ear. Andrew's eyes slam shut as his chest expands. The air in the room is thick, the heat is electric. My heart's pounding at the sheer intoxication that's unfolding, even Marcus and Rosa can't tear their eyes away.

Her dress rides her thighs as she straddles him. His upper body stiffens as she grazes her teeth along his jaw making his Adam's apple bob with a hard swallow. His eyes are hooded with lust, confusion and when her lips touch his Andrew retreats slightly before a seen of mouth fucking soon takes place. I'm on the edge of my seat; I can't take my eyes away. I don't want to.

"Wow, this is better than the movies." Rosa whispers.

Megan's hand tugs his hair as she rocks against him, still locked at the lips and to my surprise Andrews hands begin to roam the hem of her dress as they become oblivious to the audience that watches. I flick my eyes to Marcus who's currently sat with a shit ass grin on his face. The intensity of it all is enough to make my own arousal spike. Clearing my throat I end the sexual dare as Marcus chuckles.

"Congratulation dude, you just got hard for the first time in years." Marcus teased. Neither of them speak, just focused on each other as they get their breathing under control. I took the opportunity to get a new round of drinks with the help of Marcus and Rosa, because I knew sure as shit Andrew had a hard on.

"What the fuck was that?" I whispered flabbergasted by the scene.

"I think that's the start of a beautiful relationship."

Rosa said pour a glass of wine.

"You can't be serious; she annoys the shit out of him."

"Clearly his mouth disagrees." Marcus chuckled as he wraps his arms around me, planting a kiss on my head. "She said she'd get him hard."

Andrew has hardly said a word since his and Megan's little tongue twister. Megan on the other hand has been like a kid on a bouncy castle with endless amounts of adrenaline running through her body. Rosa had done the motherly role of preparing snacks for us all and a huge chocolate cake with candles.

"Right, Amelia, it'stime for you present." Megan announces.

"You already got me a present."

"Tequila doesn't count. Close your eyes and don't move."

"It's not going to freak me out is it?" I close my eyes feeling a little uneasy. Marcus takes my hand with a squeeze, reading my nervous like always. She knows I don't like surprises.

"Just trust me… and no peeking."

There's lots of whispering coming from the kitchen as I bite my lip with anticipation. Last year's present was jelly sweets, a vibrator and a year's supply of male magazines, which she ogled more than I did. And if the Tequila wasn't my present than god only knows what I'd get this year.

"Ok, you can open now."

I blink my eyes open a few times before they widen instantly to the sight up ahead. "Lucas!" I squeal, flying from the sofa and charging towards him to leap into his arms, wrapping my arms and legs round him in a big bear hug as his deep laugh vibrates through my chest with his tight embrace.

"Hey, how's my Ginger Spice?"

"God I've missed hearing you say that."

"I've missed saying it." He looked incredibly sexy as ever. His chiselled jaw was working the day old scruff as his bright blue-green eyes sparkled against the light. The thick muscles of his arms secured around my body and as my leg wrapped around him his waist was just a broad. He was a fine figure of a man. My beautiful non blood brother and fuck me I'd missed him. Tears swelled my eyes with happiness as I squeezed him tight.

"I've missed you so much."

"Hey, no tears on your birthday, beautiful," brushing his hand over my face and kissing my forehead. "You look happy," he whispered in my ear.

"I am." He's yet to be introduced to the rest of the room and I know all eyes are on us. If not all then definitely one set. I can feel them burning into me from across the room.

"Everybody this is my big brother Lucas." Megan says, introducing him to the others. As soon as Megan mentions Marcus's name, Lucas puts me down and strides over.

"So you're the one that's been sniffing around my girl?" He said sternly, folding his arm and giving the death stare as intimidation runs off him like heavy rain drops. The room falls silent and Megan shoots me a smile. This is typical Lucas, all hard ass and protective over his blue-eyed girls, only his composure won't last for long and his sternness will fall. However Marcus is unsure how to respond and a look of uncertainty if not anger washes over his features as he stands to measure himself up to the brick of muscle in front of him.

Lucas lets out a deep chuckle and holds out his hand.

"Just kidding man good to finally meet you. I've heard a lot about you."

"Nice to meet you too. Amelia often talks of you." Marcus accepts his hand shake as his body relaxes.

"Glad to hear it." Lucas says with a wink in my direction.

"I don't believe we've met. I'm Rosa, Marcus's mother." She smiles bringing Lucas in for a hug and mouths *'He's gorgeous'* to Megan and I making us giggle.

"This calls for a new round of drinks." Megan squeals as I help her out in the kitchen while the rest get to know each other. My grin is a meter wide as I stand looking towards the room of people. Reality hitting my chest with an overwhelming feeling I've never experienced.

"There all here for me." I whisper as Megan comes up beside me wrapping her arms around my waist.

"Of course we are. It's because you're special."

Tears glass my eyes; I've never had this feeling before. A feeling of unconditional happiness and affection. All of which I give and get back from the people that are under this roof. The feeling is almost suffocating. "Thank you, Megan. Not just for today but for everything. I wouldn't of gotten through these last few years if it wasn't for you and Lucas. Nobody knows what it's like to be so alone it feels as though your soul is dying. But you stood by me and helped me though that. I forgotten what it was like to be wanted and cared for. But the four people in that room have shown me what I've been missing. You don't have to be blood to have a family and that's what you and Lucas are. You're my best friend and my soul sister and I love you unconditionally."

"Loyalty makes you family. Lucas and I only did what

any other person who loves you would do. You're the one that's done the rest. You pulled yourself through no one else, and I love you with every ounce of my body. But promise me whatever happens you will never leave me. I need you just as much as you need me."

For the first time in all the years I've known this blonde beauty there was a look in her eyes that told me she was fighting a demon that was undiscovered to me. Megan is one of the strongest people I know, she's always had my back and fought for me, only now it seems I should been fighting for her as I can see a vulnerable side behind her ice blue eyes that sparkled with her tears.

"I promise I will never leave you babe." I wrap my arms around her as Lucas joins us for a group hug and kisses us both on the head. It's so good to have him back, to have my family back together. Nothing will ever break the bond that we three have.

Chapter Twenty-Four

Amelia

"How long are you here for?" I ask Lucas as I lean against him in the kitchen, everyone else is in the other room chatting and Marcus is currently burning his eyes over my body. The same look he's been giving me all evening only now it seems a little more intense.

"Just a few days. Got a couple weeks off but I need to sort stuff out before my next contract begins. It's only a few months at another sugar daddies string of conventions. Then I pack up and move on after that." My heart falls a little at the thought of him moving on. Lucas works as a personal body/security guard for big events in LA. He has worked with a huge number of celebrities over the years and more often than not hooked up with rich girls for naked pool parties after working hours. He loves it over there so it surprises me that he's planning on leaving.

"But you love it there. Where you heading this time?"

"I thought I'd give Spring Rose a try," he grins.

Excitement automatically hit me and I grasp his arm, jumping like I've just been given a puppy. "*Really*? You're coming back here?"

"I love it there but I miss my girls. Besides someone's got to keep an eye on my crazy ass sister."

"Heard that asshole!" Megan shouts from the living room.

"Megan did you know about this?"

"Course not. He tells you more than he tells me."

"That's coz she's special." He chuckles, stuffing crisps into his mouth and lifting his arm around my shoulder. I flick my eyes back to Marcus and smile; his stare sends a shiver down my spine. I've kind of abandoned him the last hour or so, not intentionally but when you've not seen someone special to you in months you tend to want them with you every second. I left the grip of Lucas and go to him, curling my body into his lap. His hand slides up my thigh and under my dress. Now the stare on me has reversed and it's Lucas that watches.

"You ok? You seem a little quiet."

"I'm fine."

"I can't believe Lucas is here. Did you know he was coming?"

"No."

I place a kiss on his lips and smile. "I'll glad you had the chance to meet him. He's an important part of me. This has turned out to be the best birthday ever. Thank you for being part of it."

"Who's up for Tequilas and table dancing at Rubies? I

want to get shit-faced." Megan shouts into the room wearing a party hat she got from somewhere and causing everyone to laugh.

Like any other night Rubies was packed. The loudness of the music hit your chest before you even walked through the doors and bodies locked with each other on the dance floor. Jack and Nathan were rushed off their feet and couldn't serve so Marcus stepped behind the bar to get the first round before bringing them back to the table that was sectioned off from the dance floor, enabling us to talk without shouting for survival. Rosa said her goodbyes and headed back to Marcus's once we left mine and as soon as we entered the building Megan was off on the dance floor looking for love.

I returned from the bathroom just as Lucas was coming back from the bar. Taking my hand he twirl around and into a hug as hazel eyes from behind him watched our every move. Marcus hasn't been his usual chatty self since Lucas arrived, however I can't complain as his eyes are never far from me which is making my body react in a way that's driving me crazy. My panties are no doubt ruined and I'm fighting the urge not to pounce on him right here in full view of others.

However I feel an air of tension around us and I'm unsure which direction it's coming from. Since the truth or dare kiss, Andrew has been even more subdued than normal, if that's even possible and Megan is knocking back the Tequila's faster than she's ever done before.

"Are those two alright they seem a little troubled?" I ask Marcus quietly once sitting beside him and entwining our fingers.

"No idea." His response was clear cut as I look at him

with narrowed eyes. Ok so maybe the tension was in fact between us as he's getting frostier with me as the night continues and I can't help the feeling of annoyance that's beginning to thicken in my chest.

"A blue lagoon for my blue-eyed girl." Lucas smiles returning to the table; Marcus's grip tightens on my fingers. "So, Marcus, Amelia says this is your place?"

"That's right."

"It's a nice place, I like it."

"Thanks." Each response to Lucas was abrupt. Lucas was clearly unaware of his change in attitude but I knew this wasn't the man I was with just hours ago. The man I wanted Lucas to get to know.

"We first met here when Marcus saved me from a drunk that was after my ass. He was my hero." I smile, trying to soften the tension but only getting half a smile back. I narrow my eyes at him, what was his problem?

"It's good to know someone's out to look after my girls when I'm not around." Lucas said brushing his hand over my knee.

The pressure on my hand was now beginning to be too much so I lean into him towards him. "Marcus, you're hurting me." He looks at me with unreadable eye and flashes them down to our joined hands. Loosening me from his grip he pushes back in his seat and heads out past the bar, completely ignoring my calls. Giving Lucas a reassuring smile and making my excuses I head in the direction of the office. Anxious to see what I might come up against on the other side of the door.

"Marcus are you alright?"

He spins making me flinch. "I don't share my woman, Amelia!" he growled. His eyes were dark, hurt. But it was his attitude I was more pissed off with.

"Excuse me?"

"I. Don't. Share."

My mind flashes to Lucas and everything begins to fall into place. My eyes-widen in disbelief and I step further into the room. "Are you jealous, Marcus?"

"Can you blame me, you've been all over him since he got here." So, he is jealous.

"You've got this all wrong."

"Have I?"

Surely he can see there was nothing between me and Lucas, not in the way that he thinks, not when I have him by my side. Lucas is like a brother and maybe I should have warned Marcus of my close connection with him. But in my defence, I didn't know he was coming and the thought of not being allowed to be myself around my friends unsettles me. I didn't think Marcus would be that guy.

"You're being ridiculous." I reach out taking his arm only for him to withdraw it from my grip.

"Oh, so it's my fault?" his raised voice and sour expression caused me to step back.

No one comes between me and my family, not even Marcus. I stand my ground as my own voice rises to match his as we fill the confined space of a darken office with our frustration. "Jesus Christ, Marcus, we're just friends."

"I'm friends with Megan; you don't see me rubbing up to her."

"What is your problem?!"

"My problem is the fact my girlfriend is paying more attention to every other fucking guy than the one she's meant to be with!"

Girlfriend? He's kidding me right?

"How the fuck can you class me as your girlfriend when you're planning on leaving in a couple of weeks. You need to rethink your choice of words before spitting them out at me."

His eyes flashed with something I couldn't recognise, the vein in his neck began to throb as his face reddened. I hated situations like this and I've been down this jealousy rage before. Arguing with the ones that are supposed to so call care for me while I wait anxiously to see how unpredictable they actually are. He stood looking at me as his chest rose with his heavy breathing before his eyes fell to the floor.

"I don't want to fight with you Amelia." He said softly. This only enraged me more. He started and clearly wanted a fight to begin with and he's now backing out, after practically accusing me of dry humping my best friend's brother. My anger bubbled quicker that I thought it would and my Tequila fuelled body found courage to get up close and spit out the words I never wanted to hear myself say.

"I don't want to fight with you either, Marcus, so you leave me no other choice. I think it's best that we call whatever this is between us a day as you're clearly overreacting and I can't deal with shit like that."

He grabs my arm as I move to leave, "Is that what you want?" he barked.

I look at his hand that's taken my arm and flash my eyes at him. In a normal situation like this, a man's grip would have sent fear cascading down my spine. But with Marcus I'm fearless. If anything my anger towards him is creating my sex drive to soar. I lower my voice but still leave another power behind my words. "Lucas is my family and as long as he's here I want to spend as much time with him as possible, and if you can't cope with that I see no other option." I tug my arm free and head towards the door, stopping to turn back as my emotions begin to build in my throat. "Besides in a matter of weeks you won't be here anyway." I head out in the direction of the people I know won't make me feel bad about being myself and try to enjoy the rest of my birthday that's suddenly gone south. Fighting back the hurt that's currently lying heavy on my heart.

The shot I ordered is down and I'm ordering another two before Jack even had chance to turn. I sniff back my tears before anyone saw as I clocked Marcus heading out the door with Andrew without even saying their goodbyes. Assholes! Why do men always have to jump to conclusions and accuse you of shit you've not done just because their ego is dented for a few hours. It pisses me off.

"Steady Ginger Spice. I don't want to have to carry you home and have your man thinking I've led you astray."

"Why are men such hurtful inconsiderate pricks?" I shot at him. "And he's not my man."

"Ok what's he done?" Lucas asks on a sigh.

"He more or less thinks we're fucking."

"Ah, I see. He's jealous, that's good. Shows he has feelings. Shows he cares."

I snort throwing back another shot. "He doesn't care. He's leaving me in a few weeks. I'm nothing more than his summer fuck buddy with the added bonus of being on his payroll."

"Oh he cares. I've seen the way he looks at you."

"How the hell can you work that out, you've only been here five minutes."

"Guys intuition." He grins.

I roll my eyes and order another drink. Lucas quickly

cutting me off and suggesting to Jack water would be better. So the big brother routine finally kicks in and puts a stop to my night of getting shit-faced to forget a man I desperately wish was by my side.

Turning on my stool I look out over the dance floor, smiling at Megan as she parades on the table in the corner that's now become her permanent stage on a weekend. A wave of anxiety churns my belly as my leg bounces on the footrest of the stool. That's when it hits me. I've not been anxious in weeks. Not since the first time I removed my clothes for Marcus. If he goes back where would that leave me and my state of mind? Maybe I need him more than I realised. That caused my gut to cramp at the thought of what this could mean if he stayed. Yes my feelings for him have changed, but they can't be any more than just a desire for sex as that is all I can give him, anything more than this doesn't even bear thinking about. *That* word changes things. It changes people.

"I've already been broken once, Lucas. I can't go back there again."

"Babe, it doesn't matter who broke you and brought you down, what matters is who made you smile again and we both know it's him. Talk to him; find out what will happen once he returns. Long distance works for some people but you won't know if you don't try." He throws back his drink and licks his lips. "Now, dry your tears because I know you've been crying and put a smile on that pretty face or yours and follow me. I want to take advantage of those legs while I can."

I take his hand and follow him towards the dance floor to meet Megan who jumps into his arms from off the table. The three of us take over the floor in style, laughing and goofing around without a care in the world as the ladies swoon over Lucas. My laughter leaves my lungs but inside I'm anything but happy and if I feel like this now I dread to think how I will cope when Marcus has gone.

Chapter Twenty-Five

Marcus

Top marks for acting like a complete dick head.

My fucked up insecurities soured and empowered my mind with unwanted questions I already knew the answers to. That said, I still couldn't push them aside. I've never been the jealous type and if that was a first class act of jealousy I fucking hate every minute of the feeling that runs through my body and mind. The words that left Amelia's mouth shook me; I never imagined her to say them and never imagined her to leave me gut-retched in a darkened office like a kid whose favourite football team had just lost the world cup. Today was her day, full of excitement and surprise guests and there I was playing the dick that ruins the party and gets everyone talking. I knew what Lucas was to her yet I couldn't help the rage I felt every time I saw his hands on her. She was mine; I want her to be mine.

Time and space was what we needed regardless. I left early as my mood would only increase the more I saw them together and I didn't want her upset, but I couldn't leave her alone any longer than I already had. It killed me to leave her behind; I didn't want to go home to an empty bed unless she was with me.

Getting the spare key from Megan along with an earful, I waited at Amelia's for her to come home. This gave me chance to cool off and think shit through. Try and work out what the fuck I'm going to say and hope she accepts my apology for being a total ass-wipe.

It was after midnight when I heard the door go, shouting her goodbyes in giggles to her friends as her heels click along the floor. Sitting back in the living room chair in my shirt and boxers I take in the scent of the flower that fills the room as I watched her. Her face was priceless this morning when we came home and she found her house decorated into her very own meadow. I love how her face lights up, the way her eyes close as she inhaled the scent and the little hum that leaves her afterward.

She works her way round the kitchen slightly unsteady on her feet as she takes off her heels before getting a glass of water and checking her phone, only to throw it down on the counter with a sigh. I turn on the living room lamp as she walked towards the bedroom; causing her to jump "Jesus, Marcus, what the fuck!" she holds her hand to her chest. Her once neatly fixed hair now sagged from too much dancing, creating wispy strands to fall around her face, her perfectly applied make-up now smudged a little under her eyes as her pale lips showed evidence of blue lagoon cocktails. My dick twitched to attention. She really was pure perfect; this woman could make wearing rags look sexy.

"Amelia, come here please." My words were a little more forceful than intended. Her body instantly went ridged; hesitation covers her frame as she stands looking at me and fingers twisting her ring.

"Are you angry with me?" she murmured.

Even after the time spent together there was often times my words would shake her in a way I didn't like. Her eyes would darken with uncertainty and dread as she gripped her hands in tight balls to stop the shakes. One night when getting all sexed up her body shuddered when I without thinking removed my belt from my jeans in a swift action. Making me aware once again that this strong woman that stands her ground at times was still so fragile. I soften my voice to reassure her panic. "No baby, I was never angry with you. It's ok, come here."

Slowly making her way over I pull her down to straddle me. She'd been crying. My heart burned as though a knife had been ripped though it at the thought of making her cry. I only ever want to see her smile. My hands run over her hair and body before resting back on her jaw. I'm lost without this woman, but I don't know who I am when I'm with her. She takes over my mind, body and soul in the most endearing way it chokes me. "I'm sorry for acting like a complete prick. I never meant to upset you."

"Marcus, me and Lucas have history but not in the way you think. He-"

I go to speak but she places a finger on my lips. "Hear me out please. Lucas plays a huge part in my recovery. After him and Megan got me out I was all over the place, I was scared to be on my own and scared to sleep alone. I'm not going to lie and say we haven't slept in the same bed because we have, but only so his strong arms cradled me for as long as I needed them. That was all it was. Marcus, Lucas pays for my therapy sessions. I have and always will have a special bond with him because of what he has done for me. He's like a brother I never had and I love him dearly. You have nothing to be jealous of baby."

Ok so now I feel the biggest prick ever. Why didn't she just tell me this before, it would of saved all of this. "I'm such an ass. I just saw you together and thought... Shit; I don't know what I thought. But I didn't like it. I don't even know what to say." I sighed.

"You don't have to say anything, I understand your reasons. Insecurities can be a bitch at times but you just have to try and get past them. Talk about them. Don't be afraid to tell me how you're feeling, I can't help if I don't know."

Fuck can she get even more incredible. Here she was constantly carrying the anxiety torch and made it flash every once in a while yet she's here offering her support and wanting to fix me and my shitty ways. "You're adorable you know that?"

"Although I must say, the thought of you jealous did kinda make me feel horny," biting her lip.

"Oh really. So does this mean we have a little making up to do?"

Her grin was sinful as her eyes flashed with lust. Trailing her fingertips along my jawline causing a shiver through my body as she dipped her head to meet my lips. Her tongue tasted of a mixed flavoured mini bar, her lips sticky with fizzy drinks as her vanilla and honeysuckle scent merged together with post-dance sweat. She tilts her head back as I kiss along her jaw, a soft whimper leaving her throat as I reach her weak spot on her neck. The little whimpers that often drove me wilder than her screams as I tantalized her body.

"You intoxicate me, Amelia. I can never get enough of you."

I drive my tongue back into her mouth to play with hers, sex with Amelia was incredible but her mouth done things to me that I never thought it could. It's like an addiction, a never ending drug, constantly on a high and craving for more as she engulfed me with everything she had. I love the way I feel when I hold her, touch her, taste her. Her delicate traces of her sweet tasting tongue on mine sent my body into a frenzy just as much as the hard strokes she provided when her own mouth was hungry.

"Marcus?" she whispers.

"Tell me, baby."

Taking my jaw in her hands her thumbs smooth over my face, her chest beginning to dust pink, a sign I knew she was losing control of her emotions that slowly take over her big blue eyes. "I don't want you to leave."

My gut twisted with her admission as a single tear slid down her cheek. This whole situation had been crushing me since the moment I laid eyes on her. I've never been so afraid of leaving someone like I have Amelia. She does things to me that scare me shitless but I wouldn't change it for the world, my feelings for her are deepening by the day. She's all I think of first thing on a morning and the last I see at night, and I know my days won't be the same without her in them.

"I don't want to go."

Her mouth collided with mine in a desperate need of hunger, our moans play into each other as her hands take the hem of my shirt to remove it. Her kisses pepper my neck, teeth pinching the skin on my collarbone triggering a growl from my throat as she rocks against me. Her arms stretch up as I pull her dress over her head, unclipping her hairpin for red locks to cocoon around her face, lacing a thick ribbon between my fingers and breathing in the honey scent.

Her eyes never faltered from mine as she slowly glides her fingernails down my front and enters my boxers. My eyes drifted closed, a throaty groan escapes my lips when she strokes her hands along my shaft. I love how her confidence grows each time we're together. Not afraid to let her hands roam my body. It's like she need constant skin on skin connection in order to breathe. Shifting her hot pink lace aside I slip my fingers into her wet pussy as the scent of her arousal lingers between us. She's always ready and waiting for me to take her anyway I want.

"I love that you're always ready for me, Amelia. It drives me crazy."

"I've been ready for hours." Her hooded eyes are full of heat and desire, changing her bright blues to a sexy royal blue as she holds my gaze that burns into hers. I don't think I'll ever get over what this woman does to me-my body, my soul. My constant need to touch her is sinful, an aching need that never ends. It's only been a few hours out of her embrace but it feels like a lifetime.

I take her by the waist and stand, shifting out of my boxers and pushing her back against the wall. Her legs wrap tight around me as I kiss the sensitive spot behind her ear, sucking hard and nipping her skin to mark her. Her moans hit my ears as she bucks her hips, telling me what she's after as my hands fall to her pink lace and in one quick sweep I tear it from her body.

"I liked those." She gasps with a flash of excitement in

her eyes.

"I'll buy you more." I can't wait another second, I slam into her, resulting in her to cry out as her nails dig my shoulders. The relief is welcoming, my veins funnelling with intense lust as my eyes fall heavy.

"Fuck me hard, Marcus. I want to feel you for days."

Her eyes tell me she meant every word and I pull out slightly only to slam back in, gripping my hands under her thighs as I fuck her hard, hitting the spot I knew drove her wild as her cries play out into the room. My blood soured its thick heat in every vessel, unearthly grunts leave me as I rock our bodies hard against the wall. When we fuck I know the limits with her and she trusts me. Sex is a massive deal for Amelia as power and control can change instantly, leaving her vulnerable and defenceless, but every once in a while her confidence rockets and no holding back is need. "Look at me baby."

She tightens around me, the rush of my orgasm about to boil as it burns its way through my own body. This wasn't love making, it was pure hard fucking. Amelia's face contorts into a wail as she milks me with her violent climax that tore through her. I fucked her with every ounce, whimpers and cries left her sexy lips as the fire inside me ejects deep inside, coating her walls with my white heat.

"Amelia, fuck." Stars dance in my eyes as my orgasm continued to rip through me like a fire-ball. Our eyes lock, hearts beat fast as sweat peppered our skin. Taking her hands above her head I kissed her like I meant it, giving her everything I owned and everything she needed as I pull her lip between my teeth. "Thank you." I exhale. More often than not Amelia was the one that always thanked me, anything I did no matter how big or small, whether it were a gift or a cuddle she would always thank me. Only it was my time to thank her for everything she was making me feel.

She giggles, her lips red and swollen. "Sweet Jesus, we should fall out more often."

"You said you wanted to feel me for days. Did I hurt you?"

"Only in the best way, I love the way you make me feel." Her eyes flash with something but they dart from me before I had chance to read them, wrapping her arms tight around me to bury her face into my neck. I love the way I make her feel too, she doesn't have to tell me anything I don't already know, that I don't already feel. I turn us round and lean my shoulders against the wall, catching the reflection of us in the living room mirror. The red locks coat her back as she holds me close, her fingers trace and twirl in my hair, relaxing my body into her touch as her breathing beats against my skin.

When I first met Amelia I had no idea she would grow to be so important to me, she's changed the person I was and made me a better one. Her existence is a gift, her embrace is my shelter and her eyes have become my new home. I can't see life without her, I don't want another day spent without her. My heart skipped a beat as the feeling that has overwhelmed me all these weeks becomes clear. I'm in love with the angel that stole my breath and etched her beauty into my heart.

Chapter Twenty-six

Marcus

I love to watch her sleep, to run my eyes over her body. I don't think she has any idea how many times I've just laid watching her over the last couple months we've spent together. The mornings that I spent with Sadie were a quick case of satisfaction, shower then head to work hardly saying two words to each other. With Amelia its total different, we spend time with each other, get one another off, talk, touch and listen to each other breathing as we lay close. It's like each second is precious. I love wasting time as long as she's with me.

"You're doing it again, Mr Matthews," she mumbles in her groggy voice, burying her face into the pillow.

"Doing what?"

"Disturbing my sleep with your wandering hands."

"I thought you liked my wandering hands?" I chuckle softly.

"Oh, I'm not complaining I'm just saying you're doing it again." I run my hands down her back and over her bare ass giving it a little squeeze as her sleepy eyes flutter open. After our make-up sex last night we held each other for hours as I tried to comprehend everything I was feeling for her and everything she's done to me since arriving. I just have to pick my moment in telling her I want her forever and I can't see a life without her in it.

"You look tired." I murmur as I tuck the hair behind her ear.

"My head hurts."

"Too many Blue Lagoons and Tequilas?"

"Ugh, tell me something I don't know. I kinda hit the shot selection after you left too. That was until Lucas went all big brother on me and put a stop to it." Remorse hit my gut at the thought of her drowning out my shitty attitude towards her friend with booze, I never wanted that, believe it or not I like the guy, I just acted like a prized prick swimming in jealousy. "You are alright with him being around aren't you? I don't want any bad feeling from an-"

I place my finger on her lips to stop her talking. "I'm fine, we are fine, and everything is going to be just fine."

"Hmm, well in that case go make me breakfast, I need calories in the form of chocolate." she groans, placing her arm over her eyes.

"What the lady wants." I get out of bed and stretch letting my muscles wake. Slipping on some jeans as my phone buzzed with a message.

Megan: Morning you sexy beast...I mean Marcus.

Please tell Amelia it's rude to not answer my calls, I'm only her best friend!

Me: She said sex is more important than your calls.

I teased with my reply.

Megan: Like fuck she did, I'm irresistible. Whatever your plans are for today change them. Everyone is hitting the beach for the boat race and that's where you'll be heading too.

"Megan's just text, everyone's meeting up on the beach later. You feel up to it?"

"Will there be cheeseburgers?" she yawns, sitting up and rubbing her eyes.

"There will."

"Then I'm up for it."

Me: Meet you there.

***

"Now this is why I come home earlier than planned. Who wants paperwork when you can have sweaty tanned men in Speedos to ogle over?"

"Mum, please, I may be a grown man but I'm still your son, hearing you say shit like that is creepy."

"I'm only saying aloud what the other ladies are thinking, isn't that right girls?"

Amelia says nothing just giggles; Megan however is looking over the top of her shades towards a rather toned man fixing his boat trailer as she bites down on the straw to her coke. "Megan, do you know him?"

"No, but whatever he's fixing, mine just broke."

I shake my head amused as the women that's within my company cackle at her sassiness.

Like every year since I were a young boy holiday weekend in Spring Rose was dedicated to yearly boat races, surfing competitions, BBQ's and music blasting out across the bay. Regulars put their daily chores aside to hit the water and holiday makers drank in the atmosphere. The whole town was buzzing and looking forward to the day ahead. Even Andrew graced us with his presence.

"How are my blue-eyed girls?" Lucas shouts making his way over to the group shirtless and causing every woman's eyes on the beach including my mother's to pop open. His physique was thick, tanned and had abs like a washboard. Tribal tattoos down his arms and shades that reflected the whole beach in the lenses. "Ginger Spice, how was the head this morning?" He asks, planting a kiss on her cheek followed by Megan's.

"A little sore but better once Marcus made me breakfast, and I've just had a cheeseburger. I'm officially hangover free."

"Good to hear. Did she have you making her Chocolate spread on toast, Marcus?"

"She did yes, although it was more spread than toast." I hand him a beer and sit down beside Amelia, helping her rub in her sun lotion on her leg.

"Chocolate spread is awesome, even better with strawberries on top. I never tried it till I become friends with those two." Amelia replies, nodding her head toward Lucas and Megan and starts rubbing the lotion on her other leg.

"As kids, Megan and I use to fight over who licked the jar clean once at the end."

"I've not had chocolate spread in years," Mum adds. "The things you could do with that as well as have it with food."

"Mum!"

"What? I'm just stating a fact dear. You know one time me and your father were-"

"Please, enough already." The group broke into laughter at my mother's dirty talk, and I needed her to stop as the intrusion of unforeseen images flashed in my mind.

"Oh, Marcus, you're so easy to wind up. Come on girls; let's go find some hot guys that need their lotion rubbing in." She gets up placing her oversized sun hat on her head as Megan strips out her dress to just her bikini, clocking Amelia watching Megan's every move as she runs her eyes over her body. I know what she's thinking, it doesn't take a lot to realise she's the only one on this beach that has her midsection covered. She wants to be free just like every other woman and the only time she doesn't feel she has to hide is at a beach that I own and no other person steps foot on it.

"I'll see you in a bit." She kisses me before they make their way down the beach, laughing at my mother who's currently trying to gain every man's attention in any way she can.

"Dude, I wish my mother was like yours." Lucas chuckles.

"You won't be saying that when she's half way through the Brandy bottle."

"I'm surprised she's not yet been arrested for indecent exposure." Andrew replies pulling off his shirt and heading down to the water leaving Lucas and I with all the belongings.

"She sounds like my sister, only older. Has Megan gained a reputation here yet?"

"You beat, she's the dancing queen. She's a great girl, her and Amelia are inseparable."

"Ugh, tell me about it." He laughs, looking down to where the girls are kicking water at Andrew. "Look I just want to say that whatever you're doing with Amelia, keep doing it. I've not seen her this happy in years. She's been through some shit in her past, which I know you're aware of. I can't lie, I hated the thought of her with someone when Megan said you were seeing her, but she's happy. But I'm warning you, Marcus, you fuck this up, I swear to god I will hunt you down and burn off your balls."

I knew I'd get some kind of warning from Lucas given the fact he and Amelia are so close, but in all honesty I was imagining being push against the wall by the scruff of my shirt and my balls squeezed in his hand. Even though there was a slight aggression behind his tone it was relatively friendly.

"I had a similar threat from your sister, is there some kind of Simmons ritual?"

He chuckles. "I taught my sister well. Anyone hurts either of them they won't know what's hit them. I'm like the Tasmanian devil when it comes to my girls."

I had the upmost respect for Lucas and everything he's done for Amelia; I had no intention of hurting her. "You have my word. For both your girls."

"Good because I'd hate to kick your ass. Now what's life like here, I'm planning on leaving L.A and heading back. Please tell me the surf is just as good in the winter."

"It's better. And if you need a place to stay, I'm your guy."

***

The beach was swimming with people all day, kids ran around covered in sand as their ice creams dripped down their arms whilst the adults played beach sports and enjoyed the sun once the races and competitions had taken place. Hundreds of local men and women took to the water in their choice of sport and showed the gathered crowd actually why they should be in there. Drinking in the adrenaline from the roar that chanted and cheered.

It was just after sunset and there were still people and holidaymakers on the beach. The music coming from Rock Waves Diner was blasting out across the sand and the lanterns placed around the groups set off a warm glow. Megan and Lucas had gone to get us all pizza whilst Mum sat deep in conversation with Andrew.

"I've had fun today; everyone gets on so well, it's refreshing." Amelia says as I hold her close, dancing to the music.

"It's been great; surprisingly my mother hasn't been too bad either."

"Your mother is amazing," she chuckles, "I feel like I've known her for years and can tell her anything,"

"She's always had that effect on people, growing up as a kid all our friends use to go to her with their problems rather than their own mother."

"I can see why."

We fall in our comfortable silence as we dance, taking in the words to the song that made me think of the woman

I'm holding. It represented love like a flower-a rose and the person being the seed that needed to learn how to grow and acknowledge that love can be painful and can leave you feeling hurt and vulnerable. But the breathtaking moments you might miss out on if you never take a chance, and encourages you to always remain optimistic.

"This is nice, Marcus."

"Dancing or holding me?"

"Both," she sighs, running her arms high up my back. "I like it when you're close to me." If Amelia was a kind of woman that played a man and guilt tripped him into staying she was saying all the right words. But she wasn't like that, she only gave so much away and when she gave something it rolled off her tongue with ease and had no intention behind it. Or it could be because I was already making plans on staying, after talking to mum the other day and Amelia saying last night she didn't want me to leave and the fact I love her, my mind was made up. London isn't that far to commute and I do most of my work via computer anyway. It's a done deal.

"Thank you, baby."

"For what?" she questions, looking up at me with a smile.

"For making this the best summer I've had in years." Her eyes turn sad, the corner on her mouth ticks up to a smile but quickly disappears.

"What will happen?" she whispers. "What will happen when you leave?"

I tuck her hair behind her ear and cup her face looking deep into her eyes. Worry and confusion coating her beautiful blues with the uncertainty of what's happening between us "I'm not going anywhere just yet baby." I place my lips to hers, coaxing them open to meet the tip of her tongue whilst pulling her close to absorb everything she gave while the world spins but we're stood timeless in our embrace.

I rest my head to hers. She never questioned what I said but I knew there were questions on the tip of her tongue, her eyes told me as I focused on them. The air that charged between us had changed. It ran deeper-stronger. I felt it. I knew she felt it. No words were needed as her single touch alone roared through me. I'm lost in her, I can't breathe without her. Her eyes are my light that shine deep into my soul.

"I love you, Amelia."

Like ice creeping its way up a living being she froze, her desire filled eyes turned with fear like I'd said the worse thing in the world and I swear I could hear her heart pounding hard against her chest. Her silence was deafening and the longer it went on the more it crushed me. She steps back and goes to speak but no words leave her lips, her eyes sparkle against the light with tears, her neck begins to dust pink with her panic and I can see the walls I broke starting to work their way back up. I know she's afraid, but I also know she can't deny her feelings. I can't love her as much as I do and know she doesn't not feel the same. She has to feel the same.

She retreats and I step forward, taking her arm to keep her from bolting. "Don't run from me."

"Let me go, Marcus." She pleads as a tears rolls down her cheek. "I can't do this."

"Amelia, wait."

"Please let me go."

As soon as I release her she fled, sprinting across the

beach and pushing her way through the crowd as I shout her to stop, but she never did. She just kept on running.

Chapter Twenty-Seven

Amelia

I had no choice but to run.

I saw my eyes turn fearful in the reflection of his hazels as everything that's happened between us flashed like a high speed train passing through the light of the underground. The final fragments of darkness released to sail away, letting only the vibrant glow back in that's fought its way for freedom for so long. He reached me, chose me, revived me, and cherished me. Everything seems possible when I'm with him. He's everything I never knew I needed. But love changes everything. What he said changes everything. His words have the power behind them that can either hurt me or heal, and it's the unknown I fear the most.

I'm afraid to love, most of all I'm afraid to be loved. I was loved once or so I believed and it was nothing more than a nightmare of sour lies and burning pain. That's all I see love to be. All I've known it to be. A bubble of protection that grew stronger around me made me feel safe, yet the same bubble can be destroyed just as fast as it was built.

I'm scared to love, but more afraid to walk away because I know Marcus is different, he's proved this already. There's no better feeling then when someone appreciates everything about you that someone else took for granted and he does that. Marcus does that and it scares me. The fear is choking me from the inside as it leaves my mind a web of unanswered questions and scars which are still healing. I can't let my guard down and fall into that trap again.

Only now I'm more confused than ever when I find myself outside his house. I had no intention of coming here, I was letting my feet carry me to my place as I sprinted barefoot along the pavement but I ended up here. My chest burns with the pressure that conceals my emotions, my head hurts with the uncertainty and my gut twists with regret for leaving him stood there after hearing his declaration. A declaration I wanted but needed not to hear.

I slide my back down the door as my exhausted body greets the ground, cuddling my knees I bury my face and let the tears cascade from my eyes. Why did he have to say those words? Why am I here? What the fuck is happening to me? I don't know who I am anymore but I like the person he's making me become.

My sixth sense told me he was close, the instant feeling of relief funnelled through my body like it always had when he was near, but when I looked up that soon was replaced with something else, something stronger. He stood at the end of his driveway watching over me like an Angel, holding my sandals by the hocks of his fingers. There is no denying my feelings for this man, when I see him I come alive. He's brought me back to life. He's strong, trusting, and beautiful. He's even patient with my anxieties and shitty ways in life. But I terrified to speak the words he longs to hear.

"I don't know why I came here." I sob.

"You came here because it's where you want to be, it's where your heart knows it belongs." He doesn't come to me he just stays at the far end of the driveway and knelt down to my level as his voice was coated in serenity.

"What if I don't know where I belong? What if I don't know anything anymore?"

"You know more then you give yourself credit for, you just need to not think, over thinking can course you more confusion and negativity. You just need feel Amelia. Tell me how you feel."

I wasn't supposed to feel. I wasn't supposed to trust. Fear and solitude was all I had. All I was used to. Now I'm suffocating with those feelings and the ones I have for Marcus. He said he would fix me, but in the reality of it he's only breaking me more. My guard has fallen, my heart has been put back on the line and I need to gain back my control.

I focus on my sandals in his hand, too frightened to look as him. "I don't feel anything."

"You know that's not true. You feel, Amelia, and that's why you're scared. When you smile you feel it. When I kiss you, you feel it."

"Don't." I murmur.

"When you're with me you feel it." I wanted him to stop because everything he was saying was true, everything

I do with him I've felt right from when he first took my hand in Rubies. The flutters in my heart when his lips are on mine, the imprints of his touch that last for days. I felt every goddamn thing that this man does to me and I feel sick because that last part of me that I was desperate to let go of and feel what I've craved all this time wouldn't fucking let me. Love is for the lucky and the strong. I'm neither of those.

"When I hold you, you feel it."

"Stop, Marcus." My anger's tight in my chest and bursting to come out the more he speaks. I want him, I didn't want him. I love him; I hate him for making me love him.

"When we make love, Amelia, you feel it."

"Stop saying that!" I stand as my rage now leaves my body in yelled sobs. "I've spent time with you. Let my guard down for you. Told my history to you. Everything I've done it's been for you. What else do you want from me Marcus?! I have nothing left to give you!"

"Give me your heart!" He begs, pain now clouding his face as he takes a step forward. His eyes desperate to save me from the hell that's choking me as my body falls heavy to fight the never ending battle between torture and love. "I want you to let me take care of you. Be with you. Love you. And I know you want the same."

"No."

"Yes, Amelia. You want it."

My eyes closed at the unwanted rawness those words brought to my heart. Everything he said I believed and wanted more than anything but my heart and mind felt as though they were at war over the authenticity of what was really happening between us.

I sniffed back the new tears that threaten and force my

voice to be direct, spitting out the words that shredded my insides as I spoke them. "You don't love me, Marcus, and I. Don't. Feel. The. Same."

"We both know that that's not true." He looks away from me; the deep sigh he gave proved his patients was slipping. "Jesus Christ, Amelia, what are you so afraid of?"

"EVERYTHING!" I yell, this time finally losing it. He's now closer and despite my yelling he remains in control, which pissed me off more as I'm not use to that. The last time I yelled at a man I got a fist in my face so maybe my uncontrolled yelling was a test to see his reaction, see how far I needed to push him. Only his test on me of remaining composed never faltered, so I continued to yell.

"I'm frightened of giving my heart that's still learning to recover. I'm frightened because in my heart I know how I feel and know what I want, but that confuses me because I've never felt like this before. I'm frightened of reliving history, Marcus, because love is also rejection and betrayal. It's having bottles and glasses thrown at you because in his eyes I dressed like a slut. It's being beaten when you say the wrong things!" I step back as he moves closer, tears now free falling my cheeks and I make no attempt to wipe them in the hope that each demon I yell will run free like I've wanted them to for so long. "Love is being held down while he fucks his anger out of you. Ripped apart as your body is tortured. It's when your heart and soul feels like a razor is making it bleed and there's nothing you can do about it. That's what love is. That's all I know, Marcus, and I don't deserve the kind of love you want to give me." I cry.

In two strides I'm pushed against the door. His eyes look just as broken as my own anguish; the hurt that runs through his hazels is not from me it's for me. He doesn't just see my pain he feels it. Cupping my wet face his hands instantly soothe my soul and battered heart, his eyes soaking up every last fragment of my anxieties that I began losing control of when I ran from him. It's not just his arms that protect me, it's his whole being.

"Love, is protection, loyalty and passion. It's holding you when you're scared, kissing you when you're sad and loving you with every ounce of my heart and soul until the day I die. Love doesn't hurt when you know it's with the right one. It's loving the wrong person that causes all this pain. What you had with him wasn't real. What we have is, Amelia, and that is what's scaring you. You deserve this more than you know, you just need to find a way to let me in and set yourself free from bad memories."

"But I don't know how." I weep. Because I really didn't know how to let go of the final part that I could have control over.

"Then let me help you." He wipes my wet face and kisses away the tears that continue to fall, making my eyes close with his gentle touch. "Let me love you, Amelia. I'm not going anywhere, not now that I've found you."

"This isn't easy for me, Marcus. I need to be sure. But what I do know is I don't want you to leave me, I can't breathe when you're not with me. I just need time, please give me time." He presses his lips to my forehead and holds them, telling me without words everything I already knew, that he understands my fears and will protect me. That he loves me.

"I'll give you all the time you need. I love you."

"I know." I wrap my arms around his shoulders and hold him like my life depended on it, showing him with my strength the words I couldn't yet say. The words I was too frightened to say.

***

Now I understand the meaning behind Dr Thomas's words. The confliction between the heart and mind. A war between the two. I'm in that conflict right now.

I lay listening to the soothing melodies of Marcus's breathing and the flutters of his heart that press against my ear as I rest on his chest. My head is pounding, my eyes puffy from my tears and sleep was not happening anytime soon. Waves of anxiety hit me on occasions but I wasn't feeling as afraid as I had been a few hours ago. Maybe that's because of the arms that envelop me as we lay in bed. He's held me for hours, once he took me in his arms outside his house he never let me go, just laid down with me and soothed his fingers through my hair, reassuring me that everything is going to be alright.

Marcus made me fearless, he broke through my darkness and he reach me and in his own way without me even realising he's made me stronger. I'm a stronger person now than a few months ago; I just have to be fearless when it comes to love.

I tip my head up to look at him, his lashes rest on his beautiful face that's relaxed in his sleep and his hair still salted from the sea water. His was a strong passionate man and he wanted me. He loves me. I'm still yet to look inside my heart to see what he can see, because all I see right now is a woman still living in her tainted past afraid it will happen all over again, but also knowing that it won't because of the angel that holds me close.

I slip out of bed and tiptoe into the kitchen needing some water. Rosa was sat at the breakfast bar reading a magazine in her robe, and clutching an empty glass that's no doubt had a shot of Brandy in.

"Rosa, what are you doing up at this hour?"

"Age. I tried convincing myself when it first happened that I was having some sort of midlife crisis, but six years later I'm still here. Can't sleep either?"

I give a half smile whilst pouring my water and sat down next to her as she flips the page she's looking at. Her brief look at me clearly told her I'd been crying.

"He talks about you all the time you know? No matter how the conversation starts it always ends with you. I've seen a change in him."

I'm exactly the same when with Megan, I can't stop talking about him, I can't stop thinking about him. It's not just him that's changed. I sip my water and avoid her eyes.

"Sometimes I feel like I'm dreaming and everything is bright and uncomplicated, that nothing bad will even happen. But if I let my feelings take over me I'll wake up and everything will become dark and cold again. How do I stop that from happening, Rosa?"

She closes her magazine and turns towards me, a sweet smile graces her face as her dark hair sits up in a clip. "Someone once told me that the word fear represented two different meanings. Forget everything and run, or face everything and rise." She takes my hand. "Like you I was once broken by a man, granted it was completely different but he still broke my heart. But what you have to remember is they are not all the same and that it's ok to open you heart and let someone in. Love is like a flame but it doesn't mean you're always going to get burnt, Amelia. Don't let the fear decide your future. Listen to what your heart is telling you, not your head."

Her words hits me more than I thought they would, here was the mother of the man I'm wild about giving me the same advice I knew my own mother would, clearly all mothers carry the same handbook. Even though Marcus said similar words and I understood them, I felt as though Rosa clarified the questions I was constantly trying to answer. Maybe it was because she herself had been through the actions of a disloyal man.

"Marcus means more to me than anyone ever has. He's makes me breathe and I don't want him anywhere else but with me. It's just…" My emotions got the better of me and my eyes glassed over.

"Go on."

"I'm scared, Rosa."

"Oh sweetheart come here." Her arms flew around me as I cried into her shoulders, providing a different sort of comfort to what Marcus, Megan or Lucas could bring. It was the comfort I longed to have for many years, the comfort and love you got from a parent whilst they provided you with advice of their own experiences. That was when I knew that no matter what happens between Marcus and me, I'd always have Rosa.

Chapter Twenty-Eight

Marcus

"So, I've spoken to Amelia and everything is underway for the Wedding on Saturday, and the staff has been informed of the protocol during their stay. Lenton's associates are currently downstairs setting up the function room, why they have to set it up two days prior god only knows and-are you even listening to a word I fucking say?" Andrew's hard slap on my desk drew me out my thoughts, my thoughts of Amelia. It's like she's brainwashed my mind with her existence. Her reaction to me declaring my love for her didn't go exactly how I planned; truth was I didn't know how I wanted it to go. Her vulnerability ripped me in two as she divulged her fearful admission. Not only has that asshole made her fear men, he's made her fear the one thing that will set her free.

"I told her I loved her." I continue to draw random marks on the papers in front of me with my ballpoint, noticing Andrew placing his files on the desk and sitting back in his seat.

"And do you?" His deep raspy voice questioned me like some fucking head teacher disapproved of my actions towards a member of his staff.

"Course I do, I wouldn't have said it otherwise."

"So what's the problem?" gesturing with his hands as they rest on the arms of the leather seat.

"She can't say it back." Ever since that night on the beach apprehension has often crept through my body wondering what will happen between us. She's been close but yet distance and I know this is a big deal for her and that I need to be patient but fuck me it's so hard being patient when I know she feels the same. "What gives a man the right to treat a woman like shit, sabotages her beauty, ruins her self-esteem and makes her believe that every man she falls for is just like the last fucker?" My aggression was constantly clawing in my chest, it was never towards Amelia it was towards the bastard that had destroyed my girl and caused her the troubles she faces.

"What do you mean sabotages her beauty?" He sat forward, narrowed brows covered his green eyes. I was always under the impression Andrew knew of Amelia's history but judging by the look on his unshaven face he had no idea. Pushing back in my seat and standing by the window I overlook the bay. Even on dull and overcast days, Spring Rose was still a scene of attraction.

"The reason why you often heard her crying in her office was because she's been battling the actions of a violent piece of shit that was meant to love her. He abused her in every way you can imagine. It was weeks before she let me touch her, even longer to get her naked because of the scars that line her skin and she can't even fucking tell me how she feels because she terrified it will change what we have."

"Fuck, I had no idea. She just told me of her dad nothing more." My eyes fall to a shimmer of orange flame exiting the car at the front of the hotel foyer, her body hugging that bottle green dress I love seeing her in as her big round shades rest on top of her head, organising the staff that are test running the red carpet for the Lenton wedding as she makes her way inside the building. "So now you're pissed because she won't tell you the words you want to hear?"

I spun around in fury. "I'm pissed with the whole situation he's put her in."

He shakes his head and points his finger in my direction. "No, you're pissed off with him understandably, but you're more pissed with yourself because you know you're nothing like him and even though Amelia knows this, she can't tell you what you want to hear and *that's* pissing you off more than anything. You're pissed with yourself."

"You're wrong."

"I'm not wrong. I've known you long enough to know when sometime is eating away at you and you have no control over it. You want her, you love her, she feels the same but in order for you to know exactly where you stand with her you need those words she fails to give and that's what is pissing you off."

Anything was always clear cut with Andrew, that's why I respected him and is one of my greatest friends. But sometimes his knowledge of me pissed me off. "Fine, you're right! But can you blame me?"

"No, it's completely natural but you're forgetting one important factor here."

"Enlighten me." I sigh, sitting back in my seat and picking up the pen to roll it between my fingers.

"Amelia spent years with a violent man who only showed his feelings with action. Then you come along and create this new Romeo and Juliet fucking lifestyle and change everything she was ever use too. Give the woman chance to get her head round that. You have to give her time."

He was right. Although I knew Amelia had feelings for me, I never considered the fact that her head would be spinning with a different state of affairs, I just jumped right in without thinking wanting to hear the words I longed to leave her lips. I throw the pen back on the desk and sighed with a low growl, "Your right."

"I'm always right," he grins.

"Yeah, and you're also an asshole."

***

"Did Megan and Lucas get off ok?" Mum asks as Amelia and I head in through the door.

"Yeah, I miss them already."

"Oh sweetie it won't be long before Megan is back dancing on tables again." She says giving Amelia a hug along with a glass of wine before going back to her Brandy. Megan and Lucas have gone to visit family in the city before Lucas heads off back to L.A. to finish his last few months of work before moving back to the coast. His last few days here have provided us a chance to get to know each other better and for a twenty-nine year old that's obsessed with women, exercise and lounging on the bed with his two blue-eyed girls, he's a great guy to which I now consider a friend. I feel like a jack-ass the way I behaved towards him when he first arrived but when you have some guy you don't know over your woman it does shit to the brain you can't control.

"So, I've cooked dinner for us all and thought we would sit down together and talk."

I look up from my phone to where she stands in the kitchen dishing up the food. When mum cooks dinner that's the norm but when she says about sitting down and talking it means there's something on her mind.

"Rosa, this look amazing."

"Thank you dear." She smiles serving Amelia her chicken salad and sitting herself down.

"What's on your mind mother? We only sit at the table altogether when mum needs to talk; it's an old school family thing." I say to Amelia taking her hand to entwine our fingers.

Mum's silence caused a sign of concern in me as she placed her fork down and picks up her Brandy. "I'm seeing someone."

My stomach dropped and my hand tightened around Amelia's, I wanted nothing more than to see my mum happy again but at the same time there was a guy sniffing around my mother and my protectiveness quite rightly soared. "Ok, tell me more."

"He's your age."

"WHAT!"

Amelia choked on her wine as Mum's laugh filled the

room in an uncontrolled form, how the hell is this a laughing matter? "Marcus, you're so gullible. Of course I'm not seeing anyone. Although having said that if he was your age I'd hardly tell you."

Amelia's giggle soon followed along with mum's joke as I looked dumbfounded at the two of them whilst they yet again enjoyed my torment, trying their hardest to get me to crack as mum tickles her nails along my arm in her playful mood.

"Don't fuck about with shit like that, it'snot funny." I smirk. "Now be serious."

She wipes her mouth with her napkin. "I'm heading back to London in the morning."

"What? Rosa, why so soon?"

I knew exactly why and it pissed me off that after all these years one household name still controlled our family like we were their lapdogs waiting to be petted. Once this fucking wedding was out the way and everyone could get back to normal the better.

"I'm sorry sweetie, but I can't stay around here knowing that family is in town as I'm likely to be arrested. Beside I need to run a few errands back in the office for Marcus as he needs to be here. I'll be back in a few days as I'm technically due a holiday."

"You've been here two weeks, this is your holiday." I chuckle.

"No, Marcus, this was just an unexpected mini break that Rosa's had to cut short because of the Botox queen's arrival, she's due a proper holiday."

"Exactly. Thank you, Amelia." Mum agrees clinking her glass with Amelia's. These two have become thick as thieves the last couple of weeks but I wouldn't have it any other way. I love the fact they get along and feel completely comfortable within each other presence.

"You're abusing your service to my company Mother."

"Then fire me." She jokes as I get up from the table collecting the plates, knowing full well I can't fire her because I need her more than ever if I'm planning on setting up back here with Amelia.

"So going back to our earlier conversation, Marcus," she says raising her voice from across the room. "Out of interest, do you have any friends your age that are available?"

"Mum!"

"Ok, I'm sorry I shouldn't have asked," she waves her hand and sips her Brandy. "I'll just scroll through your Facebook."

***

The tension was running high at the Hotel, word has it Nadia had turned up to check on things and was working her way through insulting the staff and reorganising them to do things her way. Amelia's neck was constantly peppered in pink with her stress levels and I chose to hide out in the office for as long as I could. Once the wedding takes place tomorrow and she uses our building for the after party the sooner we can relax and mum can return back to enjoy her break.

"So, it is you then. I saw you on the web winning that award and I don't know whether I'm more pleased because I now know who I'm dealing with or more pissed off because of who you are, thank god my father isn't here yet." Her voice grated on my nerves as she forces her way into my office uninvited, crossing her legs and tapping her fake nails on the arm of the leather seat she's just helped herself to.

"You mean your research team failed to make the connection with me to this place when dealing with your demands in finding you a reception location? Jeez someone's gonna get fired."

"Don't fuck with me, Marcus; I can pull out of this any time I want!"

"And have your name plastered across the papers for possible pre-marriage problems? Yeah I can really see Daddy letting you do that, Nadia." Her glare was as sharp as a knife under her thick black lashes, make-up plastered on her face while her big gold earrings showed from having her blond hair tied back. Even dripping in expense she still managed to look fake.

"What do you want, Nadia?" I sigh. "Because believe it or not I have work to do."

"I have a few things that need to be put into place. My hired team will arrive an hour before us to make sure everything thing is in order."

"Your hired team?" I raise my brows in question.

"My extra security team that will be working for James and I during our time at The Grand, our safety is essential, Marcus."

Hiring an extra entourage, is she for real? Where the fuck does she think she's coming to, the Bronx? "Nadia, the Hotel has a high level of security in place already; I can assure you that you'll be fine."

Her deathly stare was doing nothing to me; I'm use to this woman and her attempts of trying to bring people down with just a look. "I want that Weston woman that's supposedly in charge of the day but is wondering around like she's just left high school to report to my head of security with any idiotic problems she can't deal with. Lord knows how she's managed to pull this off."

My irritation towards her was growing by the second and with talking of Amelia that way, it only made it heighten. "Her name is Amelia, and believe it or not she's worked her goddamn ass off for you these past few months, give her some credit."

"She's a redhead, Marcus, they don't seem as intelligent and capable as blondes and brunettes in my book. That's why you don't see many of them around, better off out the way if you ask me."

Fucking bitch! I jump up from my seat as the burn of my anger towards this vile woman runs through my veins. I'd love nothing more than to slap her right now but I don't do shit like that. I rest my balled fists on the desk and try and control the aggression behind my words. "Who the hell do you think you are? You come in here throwing your demands, abuse my staff with your inappropriate comments and have the audacity to accuse Amelia of not being capable of doing her job because she's a fucking ginger?"

A smug look plasters across her face as she sits forward, "You're fucking her aren't you?"

"Close the door on your way out!" My own glare was now as sharp as hers. Collecting her Prada bag she struts towards the door like a Hollywood Supermodel while the bracelets on her wrists clink as she strides.

"Oh, Marcus, one last thing. Anyone of your people step out of line, they'll find a lawsuit slapped in their face before they've chance to speak."

Five minutes of seeing Nadia has brought back the

history of what my father and her mother had done to our families with their infidelity and lies about my mother. If I don't get my shit together and fast, I don't think it will be my staff that will be facing a lawsuit- it's likely to be me.

Chapter Twenty-Nine

Amelia

As soon as I pulled back the bedroom curtains, I couldn't help the deep uncontrolled giggle that rumbled through my body. Today was Nadia Lenton's wedding day and Mother Nature sure as hell knew how to piss her off. The sky was grey as the heavens opened, coating the pavements of the coast with its summer rain as the rumbles of thunder played out in the distance. A storm had been brewing for a few days as the humidity had doubled and the winds had picked up. Seeing Nadia dripping wet and mascara running down her face would make my day. I can almost hear her Bridezilla scream from the happy place of my bedroom.

"You shouldn't be laughing. No one wants it to rain on their wedding day." Marcus chuckles, walking into the bedroom in just a towel, water dripping off his chest and making butterflies take flight in my belly.

Jesus that man is too damn sexy.

"Uh hello, this is Nadia we are talking about?"

"Hmm then again on her wedding day, rain is pretty fucking awesome." He comes and wraps his arms around me, sticking his wet body against my nightshirt. The intimacy between us since announcing his love for me has got stronger, yet my stress with organising staff rotas for the wedding has made me aloof on occasions as I drift into my world of living on my nerves from the pressure I'm under today. As well as that I feel as though the unit of people I had around me just a few days ago is slowly disappearing. Having Lucas around made me realise just how much I actually miss him, and Rosa has been like the mother I've needed since my own mum died and has supported me like I'm her own. Now they've gone their separate ways for a while, along with Megan I can't help but feel lost. If it wasn't for Marcus and Andrew keeping me grounded over preparations for today, I'd no doubt be rocking in the corner with a bottle of Tequila.

"Tell me something true," I coo as he nuzzles into my neck.

"I love you." I knew that was coming, it seems to be dropped into every sentence with him lately along with the beautiful. Like as though he has to keep reminding me of what I mean to him.

"Hmm, I know. Tell me something else that's true."

"Um? I hate cold pizza."

"What!" I turn my head to look up at him in horror. If Megan was here now she would probably slap him, she's obsessed with cold pizza. "How the hell can you not like cold pizza?"

"I just prefer it hot."

"Jeez, I learn something new about you every day." He kisses into my smile and runs his hands up the front of my shirt to play with my breasts.

"It'snot just pizza I like hot?"

"Care to clarify that a little better Mr Matthews?" I grin.

"Well, you're like my personal slice of Pepperoni, hotter the better."

The giggle left my belly as I spoke, "You really need better pick-up lines because that was the cheesiest one I've heard."

He removes my shirt so my back feels the bareness of his chest, as his hands glide down to take hold of my panties, pushing them from around my ass to fall to my ankles. My greed for him to touch me ignites as he runs his fingers up and down the inside of my thighs, teasing me as he kisses the weak spot on my neck, the one that with just the sweetest of a kiss will set my body a flame.

"How bout I ditch the pick-up lines and just make you cum?" He whispers.

"Sounds like an excellent idea."

I moan as his fingers greet my clit, circling the swollen bud before thrusting a finger inside me. I can never get enough of how our bodies respond to one another, Marcus just has to look at me and my panties are soaked and I hardly have to do anything and his response is evident. Over our time spent together he's made me love my body in a way I never thought I ever would again. He's made me love myself as well as another, making me feel beautiful and sexy within and out of his presents. Every woman deserves a man that makes her forget her heart was ever broken and Marcus is that man for me.

"Tell me something true." He mumbles, holding me up by the waist as my legs begin to weaken with the electric currents that are funnelling through my body.

"You drive my body insane," I gasp, digging my nails into his skin. "Your turn, tell me something true."

"You're going to be late for work."

"Who gives a shit; I'm sleeping with the boss."

"But I'm not your boss, Andrew's your boss remember?"

"Don't say that!" I breathe, unclipping my hair and letting my red locks fall down around the pale skin of my shoulders, knowing that is what Marcus likes to see when he has me.

"Don't say what? That Andrew's your boss?"

"His *name*. You can't bring another man's name into the equation when you're trying to make me cum."

He chuckles against my ear as he tweaks my nipple between his fingers. I push my chest up into him and hook my arm around his neck for extra support as my legs tremble beneath me. I begin to tighten with the added pressure of his thumb that rubs over my clit, working my walls, clit and nipple in unison with his hands and creating the fire within me to explode.

"Who you thinking of now?" he sniggers.

"Oh god! Only you. It's only ever you." I exhale in a cry as the most delicious shockwave rips through my entire body to coat his fingers with my orgasm as he takes my weight in his arm. I turn my head to the side and bring his mouth down to mine to slip my tongue in to devour his mouth.

"Now that will keep you going for a few hours." He smiled kissing me nose.

If there was one thing I loved more than anything about this man was that he never expected anything in return. We'd fuck each other senseless and get one another off, but then there were times when he'd torment and tease my body in the most enduring ways and got just as much satisfaction from that then when we fucked.

I rub my thumb over his cheeks as I stare into his hazel eyes thinking just how lucky I was that I was found by him when I was at my weakest. "Just because I haven't told you the words you're yet to hear, does not mean that I don't feel anything for you. You know that right?"

"Of course I do," he replies with a kiss. "Just answer me one question."

"What?"

"Were you really thinking of Andrew?"

My giggle erupted from my belly as his arms tightened around me.

***

Myself and Andrew wait in the staff conference room as the employees of The Grand enter and take their seats. Each month a meeting is held purely for Management but today Andrew has scheduled one so every staff member available knows the protocol.

"Ok, so Lenton's hired team is due to arrive within the next two hours once they have married at Whistmen Cathedral. From that point on any issues you may have must be informed immediately to Miss Weston who will then report to Nadia's management team with any enquiries and problems etc. The first two floors have been signed off to her guests along with the double Honeymoon suit, and we have strict orders that no one is to speak with any of the Lenton family during their stay here at The Grand, if they need anything it will be run though their team. Is that clear?" The group of staff members sat in there tailored uniforms look just as terrified as I feel. I thought Nadia was bad enough when dealing with her over the phone but she's an even bigger dragon in person.

"Will Mr Matthews be attending today?"

Marcus decided it would be in everyone's best interest if he stayed away from the reception as the likelihood of bumping into Nadia's father would be inevitable. Although Marcus was in some respects on speaking terms with Nadia, Harry was another matter altogether due to his wife having an affair with Marcus's father. The fact that neither Harry nor Marcus was responsible for the affair didn't come into the equation. In their eyes everyone was responsible with the breaking of two families.

"Mr Matthews has business elsewhere today so all reports are to be taken to either myself or Miss Weston… Amelia?"

"Thank you, Andrew." I step forward to take over. "Now the sheet of paper you were all giving on your way into the meeting is a timetable in which will be your best friend for the next forty-eight hours. Do not lose it! Where your name is highlighted will be your duty of work within that timeline stated. Now I appreciate some of you may not have the expertise within some of the areas listed but that's where you'll be for that period of time. It has been worked that those who have the knowledge will be on show during the Lenton's stay here."

"So basically what you're saying is those of us who fail in some areas get put out the way until they leave?"

"Exactly." Andrew replies to Claudia.

I sigh hating every bit of this and long for a Tequila when it's not even noon yet. "Look Claudia, we hate this as much as you do but there's no other alternative. The Lenton's are one of the biggest and wealthiest families in the country and will bring a huge amount of popularity and status to The Grand along with further high class celebrities to the coast in the near future. We have to work as a team here in order to pull this off understood?"

The group of uniforms mutter their response in an unenthusiastic way that wouldn't give an onlooker any form of confidence what so ever, but I knew I had their trust. Once the ball gets rolling they switch gear and provide the professionalism they're paid to do and treat the job and guests with the utmost respect. Their mood now wasn't because they didn't want to work; it was because of who they'd been running around for. One thing I noticed with Nadia whilst at The Grand yesterday throwing her demands was that she seemed to leave a trail of glumness behind her as she walked around with a stick up her ass. You just had to look at the woman and your instant happy mood was sliced apart in seconds.

"Right, well you're free to go but remember two important factors here people. Professionalism is key and nothing must go wrong."

I close the door to my office and collapse on the sofa for a break I should have took two hours ago, kicking off my shoes that are biting my toes as I munch on a bag of crisps and a chocolate bar. Calories are needed if I need to get through the rest of the day without Marcus or Megan here to hold my hand, and there was nothing I wanted more then to see them right now. My head feels like a vice is pressing against it and my body is already exhausted. Swiping the screen on my phone I give Megan a quick text.

Me: I need Tequila! How's the family?

Her reply was instant.

Megan: Irritating! I'm currently getting the third degree from Gran about how I need to look after my liver; too much Tequila is no good apparently. I've never heard such bullshit in my life. Ha!

Me: Wait till she knows your love for a good hard surface to dance on, whilst guys look up your skirt.

Megan: Hmm best not tell her that, she might have a cardiac arrest.

I was just about to reply when my desk phone rang. Growling out loud at whoever was disturbing my quiet time.

"Amelia, Miss Lenton's security manager has arrived."

And so it begins, nerves double in my belly as I'm now responsible for running one of the biggest Wedding Receptions this hotel has seen in a long time. "Thank you, Felicity. Where is he?"

"He's waiting at the desk with me now."

"Ok, I'll be right down." Checking over his name on my computer I quickly put a brush through my hair and top up my lip-gloss, making sure I look presentable before heading down to the ground floor. Nadia will be here in just over an hour and I had to make sure the final preparations were in order. I can see why wedding planners hit the bottle after the big day they organise takes place. It's been stressful enough running around after Nadia when it comes to hosting her reception, doing it full time along with every other detail will be enough to push me overboard. Megan however loves things like this, all the arranging and organising. She would make an excellent Events Manager.

Rounding the corner my belly flipped with anxiety at the sound of voices at the desk. A tall well-built guy known as Lloyd was in deep conversation with Felicity as she giggles at whatever he said. With her nod of my arrival he turns and I freeze. The man stood in front of me was not known as Lloyd.

I knew him as Daniel.

Chapter Thirty

Amelia

My back hit the wall of my office with a harsh thud, legs struggling to hold my weight, lungs convulse and fight for air as my palms become clammy with my body's reaction of panic. My legs carried me as I ran through the lobby but I felt as though I wasn't moving. Tears burn my eyes as the heat rips through my body, burning every nerve ending as my heart pounds its erratic beat. Why is he here? How did he find me? I feel sick and sweaty, squeezing my eyes closed trying to control my body and fight against it leaving me.

I can't breathe. I can't breathe.

"Amelia, could you please go back-" I whip my head round only to see Andrew running towards me as he entered my office and throwing his files at my feet. "It's ok, just try and stay calm. I've got you." Getting his phone from his back pocket he scrolls the screen knowing exactly who he's wanting to call whilst trying to calm me.

"No," I try to speak but harsh gasps leave my dry throat as I grab at his arms, "Don't."

He can't see, I don't want him to see. It will lead to questions I don't want to answer. Question that will make what I've just witnessed a reality. It's like he's here to remind me of what I can't have, what I don't deserve to have.

"Amelia, he needs to be with you."

I shake my head pushing the phone away from him. "No."

I've not had an attack like this in years and it's hit me like a fucking freight train as it sucks the life out of me. My hands cling to the deep ache of my chest as I lean over trying to find a position that is comfortable, but fail. My stomach muscles spasm through fighting, heart racing a mile a minute as pins and needles prickle around my mouth. It's killing me.

"Look at me. Focus on me, Amelia, follow my rhythm." I flash my watery eyes to Andrews as he cups my face, his green eyes channelling into mine making me focus, as I look for that bit of hope in helping me get out of this torment my body is under. I feel trapped.

I can't breathe as there is no air, flashes of Daniel's face are vivid in my mind I can't shake away and my heavy tears cascade my face choking me as I fight. I don't understand, how did I not know? Everything I was afraid of happening with my future has come back to haunt me like a ghost of the past.

"Breathe in and out, in and out." I follow Andrew's

lead inhaling as much as I can muster and blowing it back out, clutching his arms hard as my nails pinch his skin. But it's no use. I shake my head at him as the burn in my chest doesn't seem to subside. My body's fighting between fear of the past and fear of losing breath. But I won't let him do this to me, not again. I won't let him win.

Andrew takes my hands and cups them over my mouth to form a mask, inhaling and exhaling to the rhythms of his guidance. "Good girl, keep going. In and out," he murmurs through his raspy voice. His fretful eyes never left mine as we repeat each other's patterns over and over, bringing me out my panic and gaining back the control I lost. Minutes feel like hours and I feel like a fucking idiot for losing it. My chest starts to ease, the numbness subsiding and my legs attempt to make a step forward, leaning into Andrew as I rest my head on his firm chest. But there's nothing that will stop the tears that fall heavy from my eyes. I always feel battered after an attack, sometimes that's more of a challenge to fight. Not only are you recovering from the aftermath, it's also psychological fight of your emotions and I know this time it's going to be a lot harder to fight.

"I'm sorry. I'm so sorry," I cry.

"Shh, it's ok. Just focus on your breathing."

Why now? Why here? Why today on the biggest days of everyone's life did he have to rear his ugly head like a cancer, spreading his evilness over my place of peace. What will I tell Marcus? What will this mean for us? Several minutes pass as I rest against Andrew, still repeating the techniques as I finally gain control of my breathing whilst he strokes my hair and holds me close.

"Thank you," I whisper.

"Where did that spring from?"

Downstairs in the Reception area, I thought to myself. I don't answer right away as I try and find the right words in which to say. "I-I'm not sure. I just…I don't know."

I want to tell him but I can't bring myself to speak the words.

Andrew helps me to the sofa and gets us both a shot of whiskey from my secret stash I didn't think he knew about, kneeling down in front of me and stroking my hand. "Amelia, are you sure there's nothing bothering you? Marcus has told me everything. If there's a problem I want to help."

Why hasn't this man got ladies swooning at his feet? If only he'd let people see the real Andrew Harris and not the dark and mysterious one he likes to play. He's like a gentle giant all muscle and rocking the jaw scruff. Thirty-two and still confined to an office when he should be with a woman that puts a smile on his face.

"No, I'm fine, nothing's bothering me."

The look in his eyes told me he knew I was lying but he never pushed me. I hate myself for what I'm doing, within minutes of seeing Daniel I've already started hiding the truth from those close to me, just like I did for him all those times he bruised my body. I hated what he did and I hate that yet again he has this control over me that I can't seem to fight.

My office phone was constant with incoming calls and I knew it's likely to be Felicity wondering what the fuck I ran for. Nadia was due in just under an hour and I knew I had a job to do even though I was terrified of leaving my office. With me and Andrew both hid away drinking whiskey it meant that no lead of authority was on the ground floor and I couldn't let Marcus down.

"I should get back." I mumbled, hating saying the words that let me. I go to stand but my legs give out with their continuous shake and I fall back to the sofa.

"You look terrible. You're not going anywhere other than home."

"Andrew, Nadia's security is down stairs. We had a function to manage."

"And I will handle it. I can't have you working under pressure when you not well, you're going home, Amelia, no arguments."

His hard stare told me I'd lost the fight and to be honest I was too exhausted to continue doing anything. I physically couldn't do anything and emotionally I was a wreck as my mind was on overdrive with panic. All I wanted was Marcus.

"You can call him now." I whisper as I lay and curl myself on the sofa, wanting nothing more than his strong arms that protect me, to cradle my vulnerable body and bring the warmth back into my heart that suddenly felt ice cold. I close my eyes and try to block out the image of evilness as the tears slip out from my closed lids in the hope that this was all just some fucked up nightmare and I'm soon to wake up.

***

"Amelia, baby?" my eyes fluttered open to catch the sight of hazels I loved to see and forever kept me safe. "Hey, what's all this I hear about you freaking Andrew out? It takes a lot to scare him." His voice was gentle as he smothered his hand over my hair. I'm still laid on my office sofa and Andrew was still nursing a glass of whiskey. The heavy feeling of fear still pumping its way through my veins.

"How long have I been asleep?"

"Not long." Andrew replies, throwing back the rest of his drink. I place my hand on Marcus's face and drowned in the sparkle of his eyes. He's like my ray of sun, surrounding me with the brightness of his embrace and burning its way through the darkness that's consumed me to fill my heart with warmth. I really don't deserve him.

"I'm sorry, Marcus."

"What for?"

"Everything. I can't even run a fucking wedding reception without freaking out. I'm such a mess." I choke out as I try to hold back my tears.

"It's just a wedding party babe, you're more important than what's going on downstairs," the softness of his lips on mine caught my breath, ever so often he would remind me with his angel like kisses just how precious I was to him and him to me. The tenderness of his touch would take my breath but somehow keep me breathing.

"You would tell me if there was anything wrong wouldn't you?"

Even though Marcus was close I still felt so exposed, like every part of my heart and soul had been ripped from me all over again and hung up on a line waiting to be battered. Waiting to take it anyway he wanted, and I knew that as long as Daniel was here in Spring Rose I was not safe and everybody's life that was connected to me was in danger too. I knew his games well and knew that everyone's life was in his hands for him to manipulate anyway he wanted. My job in the past was to protect my best friend, now I have a unit of friends around me I loved and didn't want anywhere near his dirty hands.

"I promise."

"Let's take you home beautiful."

I heard his repulsive laugh before I saw him. Felicity's giggle bouncing out against the wall of the foyer as he worked his putrid charm and hated that she's just as blind as I was. I saw my own reflection in her as he ogled her like the grand jewels, no doubt acting like a true prince only to turn twisted evil once the door had closed. That was one thing I could never work out with him, how one moment he was everyone's favourite person providing his sweet smile and engaging others in conversation they wanted to hear, as the woman swooned around him like a flock of horny housewives, then the next I was thrown against a wall and beaten for showing too much cleavage in the dress that he bought. He was a permanent head fuck, his mind control was fatiguing and after all this time I still couldn't work it out.

My hand tightened around Marcus as we rounded the corner and just like earlier I felt like I'd been punched in the gut when he turned, feeling his eyes run over my body without even giving him eye contacted.

"Mr Matthews, I didn't think you were coming in today." Felicity smiles, lacing a ribbon of hair between her fingers.

"I'm not, I've just come to take Amelia home."

"Oh, Miss Weston, is everything alright?" she ask before quickly flashing her swoony eyes back to Captain Evil.

I couldn't be bothered to respond, a nod and smile was all I could muster as Marcus swims his arm around my waist as we make our way over to where Daniel stands.

"Marcus, what are you doing, let's go."

"Baby, I can't just ignore him. I won't be long." He smiled with a kiss on my cheek. If Marcus hadn't been holding me I'm convinced I would of fallen as I could no longer feel my legs, trying to stop myself from falling into another panic attack with the deep inhales through my nose as we got closer,

"Mr Newman, is that correct?"

"Lloyd please," even his voice caused the bile to thicken in my throat. After all these years of not seeing him and recovering from the life I had with him felt as though I'd never left his escape. His build was thicker, overgrown scruff on his jaw and had a look evil like he always had.

"Lloyd, Marcus Matthews, pleasure to meet you sir."

They shake hands. If only Marcus knew.

"And yourself, congratulations on the award, your hotel is incredible, the money that's gone into this place is noticeable, it's even bigger than I imagined."

"Thank you, I take a lot of time and thought when I invest, I knew this place was full of potential when I saw it on the market."

Stop talking, stop talking!

"Babe, can we go now?" I plead in whisper.

"Yes of course. Unfortunately Lloyd, Miss Weston is a little under the weather and needs to be taken home. Claudia has very kindly stepped in to take her place so any problems she's the one you need. Or there's Andrew the Manager on duty."

"Thank you. I'm very sorry of you sudden ill health, Miss Weston. It was a pleasure to finally meet you." Before I had chance to react Daniel takes my hand in a shake. Squeezing my hand tight in his grip and flashing my eyes to him as I try and hide the pain. The look in his eyes was one I remember well, cold and dark. It was the look of warning and the grip of his callus hand was the physical message of what he could do. There was no life in his eyes, no emotion, no remorse, just dead and cold which sent a chill down my body. A chill that laid heavy on my heart.

"Until we meet again, Miss Weston."

Chapter Thirty-One

Amelia

You can be the strongest amongst many but it only takes one person to bring you down. One person to wash away every bit of recovery you've achieved over the years. One person to set your anxieties, panic and fear rocketing to new highest. One person to destroy the life you're beginning to love and one person to take you right back to the broken fragile girl who was lost in the world of the darkness. I thought that person was no longer around to hurt me; I thought I was freed from his violence and septic words. I was wrong!

It was either nightmares or insomnia that played the nightly roll, last night I laid reliving the nightmares with my eyes wide open as I clung to my prince and not wanting to let go. I've laid here since dawn just watching him as he sleeps peacefully, thinking how lucky I am that he wants me in his life.

"I believe I have your beautiful eyes watching me?"

"How the hell do you do that?" I smile as his own mouth curves.

"What? Know that you've been watching me as I sleep? It's my special Spiderman-senses." He replies with his eyes still closed and his voice thick with sleep.

"Oh really? I thought you were Thor?"

"That to." He rubs his eyes and opens them, clearing his throat and pulling me over to lie flat out over his body. He tucks my hair behind my ears and his fingertips trace up and down my back. "Just call me the King of Marvel. I've already gone all Hulk over Lucas, only he got off lightly as I never got chance to threw him against the wall." He chuckles.

"Not to mention your Superman stunt when we first met,"

"Exactly. I'm a collaboration of Heroes when it comes to you, Miss Weston, one I never fail to get tired of."

I softly run my finger round his hairline, his jaw, over his eyebrows and down his nose. Finishing with my fingers tracing over his lips and flicking my eyes back to him as he watches. He's perfect in every way and it's still crazy to think that he can have any woman he ever wanted yet he wants me, all of me, flaws included. "I'm so lucky to have you, Marcus." I whispered. "Promise me I will always have you."

He rolls us over and rest on top of me, his hazel eyes full of integrity and promise that fill my heart with unconditional love. "You know you have me, there's nobody else I want other than you. What do I have to do to prove to you that I only want you?"

"Kiss me like you mean it and hold on to me forever."

His lips made contact with mine and he kissed me in the most desirable way, full of passion and power, running his hand over my body and cupping my thigh to lift my leg and smooth over my skin. It's moments like this that I want to hold onto forever, keeping me safe in his arms. Keeping me from falling. "I love you, Amelia."

Tell him, tell him! The words are on the tip of my tongue, wanting to tell him that he has me, all of me. But I only speak the words I know how. "I know."

***

I loved my job and everything about it, it brought me peace, happiness and kept me grounded. But right now as we leave the house and head in the direction of the hotel, I hated every second of it and wanted nothing more than to lock myself in the house with Marcus and never leave.

Dread ran over my body like mites, the bile in my throat felt as though it's choking me and I feel sick to the stomach with what I knew I had to face. Today is the last day Nadia and her people are at the hotel and once they have gone everything can be back to normal. I've not told anyone of my findings as the thought of what that would mean scares me, I don't wish to put anyone's life in the hands of a violent man but the secrecy is killing me and fucking with my head.

Maybe he's changed. Maybe after all these years he's seen the error of his ways and become the man I always thought he could be. Those questions often ran through my head the hours I spent last night staring at the ceiling, secretly crying as Marcus slept beside me. But then I remember the way he looked at me when I first laid eyes on him in the foyer and the power behind his strength when he took my hand whilst we were leaving. And even though there was a look of sick satisfaction in his eyes, there was also the look of darkness I remember all too well.

Just that split second of seeing my past, I knew without doubt where I wanted my future to be and who I wanted it to be with. I may not have told Marcus I love him yet but seeing Daniel confirmed everything in my head I was fighting against with my heart.

"Babe, I'll drop you off, I need to stop by Fitzford Hill."

My stomach dropped at the thought of him leaving me alone. I throw my phone into my bag that was in the footwell as my fingers continue to twist my ring that's beginning to chap my skin with the constant friction. "That's fine."

Opening the car door for me once at The Grand, Marcus takes my hand to help me out as his arms slink around my waist, bringing me close to him. "Are you sure you're ok? Your eyes are telling me you're not."

"I'm just tried. Told you these last two weeks will take it out on me. But least I have you to keep me together." I smile, trying as best I could to convince him nothing was wrong. He brushed his lips on mine as my body melts against him, taking the edge of anxiety that lays heavy on my gut.

"Pick you up later," he says, sweeping my hair behind my ear and kissing my forehead.

"Missing you already."

I wave him off as the ice cold shiver slowly cascades

its way down my body at the thought of going inside a building I once loved. The hairs on my skin stood tall as I clicked my heels along the marble floor trying my best to avoid everyone's eyes as I made my way into reception. Feeling even more vulnerable in knowing that I wouldn't see the face of my best friend who would kill for me if she knew what I was facing today.

"Good morning, Miss Weston," Felicity beams handing me my mail, "Andrew sent a message to say he will be delayed."

"What?" my breath catching my throat. "When will he be here?"

"He never said, sorry." Even though I heard her loud and clear I still looked at her as though I was waiting for answers. I was officially fresh bait and on my own.

"Ooo you know that sexy security guy of Nadia's? We so hit it off yesterday and he-"

"Stay away from him!" the sharp jab of my voice made her jump. "You shouldn't be getting in involved with staff members that work alongside-"

"You're involved with Marcus." She interjected. I felt like a bitch taking my anger and insecurities out on her when she wasn't even to know of my issues but I just saw red on the mention of Daniels existence.

"Marcus owns the building, Andrew is my boss there's a difference. I however am your boss and I'd like to pay you for the job you're meant to be doing rather than checking out every piece of fucking eye-candy that walks through the hotel doors. Is that clear?!"

"Y-yes, Miss Weston." I wanted nothing more than to wrap my arms around her and hug the shit out of her, Felicity like myself was easily led astray when it come to the wrong men and lacked confidence. She would hardly look at the guests when she first started and here I was knocking her down like a hammer to a nail.

I take my mail and leave her silent as I walk my unsteady legs through the hotel and up to my office, constantly looking over my shoulders for any unwanted monsters lurking in the shadows. The relief that hit me when I took hold of my office door was overwhelming, only it soon vanished and the fear returned hitting me like a wrecking ball once I walked inside.

"We meet again, Amelia." He leant against my desk in his black suit, drinking my alcohol in my fucking office. I could smell his putrid musky scent lingering up my nose whilst vivid flashbacks of his torment play in my mind as I tried to remain strong. He was drinking before noon, which meant he wasn't in the greatest of moods.

"Get out." My frightened voice is feeble and pathetic, like he always made me feel. His snigger's making me uncomfortable, his eyes are dark and dangerous like they always were as my body prickles with panic.

"I'm not going anywhere. Not until I get what I came for." The callousness of his voice grated through my bones, even after all this time the only emotion he showed was aggression and hatred.

"Which is?"

He downs his drink in one gulp, placed the glass on the desk and flashed his eyes at me that have now turned to fire as he growls. "You,"

A firm hand pinches my arm with his grip as my legs are taken from under me in my bid to escape, covering my mouth as he kicked the door shut and slamming me against the wall. "Make a fucking sound and I will hurt you!" he sneered.

My heart was rapid, chest convulsing for air as my eyes-widen in fear of the likeliness that's going to happen. The pressure of his hard body on mine was more powerful than I remember and the painful grip on my mouth felt as though I was already bruised.

"Now here's what's going to happen, so you best listen very clearly as I don't like repeating myself. Does that rich fucker you're screwing know who I am?"

I shake my head as my chest feels as though it's shutting down with the onslaught of my panic. "Good. Because I can't be responsible for my action so you're going to keep your fucking mouth shut do you hear me? Because I will hurt him, Amelia, I promise you that."

I nod, desperately wishing I told Marcus he's found me but knowing I needed to protect him. I'll do whatever it takes to protect him. "I'm taking my hand away now, not a sound you hear me?"

I nod to his order as the instant relief on my mouth causes me to gasp for air, "What do you want from me?"

He pushes off of me and steps back never taking his stone cold gaze away. In the corner of my eyes I can see the security button under the lip of my desk but it's too far. I'm closer to the door for my escape. "I've been working in security for a while, Nadia is the biggest money grabbing bitch I've worked for, the pay in hardly liveable, not for today's standard of living. Then I saw you and lover boy, collecting an award for a seven star hotel and thought I'd pay you a visit. When I found out it was Nadia's location for her reception it was a win, win. You ruined me, Amelia. You owe me."

I try to escape once he turns for another drink but he's

too quick for me, pulling me back by my hair and slamming me against the wall, gripping my jaw with his hand and smashing my head back against the bricks making my cry out with the blow.

"I'm sorry. I'm sorry." I gasp even though I have nothing to apologise for but I always felt I had to. He eyes now full of fury as he seethed his word out through gritted teeth.

"I spent years on the run because of you and you're fucking lies, changed my name, my lifestyle, and lost my friends. You owe me every-fucking-thing you've put me though. I want something in return. You owe me. 50k should do it and I'm not going till I get it."

He has to be kidding right? "Daniel I haven't got that sort of money."

"You're fucking a millionaire, you have the money!" Pain radiates in my head and neck with another hard slam of my skull to the wall, my hands pathetically try to defend myself.

I agree to his ridiculous demand in the hope it will bide me time to tell Marcus. "Ok, I-I'll get you w-what you want, I need time. Please." I beg with my hands not knowing what to do with them.

A sickening smile greeted his malice eyes as he moved forward, his voice had now lost the aggression behind it, "That's my girl. You see how easy things are, how differently they could of been if you'd listened to me," he murmurs, pressing himself into me creating a proximity that nauseates my stomach as he runs his hand up my dress. My heart is in my throat, my mouth dry.

"I'm sorry," I whisper, trying to hold back my tears. Tears that would enrage him more if he were to see them.

This was where his unpredictability came out, after hurting me he would always try and plead his forgiveness with caresses and healing words. Words and touches that repulse me as his breath hits heavy on my lips.

"I've missed this, this connection we have. I've missed you. My gorgeous, Amelia." He says above a whisper. My body burns with panicked heat when his lips hit mine trying to force his tongue into my mouth, I press my lips together firmly, shaking my head to prevent his entry. The hard yank of my hair causes me to gasp with pain as it rips my skull, gaining him access into my mouth with his unwanted invasion that robs me of my breath and abuses my mouth. I push hard at his chest to try and remove him from my grasp but he's too strong. He takes my arms, pinning them above my head with one hand while the other plays with the hem of my dress to work its way rather up my thigh, pressing his solid body against me to prevent my escape as the feel of his arousal makes me want to vomit. My body trembles with the terror of what's going to happen. My attempts to fight back begins to such down against the poisonous body that's crushing me. Not again. He can't have me again.

"Babe, you left your phone in the-" Our heads spin towards the voice that saves me, warmth and relief hitting my body which quickly turns cold as his eyes darken with anger when he sees my body entwined with another.

Chapter Thirty-Two

Marcus

Air left my lungs like I'd been winded with a solid blow. My bloodstream a mixture of ice cold and fury working its way up my body in equal measures with witnessing the unexpected that stood interlinked before me. Her lips red and swollen from the wildness I interrupted and her eyes popped out with horror from my entrance.

"Marcus," she gasps, panic dripping from her voice. "I-I can explain."

That's the line people say that automatically makes them look guilty.

"It's not what you think."

And that's the second line people say because they *are* guilty.

My eyes blaze into hers, chest expanding from rage

that's soon to erupt from my body as I clench hard on my jaw. Why would she do this? What was it with me and cheating women?

"Well this is awkward."

My eyes shifted from Amelia's to a bearded man with a smug look on his face, dressed in a black suit, the same black suit that belonged to the entourage of Nadia-fucking-Lenton and the same lapdog I spoke to just yesterday. Of all the people in the world it could have been it had to be some prick from her colony. Another one to laugh in my face. She's going to fucking love this. "What's the fuck is going on?" I seethed as I step towards them, knowing exactly what's going on.

"Do you really have to ask, surely it's obvious?" his cocky stance pissed me off the more he spoke. Hands in his pockets as he rocks back and forth on his heels without any kind of remorse. Fucking prick.

"No. Don't listen to him, Marcus. Let me explain."

"Amelia, baby what's to explain, he's already caught us, you should just tell him, now. Save all the heartbreak." He smirked. He fucking smirked.

"Stop it! Marcus, listen to me." She moves towards me, pleading with her hands but I focus on the piece of shit behind her that's clearly getting a kick out of all this. My fists clench tighter at my side as the rage becomes overpowering. Only I call her baby.

"I asked a question. What. The. Fuck's. Going. On?"

"Are you blind man, she wants me. She's well up for it."

There was nothing in his eyes other than amusement, no guilt, no shame, nothing. Just a look I couldn't work out other than enjoyment. His cold dry cackle was enough to make me lose my shit, lunging towards him and knocking him off his feet as my fist made contact with his face. Grabbing the scruff of his jacket before he had chance to recover and slamming his front against the wall as he fought against me. Amelia screaming at me to stop and I can't help but think it's to protect the piece of filth I want nothing more than to throw in front of a fucking train.

"Couldn't get what she wanted from you so she came to me."

"Fuck you!" I growl.

"Don't listen, Marcus, he's lying!"

She tugs at my arm trying to make me look at her but I shrug her off as my only focus is the bastard that's had his hands on my girl and is currently laughing at me while pressed to the wall. "Get back, Amelia."

"I love it when I make her scream for more," he grunts.

I pull him back with a spin, smacking him a second time as he comes in for his own blow, hitting my chin with a solid punch that makes my teeth smack together. I swing for another as the office now becomes a ring to a bare-knuckle fight.

"Stop it! Stop it!"

Her piercing cry should have made me stop but in all honesty I couldn't give a shit about the woman that's betrayed me right now. I needed to release the wrath of what I walked in on and make her suffer just as much as I was. Make her hurt like I was hurting as I still see the vision of her slim body up against his.

Within minutes a cloud of black entered the office in a heavy form, separating us from our conflict as I try to fight against whoever's holding me back.

"What the fuck is going on?!" Andrew bellowed, his

green eyes burned into mine as he takes in the surrounding of two men in a heated brawl and a woman curled up in the corner in a trembling mess. My gut twisted at the sight of her, frightened and confused, yet I didn't want to go to her. Comforting her would be wrong of me when she's the reason behind this.

"She can't get enough, Matthews. She wants me," he laughed, as the blood dripped from his nose. "Amelia, I'll see you very soon."

"Get him out of here!" Andrew snaps at the security holding the enemy, giving me a disapproving look and going straight to Amelia.

"Amelia, sweetheart are you ok?"

"Yes," she cries.

"Come here, its ok."

Seeing his arms around her pissed me off, not only were I mad with her, I wanted to hold her. I hated seeing her upset. Then in seconds I see them again in my mind and hate her for it. "Oh, enough with the fucking sympathy, she's the reason this has happened."

"No. No. Marcus, it's not like that."

"Will someone please tell me what is going on here?" Andrew glared, asking me for answers while he held her close.

"She's fucking her way through Lenton's Security." I gestured to her with my hand.

"No!" she pushes past Andrew and comes to me, grabbing my arms to hold me as I turn my head not wanting to look at her. "You have to listen to me, Marcus. You have to trust me."

I'm taken right back to walking in on Sadie and Sean when their dirty lies were uncovered. I'm taken right back to the feeling of disgusting disloyalty and humiliation as I stand before this woman who promised to give me her heart, only to go and jump in some fuckers pants. I thought she was different. I thought she understood the word truth and loyalty, clearly I was wrong.

"I'll leave you to it." Andrew leaves us in the silence of the room as I pour myself a large whiskey, wanting to leave but needing answers while her constant sniffles do nothing to ease my anger that's still simmering. Of all the people to do shit like this I never thought it would be her. I love her, respected her, treated her like a queen and this is how she repays me.

"Marcus, please say something."

I walked the floor in silence, I didn't want to talk, sometimes you just gotta stay silent because no words can explain the shit that's going on in your heart and mind as I tried to control the tightness in my chest. I wanted an explanation from her but I needed to calm myself. Even now I was thinking of her and her mental state, what my reaction would do. The last thing I wanted was to frighten her as that would only prove her theory on men. And despite my outburst I was nothing like her last.

"You're the one that should be talking, Amelia." I sigh, pouring myself another drink and sitting at the opposite end of the office as close to the door as I could get, I feel like I'm suffocating the closer I'm near her. She slowly moves her shaky body to the sofa, twisting the ring on her finger and sniffing back her tears as I run my tongue along the inside of my lip that's been split with the impact.

"Yesterday was the first I saw of him. He was already in my office when I got here this morning. He kissed me, Marcus; I was trying to stop him when you walked in.

That's all it was I swear. It's not what you think."

"Is that right?" I scoff. "That's exactly what Sadie said when she was fucking my best friend."

"But I'm not Sadie and I'm not fucking him," she cries, mascara running down her face as her neck becomes blotchy. "I'm not fucking him. Please, Marcus, you have to believe me. I'm yours, you have all of me remember?"

"I thought I did," I murmur.

I sit forward and pinch the bridge of my nose, squeezing my eyes shut as the pressure in my head becomes too much. Loosening my tie and top button in need of freedom.

Wiping her tears Amelia straightens herself, her voice thick with emotion but commanding, "Look at me, Marcus." I don't, I can't, because her eyes that are my home will break me and I'm afraid of what they will show. "Look. At. Me."

She comes over taking my face in her hands and instantly washing away the aggression in me with her magical touch, the touch that for the first time I disliked because she was clouding my vision with her existence. My heart ached the moment she tipped my head up and I looked into her eyes. Hurt and confused just like mine as she spoke through her sobs.

"Do you really think that after everything I've been through, after the courage I had to find in showing you my body that I'd go with someone else? Do you really think I'd do that?"

I'd like to think that she wouldn't, I like to think that everything she was saying was true but that part of my past threw up the warning sign and prevented me from thinking anything other than what I witnessed. I can't fall back into that life again.

"I don't know what to think. I can't think when you're around me; you take that ability from me, Amelia, because all I think about is you. And now all I can see is you and him."

"There is no me and him, Marcus, I want you. Only you."

My irrational mind was driving me crazy with scenarios and the same one kept repeating in my head. She's not told me she loves me because she was saving me from the fucking humiliation, only I've stumbled upon her little party like a surprise visitor. "Is this why you've not told me you love me? Because of wh-"

"Just because I don't speak it, doesn't mean I don't feel it Marcus, I've told you that. I only want you. It's just you and I."

She moves further forward, coming up closer to my body and stopping my ability to breathe. Suffocating me with her honeysuckle and vanilla aroma causing my eyes to close with the unwelcoming feeling of yearning that she giving me. I can't bear her touching me because of the feeling she creates inside. The feelings that makes my heart feel like it's going to explode because of the love I have for her, my heart is hers and she's breaking it. She is breaking me.

"Amelia, don't." I mumble.

"You know me, Marcus. You. Know. Me. You've made me come alive, made me learn to love myself and made me feel, why would I jeopardise that?"

Her eyes always told me things she never needed to speak, they held my gaze when she spoke of her fears, never faltered when she was sad and still held on when she spoke the truth. Even though I found it hard to look at her I knew her eyes were on me the moment I stepped foot in this office. And now as she held me through her tears they still locked on mine as she spoke, which only confused me more.

My body stiffened as she dipped her head to mine, my heart pounding faster as my emotions were all over the place. "Amelia, please don't do this."

"I only want you, Marcus," she whispered a breath apart from my lips. "I don't want anybody else, I only want you. Let me be yours."

Her lips touched mine and my stomach tightened. The saltiness of her tears met my tongue when she slipped hers into my mouth to captivate me. My heart and mind fighting the rollercoaster of emotions that compressed within me. I didn't want her near me, but I don't want her to leave. I want her; I hate her for making me feel the way I do. She was the best thing that had happened to me and I can't bear the thought of losing her but I felt trapped, humiliated. Hurt. A part of me believed everything she said because I did know her, but that fucked up part couldn't forgive her, the things he said kept going over in my mind.

"I can't do this." I push her back and stand. Feeling as though I'm suffocating. I needed to be away from her in order to sort my head out and have time to think.

"Marcus, please don't go, nothing happened I swear. I'm nothing without you."

"I need time, Amelia. I need to think."

"Marcus, please don't leave me on my own. I need you here with me." She begs, grabbing my jacket in desperation and resting her head on my chest as she cried. "Please. Please don't leave me on my own."

Her pleading words crushed me but I couldn't stay any

longer. Every relationship goes through struggles, but only the strongest relationships are the ones that work and I hoped that we could get through this. I needed space to sort out the shit that was running around in my mind and work out what was the right thing to do.

"I need to think, I'll find you when I'm ready."

"No. No, Marcus, don't-" I push her from me and walked out with clenched hands and a shattered heart as she cried my name over and over through her sobs. The sort of cry I knew won't leave me any time soon.

Chapter Thirty-Three

Amelia

My legs burned, my body's exhausted and my chest ached from the endless miles I've put in on the treadmill in the last twenty-four hours. When I need to think I run. When my anxieties need to be eased I run and when I'm fighting the fear of my ex, I run. Running was my freedom. Now it's only my escape. I can't work out if it's more painful having my heart ripped out from being beaten daily or from the one person I never wanted to lose.

I've not seen Marcus in two days and my heart feels as though it's shattered into a thousand pieces. The ache in my chest deepens the longer we're apart and I feel as though I'm losing the ability to breathe without him near me.

In the past few months there's hardly been a day or night without him and the thought of not having him close scares me shitless. My fears and anxieties have heightened, my tears won't stop falling and I can't seem to function. It's like he's took all the control I ever had and now I have to start all over again in order to make it through the day. Yesterday I spent the entire day barricaded inside my house too afraid to leave whilst I cried myself into the whiskey bottle trying to find answers that weren't there. I forgotten what it felt like to feel broken and now I'm right back there in the cloud of darkness. The scariest part of loving someone is the uncertainty that they could stop loving you at any given moment and I fear that this is what's happened between Marcus and me. He's not returned my calls and I've left dozens of tearful voicemails as I pleaded my forgiveness. I respect the fact he needed time but every second I'm without him, feels as though I'm drowning.

If only I could tell him the truth, then none of this would have happened and he'd be with me now. But I couldn't put him in danger, Daniel is an evil man and never one to go back on his word, if he said he would hurt Marcus he won't stop until he does and because I love him I'll do anything to keep him out of danger. Even if it meant losing him forever.

In one respect a part of me is thankful Daniel has found me, because if it wasn't for his return I wouldn't have realised just how much I'm in love with Marcus. I tried to bury the feelings I had as I was terrified of falling in love, because I knew Marcus would never hurt me and that's what scared me the most. Only now he's hurt me in other ways. Sometimes it's not the butterflies in your heart that tell you your feelings but it's the pain, and that pain is ripping through me like a hot bullet. Through my own stupidity and apprehension, I've lost the man that only ever loved me and

I never got the chance to tell him he had my heart.

I shower and dress for work as dread glazed my body, gripping my stomach with its painful twist. Today is my first day back to work after I'd called in sick yesterday and the thought of possibly seeing Marcus jabs my heart with a spike. I miss him more than I ever thought I would and as soon as I was home I knew I needed someone to be by my side as I went through this new area of torture. I called Megan asking her to come home early and gave her the rundown of the situation, and like before I never told her Daniel was back as she needed the protection just as much due to her and Lucas getting me out all those years ago. He could destroy me all he wanted but I wouldn't let him hurt those I loved.

Heading into the kitchen in search for my keys, the anxiety cripples my belly causing me to halt and hold my stomach. I hated attacks like this. It's like a decay that's slowly eating away at me and one I had no control over. Even though I didn't face going into work I knew I couldn't hide forever and right now the last thing I wanted was to be late and give him a chance to throw some form of reprimand at me.

"Looking for these?" I freeze at the sound of the male voice and slowly turn. Sat like a king in his fucking castle was the asshole that caused so much anguish in my life holding up my door keys.

"Doors locked by the way, less chance of anyone disturbing us." My eyes flick from the keys to the door. My chest becoming tight as I grip my hands hard on the counter that's stopping my legs from buckling.

Scanning the area discreetly, Daniel holds his other hand up, shaking the item I'm searching for. "Looking for this too?" he snorts before standing. "You're so fucking transparent, Amelia." Dropping my phone to the floor he stamps his heavy boot on the screen smashing it to pieces.

"There," he looks at me with cold dark eyes. "Now no one can disturb us."

"How did you get in here?" I breathed noticing the panic in my voice.

"It's not hard to have a set of keys cut and return the originals without you even realising. Maybe you should be more careful who creeps into your house uninvited."

The thought of him here now terrifies me, but the thought of him being in here unaware makes me want to vomit. This was true Daniel style and I hate myself for not thinking about his twisted games sooner.

"Why are you here?" I tried to stay as calm as possible, trying not to let on I was anything but calm on the inside as my body become more unsteady.

"You know why. I'm here for you and for my money."

"I-I haven't got it all. I could only get half of what you wanted." As soon as I left the hotel the other day I went and cleared my savings hoping that some of what he was after would be enough. Only as he walks towards me the foul look on his face tells me otherwise as the smell of brandy rolls off his tongue in an unpleasant form. Daniel was always evil but with alcohol inside him I could never stop his anger from exploding.

"Get it from your fuck buddy that thinks it's acceptable to throw his weight around," his voice gravelly and cold.

"I can't."

I dart my eyes from him as the piercing stare was making me uneasy. He grabs my wrists and begins to squeeze, I whimper as he leaned in close causing my back to arch over the breakfast bar. His eyes now darker than they were and his chest started expanding from losing patients. "You can and you will." He sneered.

"I-I'm sorry. I've not seen him. H-He won't talk to me." My breathing had become out of control as I gasped out the words in panic, knowing that I wouldn't get out of this anytime soon as the door was lock and the keys in his pocket. Constantly praying that someone will come for me.

"How'd you manage to find someone like him when you're a nobody? I mean look at you," he runs his eyes up and down my body. "You're dressed like a slut, your make-up is cheap and your perfume is not the one I like. You're a fucking mess, Amelia. Why would he want you?"

"He loves me." I snap.

"Ha! Please, he doesn't love you, he just loves the idea of you. You're just some slut to make his profile look good. He doesn't want you or he'd be here." His words stung my heart and for a second I believed him. But I now knew the difference between love and hate and the man stood before me I despised more than ever.

Like always his bipolar mood changed again as he continued crushing my wrist. His other hand slowly runs up my body to cup my cheek, my stomach tightening with the knowledge of what his strength could do as he tried his best to show me his other side. I fell for those games one to many times and I'm not falling for them today. I have nothing more to lose. He could have me anyway he wanted, but this time I'm not going down without a fight. "But me, Amelia. I want you. I've changed."

"Someone who never saw an issue with their actions will never change!" I hissed.

The flash of anger in his eyes told me I'd hit a nerve as

his jaw clenched. The want to fight him soon made me question if I were making the right choice when he growled out his words in rage. "You made my life hell Amelia! I couldn't do anything without looking over my fucking shoulder, waiting to be picked up by police and now it'stime to pay the price."

"You emotionally abused me, beat me shitless and broke my bones, yet I made your life hell? Jesus, Daniel you really are something else."

He steps away, releasing me from his painful proximity before spinning back around. His chest now expanding as far as it would go while the redness in his face increased. "I was a good man and you destroyed me, my reputation! It all went to shit with your crying over you parents and demands for fucking attention!"

My blood now boiled from his pathetic excuses. My eyes couldn't possibly widen any more than they were and I suddenly didn't give two shits about my response as my voice raised to match his with my screams.

"Oh I'm sorry I lost my mother, what should I have done jumped for joy? And as for attention we were meant to be in a relationship not a fucking boxing ring you bast-" My yelp filled the space between us when his fist made contact with my face. My hand covered my lips that stung with the pain, the metallic taste of blood coated my mouth as I ran my tongue over the split. All the while eyes of fury sprung back at me.

"You deserved that." He seethed through gritted teeth. "Just like your blonde bitch I saw on my way here. She needed a lesson a long time ago."

My blood ran cold. Everything seemed as though it had stopped and only his sick cackle from his lungs played out, tipping his head up to the ceiling and loving every minute of being in control.

"What?" I breathed in panic.

"She needed telling, so I told her."

"What have you done to, Megan?" I cry as he continued to laugh. I'd now lost all ability to hold back my tears at the thought of not being able to protect her. I never even told her he was here yet he managed to find her and I couldn't do anything to stop it happening. "What have you done with Megan?!" I screamed, lunging at him and hitting his chest hard with my fists as years of my fury towards him left my body uncontrollably.

"Oh, so now you fight back, good job. Only you forget I always win bitch."

His solid blow to my cheekbone knocked me sideways with the impact, smacking my head on the corner of the counter and falling to the floor. The pain radiated throughout my frame as white spots formed in my eyes. Using every muscle in me I scrambled my feeble body to my feet as quickly as I could. My head felt dizzy and top heavy, my eye failing to focus from the blood that laced into it. "You really are a vile excuse for a human being." I disdained, making my attempt to escape but knowing it was useless as he had my keys. But I had to try.

I cried out begging him to stop as he pulls me back by my hair, slamming my back against the wall and punching the air from my lungs. "I'll stop when I get *all* my money!"

"I. I've not-" I gasped as my lungs blazed, unable to get my words out. His hit was powerful and he now towered over me, I leant forward clutching my waist. Holding my arms out to try to protect myself but he hit again, and again. I couldn't take much more, but I knew I couldn't let him

301

win.

His yelling became white noise as my eyes clocked the empty whiskey bottle on the counter beside me. Everything happened so fast. As he lunged towards me I felt my body swerve, gripping the bottle in my hands and with every ounce of strength I had I swung my arms full force like a cricket bat to a ball. Making contact with his skull as the glass shattered around us and the traces of leftover whiskey lingered. Daniel's body twisted and stumbled back to the unit, holding the counter top startled and dazed. My body trembled with the shock of what I had done, focusing on the blood that dripped from his head as the remainder of the bottleneck slip out of my hand. Yet he never failed to let the putrid laugh leave his throat as he turns his head and smirks, "Can't get rid of me that easily. I always win, remember."

In a flash his hand struck my belly with a turbulent blow, excruciating pain ripped through me as the ragged razor sharp glass tore through my flesh. The same pain I've felt before on my back as it burns its way through my body. I cry out, my back arched and face contorted. Lungs heaved for air while my body convulsed. Before his laugh pounded my ears as he wrenched the glass free and dropped it to the floor. Hot fluid oozed soaking my dress in crimson. Even though I knew, I brushed my fingers over the wound to make sure of the reality. Deep red traced over my fingertips and manicured nails as my body become unstable. He stepped forward with an unsteady sway. Blood running onto his shirt.

"Nobody cares, Amelia. Nobody wants you."

Another blow to my face and I'm on the ground, screaming out with the pain that shot through my abdomen before I felt my bones snap with the blow to my ribs. Hit after hit, he slowly took the life from me. Every inch of my body felt as though it were failing and all I saw in my blurred vision of my mind was Marcus and that he wasn't here with me. Maybe Daniel was right. Maybe this time he really had won.

Chapter Thirty-Four

Marcus

"I'm meeting Amelia for lunch today, I've not seen her since I've come back. Will you be joining us?" Mum's sympathetic voice disturbs me from my work as she sits in the vacant seat of my office, she returned back from the city late last night after disappearing for the wedding. All of which I now face a lawsuit from for smacking one of Nadia's people.

"No, I'm finalizing work here before she arrives. I'm not ready to see her yet." Work had gone to shit since everything that happened. I can't breathe let alone concentrate and I still hadn't figured out if I believed her or not.

"Oh for Christ sakes, Marcus, have you ever been in a situation where a woman has kissed you unexpectedly?

Because that's the position Amelia was in."

I look up from my desk and shot her a look. "You believe her?"

"She rang me upset and told me her version and yes I believe her. And I also believe you do to, only you're punishing her by ignoring her calls and making her think she's done wrong. You forget that I use to do the same thing with your father."

I sigh and threw down my pen knowing she was right, only I don't know who I was punishing more me or Amelia because the longer I wasn't with her the harder it got.

"Tell me what you're feeling, Marcus."

Truth was I'm not sure what I'm feeling. I've hid away from the world, not given two shits about my appearance and as for sleep-it's non-existent. All the while I endlessly sat yesterday and the night before in a darkened room with the whiskey bottle listening to the voicemails of her own anguish. Maybe it was all him and it was just a stupid kiss that took her by surprise, but to me it meant more than that. I never wanted to re-experience what I felt when walking in on Sadie and Sean but in a flash my happiness was once again crushed by the hands of another. I never thought I'd be that man again.

"I don't know how I'm feeling. I loved her. I still fucking love her and I have a sick feeling in my gut because I have this need to save her for some stupid reason, and then all I can see when I close my eyes is them together."

"Sweetheart, maybe you need to talk to-" My office door swung open and before I had chance to react Megan's hand made contact with my face with a hard slap.

"Where is she?!"

"Megan, you're back early." I sigh, rubbing my face

from the slap I'd been waiting for.

"You know you're many things, Marcus, but I never had you down as an asshole. You promised me you wouldn't hurt her and you've pushed her right into his trap."

"She's only got herself to blame."

"Bullshit! Did you even know who he was?"

"You need to leave, I'm done talking." I command pointing to the door with my eyes; I don't wish to continue this interrogation as her eyes try to kill mine through the daggers she throws. She's here for Amelia I get that but so help me god I'll have her ass dragged out by security if I have to. I push back my chair and make my way to the window, trying to find some form of control. I like Megan but I can't face this right now.

"This is serious, Marcus, she said she'd be here, I'm worried. Rosa, he cheated his way into the Lenton work system. She's not-"

I spin as she tries to make excuses for her friend. "Fuck sake, Megan it doesn't matter who he is-"

"No, Marcus, you have to listen to me. She's not safe on her own." She interjects.

Andrew now enters my office and hesitates for a second when seeing a tearful Megan and me a raging mess. "Um, Amelia's not turned up for work and she's not answering her phone."

Megan frantically rummages in her bag to pull out her phone with shaky hands, dialling a number I can only assume is Amelia's. "I got back late, I've not seen her. She said she'd meet me here. We need to find her, Marcus."

"Megan, sweetie calm down, what are you saying?" Mum questions as I become more irritated by the second.

"Yeah, Megan, what are you saying please enlighten

us because-"

"It's Daniel!" she screamed. "The guy you saw her with was Daniel. He's back. He's found her."

I felt like I'd been hit by a freight train. My face drained in colour and my chest hurt with the impact that come from her words. The ice cold shiver that cascaded through my body was unwelcoming. My knees weaken, causing me to collapse down to the sofa as I find it difficult to breathe.

"She was protecting you, Marcus. She was protecting all of us. That's what she does when it comes to him. Why would she want him after everything he's done?" the tears fall over her cheek, her eyes pleading with me. "She never did those things, she was scared. She loves you." The anger in my body was boiling with the realisation of who that fucker was, I had him in my own hands and I had no idea. But even after Megan's admission the asshole part in me still felt betrayed. I should feel at least some sort of relief and understanding. I should be wanting to rush to her begging while I crawl on my knees for her mercy. Hurt, confused, bitter, love. I don't know which one I'm feeling.

"What the hell happen to your face?" I looked up to find Andrew lifting Megan's chin. In our fight over Amelia I never noticed the red shimmer on her cheek that was too fresh to be from a Tequila fuelled fall at the weekend. Her lip quivers as she looks up at him, answering the question I never needed her to say. "I saw Daniel on my way to work and we argued. That's when I realised what was going on. She never told me he was here. I-I didn't know what to do, Andrew. I came straight here. She said she'll met me here."

"Jesus, Megan."

Wrapping his arms around her he opens his mouth to

speak when Claudia rushes in. "Megan, I ran Nadia's Security guy through the system and it's still coming up under a Lloyd Newman, however the guy in question checked out this morning and was last seen heading towards Briston-" Megan was out the door in a flash, followed by Andrew and me. A deathly chill now gripped my gut. Briston Pier was on the way to Amelia's and in the opposite direction to any Coach, Train or Airport out of here. Adrenaline pumped my veins with dread as a thousand images invaded my mind of what or where she could be.

"Stay here." Andrew ordered when he caught up with Megan, pulling her back by the arm.

"No. Andrew, I need to find her, you don't know what he's capable of."

"Which is why I don't want you anywhere near him," he growls. "Stay with Rosa."

"Marcus, please?" she cries, her tearful eyes full of fright and anxiety.

"Megan, he's right. Stay here with mum and call the police."

"Marcus, shouldn't you wait for them?" Mum questions, dialling the number.

"We can't, we'll get the quicker. Stay here, Megan. You'll be the first to know anything I promise." She looks at Andrew who only confirms his agreement with a nod. A sob leaves her chest as I kiss her head before rushing out the hotel.

The repeated slam of Andrew's boot on the door forced it open with a swing. Barging into her house I called out for her as my heart was pounding like a bitch. Crunched glass grated under my feet and my eyes darted to the floor then Andrew. Blades of glass lined the floor with blood specs glistening on the razor edges.

When I turned to pass the breakfast bar movement caught my eye and everything stopped. Sickened by the sight in front of me a cold sweat claimed my body. Her feet struggled to get a grip of the floor as his large body straddling her small frame while she fought for breath from the hands that pressed hard around her throat.

"Get off her!" Both Andrew and I lunged towards them, smacking my fist solid against Daniels's skull to startle him as we dragged him off her. Amelia's desperate need for air comes with a harsh gasp, choking her with the invasion that consumed her lungs while I continued to beat the shit out of the fucker in front of me.

"I'm gonna rip your fucking head off." I growled with another blow to his face, blood ran down his head and the satisfaction inside me roared knowing my girl had fought back.

"She loves it rough. Even better when she's immobile." He lunges towards me with an unsteady swing. I dive and hammer him hard in the ribs followed by another.

"You sick fucker!" Making contact with his face I hit him hard. Pound after pound I let my rage burn through my tight fists as he becomes a blooded mess of dark red that's struggling to fight back.

"Enough, Marcus, she needs you." Andrew drags me off him and I gloat when Daniel's body slides down the wall defeated. A whimper caught my attention to a lifeless body on the floor. Blood oozed from her belly, soaking her clothes as she lay motionless. Her breathing, fragile and painfully raspy. The sight of her killed me.

"Amelia?" I whispered, kneeling down beside her. I wanted to pick her up and hold her but was to scared of touching her, she looked so broken and bruised as blood covered various parts of her body. Removing my shirt I cradle her limp frame, sweeping her sticky blood stained hair from her swollen face. The painful cry that left her sore throat crushed me as I pressed my shirt down on the wound to try and stop the bleeding.

"I'm sorry baby. I'm so sorry."

Lifting her head I rest my arm under her neck, the pain in my gut of seeing her like this is ripping me in two. Her hooded eyes were looking right at me, but they weren't hers, they weren't my Amelia's. Everything around me become a blur, I was numb with regret, fear and lose. She was my everything and it took a fucked up situation like this to make me realise what a prick I'd become these last few days. Now I've only put her in danger.

"You just hang in there ok? We'll get you out." My throat was thick with grief and time never seemed to tick fast enough, causing me to bellow to the ceiling for someone to fucking help us.

"Marcus?" I froze at the sound of her choked fragile whisper, unshed tears bubbled in the wells as she swallowed trying her best to speak. "You. You c-came for me."

Her raspy breathing deteriorated, chest contracting with short sharp breaths that left her whimpering in pain. Her eyes closed and panic hit me. "No, no, no, don't close your eyes! Stay with me, Amelia, open your eyes!" shaking her, desperate to see her blues as tears trickled my cheeks. "Wake up, Amelia. Please don't leave me. I love you." But there was nothing as she drifted further away from me. I can't lose her, she is my world. I'm nothing without her.

My lifeline I couldn't lose.

***

My feet hardly touch the ground as I stormed through the hospital, pushing my way through the crowd of sick people and emergency staff. People roaming their eyes over my wet blood stained shirt and hands as I reach the desk-pushing my way forward not giving a fuck who's in front of me. Demanding answers from the uptight woman who's scowling down her glasses and refusing my questions.

"Where is she?" I bellowed, Andrew drags me back with all the strength he can muster.

"Keep your shit together for fuck sake, this isn't helping anyone."

I growl in frustration, lacing my fingers through my hair and tugging hard so my scalp prickled. I felt sick with worry and wanting the nightmare I was being swallowed into to end quickly. I want to hold my beautiful girl and never let her go.

A clatter of doors and the sound of raised voices awakens my attention as a portable bed swings into view and heads down the corridor. A glimmer of red locks was all I needed to know who lay amongst tubes and wires. I bolted in seconds. "Amelia."

A tall man dressed in blue scrubs pushed me back as the trolley continued down the corridor. "Please sir, let us do our job."

"She my girlfriend. What's happening?" I step to move passed franticly trying to get near but he grabs my shoulders, forcing me to stay put as Andrew takes my arm.

"Amelia has suffered a rupture to the abdomen which you know but it needs to be assessed on the extent of the damage and any further internal injuries. I'm sorry sir that's all I can give right now. I'll keep you updated as soon as I know more."

"Please don't let her die." I beg, feeling completely hopeless before he heads out of view.

Leaning against the wall for support I focus through blurred vision on the chequered black and white flooring beneath me. "She can't die, Andrew. She can't die."

He cups my shoulder with a squeeze, looking just as terrified as I felt. Clearing his throat he indicates his head with a nod to the side. Stood small in the oversized corridor is a different broken girl altogether. Focusing on the deep red that coats my shirt and fighting back her tears from my words she's clearly overheard, her frame trembles.

"Megan." I rush to her as she crumbles in my arms, holding me close with a tight grip as I comfort her the best I could.

All we can do now is wait.

Chapter Thirty-Five

Marcus

"I'll call her father; I think it's best he knows." Mum said leaving the room. I pace the hard floor a thousand times over, looking for answers that aren't there as my gut ached with dread of words I do not wish to hear. The confined space of the family room is a mixture of heavy breathing and the snuffles of a red-eyed Megan who's curled up against a silent Andrew.

One hour turned to two and two turned to a fucking eternity as we sat waiting for news. News that had the potential to change everything. Mum has been a godsend in keeping everyone calm; her love for Amelia was strong, just like mine. She had no doubt Amelia would do anything to hurt me and warned me countless times that Lenton would come back to bite me on the ass, yet I fell right into her trap and pushed the woman I love into danger with my stupidity.

The police arrived a short time ago with questions we did our best to answer as the doctors treated the piece of shit that caused this. Along with his charges today, being on the run and other crimes from his past he's now facing a lifetime behind bars. But for me even that wasn't enough. I wanted to stamp every inch of him into the dirt along with his head that screamed for mercy under my boot. I wanted him to suffer like he made Amelia suffer from the inside out. Prison would be too cushy for putrid trash like him, a slow agonising death seemed more beneficial.

"She begged me not to leave her," I sigh, overlooking the busy car park from the waiting room window. "I should have listened and not let my own history cloud my fucking judgment."

"It's not your fault, Amelia should have told you. But at the same time I understand why she didn't. She thought she was doing the right thing in protecting you."

"From him?"

"From him hurting you. He use to threaten those she cared of if she spoke out. That's why she was with him so long, because she was protecting those she loved. I knew there was more to it when she asked me to come home early. Then I ran right into the asshole. She must have been so scared on her own." Megan's voice cracked as another round of her tears fell. Wiping her blotchy face with the cuff of her sleeve she collects her phone from her bag. "I'm going to go ring Lucas again, see if he's managed to get a flight."

I push off from the wall and go to her, wrapping my arms around her petite frame and kissing the top of her head. Even with her sassy mouth and attitude there's a side to

Megan that not many people saw. "Your being so brave, Megan." I whisper before she quickly rushes out the door releasing her sobs once on the other side.

"We need to watch her," I inform Andrew who's staring at the floor. "She needs Lucas and until he gets here, we need to keep an eye on her."

He nods looking in direction of where she'd just left with a long exhale. "It taste like shit but do u want a coffee? The machine's just down the hall."

I shake my head as he leaves me isolated in the silence of the room. I'm not one for believing in god or prayers but right now I silently pray to the angels above that I get to keep my Amelia. She's the only light that fills my emptiness. The one I need until my last breath and I would give everything have her back in my arms again. I miss her so much. I need her with me.

***

The door to the waiting room opened and the overworked bobbing of my knee stopped instantly as I shot to my feet. The doctor I saw earlier entered with a straight smile, his dark hair had flecks of grey forming at the sides, his glasses sat on the tip of his nose as patient files sat snugly under his arm.

"Please tell me it's good news." I ask as my insides clenched with fear. My mouth dry and heart pounding in my throat.

"I'm Dr Chase, Amelia's doctor. Please sit." He gestures for us all to sit as he takes a seat himself. Mum takes my hand and pulls me down to sit as my airways begin to close, my palms sweaty while a raging anxiety ran my body.

"She's responding well. Amelia has suffered numerous fractures to her ribs and one to her collarbone along with her head injury and various bruising. Our main concern was her breathing. Due to the nature of the blows to her torso, Amelia's suffered what we call a Pneumothorax."

"What's that?" Megan questions.

"It's when air escapes the lungs preventing normal function which caused her lung to collapse on her way in here. The pressure was relieved and will take a while for her to fully recover. The incision to her stomach caused some tissue damage to be affected but wasn't deep enough to cause any long term damage. She's still in recovery but is doing well."

Sighs of relief hit my ears, the words from Dr Chase repeated over and over in my mind as I focused on his white surgical shoes.

A soft touch on my cheek turned my head to the eyes of my mother, a tear escaping her and her smile reassured the words I'd heard. "She's going to be ok son."

"Can I see her?" I asked, wiping my cheek with my shoulder and coming to a stand.

"Once the nurses have finished with her that will be fine. Although one visitor at a time, she's incredibly weak."

"Thank you, she's definitely going to be ok?"

Dr Chase shakes my hand, squeezing it with confidence and looking right at me. "She's going to be fine. She's a very lucky girl."

Even though the news of Amelia would make a full recovery, Megan still cried. It was as if she'd bottled every last ounce of emotion up and as soon as the words left the Dr Chase's lips the floodgates opened and all her fears and relief came rushing out and she could do nothing to stop them. After seeing Amelia once she was back on the ward Andrew took Megan home for rest and the waiting of Lucas's arrival. He managed to get a last minute flight from L.A but wouldn't be here for a few more hours.

"You haven't gone in and seen her yet, Marcus." Mum said softly, handing me a coffee and swimming her arm around my lower back. All I've done is let the others go to her while I stood back reluctant to go through the doors.

"I can't. I can't see her laid there knowing I'm responsible for all of this."

"What are you talking about, you never caused this." Her voice was low and filled with concern and disbelief.

"Didn't I? I walked away from her mum; I led her into the hands of a dangerous man that she was desperately trying to rebuild her life from. All this pain and devastation she's been through could have been prevented if I hadn't of acted like a total asshole. And it'snot just Amelia I've hurt it's Megan too because her best friend is in that room."

She takes the cup from my hand, placing it on the table of the family room, turning me to look at her. Her eyes have the same look in them where as a kid you knew a firm talking to was about to take place.

"Do not let me hear you say that again, Marcus Matthews. You are not responsible for the actions of a violent man. Regardless as to whether you were with Amelia or not he wouldn't have stopped until he done what he intended on doing, no matter who stood in his way. Yes it's unbearable to think of what the outcome could've turned out like but it hasn't. Amelia's still here fighting. Now get your ass in that room and be with the woman you love. She may be sleeping but she needs to know you're here when she wakes."

"What if she can't forgive me?" I whispered.

"She will. She loves you, Marcus. Just give her time; she's more afraid than she lets on."

I wrap my arms around her and dip my head into the crook of her neck. No matter how old I get I will always show my mother the love in which we share and will think nothing of holding her close. After dad left and my sister fucked off abroad, mum and I ruled the world and didn't let anyone stand in our way. She is forever my rock and I hers.

She kisses my cheek and smiles, her eyes glistening with tears. "I love you, Marcus. But right now you smell and look like shit. I'm going home to get you some clean clothes and a wash bag."

"What would I do without you?" I chuckle.

"I dread to think. Now go be with Amelia."

I grip the handle to the room of which Amelia lays and slowly prise the door open. The instant beep of the monitor attached to her caught my attention and my eyes travel all around the screen as numbers flashed in different colours. She looked so broken.

"It's ok to come in. I'm just checking her Obs," the dark haired nurse spoke with a voice just above a whisper.

"Has she woken?"

"She did earlier and we had to sedate her due to her extreme anxiety, she will be sleepy for a while yet. Are you staying?"

"Yes, I've left her once already I'm not going again."

The young nurse looked at me with sympathetic eyes before they focus on my blooded shirt I'd yet to change. Finishing her notes and placing her pen in her top pocket she walks around the bed. "When was the last time you ate?"

Good question, food hasn't on my list of priorities of late and by the sound of my grumbling stomach it was desperate to be heard. I shrugged my shoulders and tucked my hands into my pockets.

"I'll bring you some toast." Before for she left the room she rested her hand on my arm. "Situations like this are hard on everyone. Physically, Amelia will get stronger. But emotionally she needs to know your close. These are just monitors that update us with her status. Don't be afraid of everything that's going on around her."

Seeing Amelia lay out like this, lines and wires attached to her body rips me in two. I did this. I may not have hurt her physically but I'm responsible for her being here and mentally that's a hard task to deal with. I knew she'd never cheat-she doesn't have it in her. And yet I still pushed her away. All those feelings and emotions from back home burned its way to the surface clouding my vision with its poison and making me loses sight of the one person that mattered, the one person that needed me most. I put her in danger with my stupidity and now she's here cut, bruised and broken, having to rebuild what she's fought against for year. All because of me. I love her and I've done this. That animal may have marked her again but it's me that's hurt her heart this time.

I'm not afraid to show emotion when it comes to those I love, I'm not afraid to hide how I feel. My mother always told me to speak from the heart and listen to your gut no matter how hard it maybe or how difficult it is. No words I say are any good right now though. I'd give anything to have her in my arms again but all I can do is let her know I'm here in other ways.

I kiss her cut lip as gentle as I could not wanting to hurt her, the air left my lungs from her touch. I've missed her so much. Her swollen bruised face was coated in colours as traces of blood still linger on her skin from her cut brow.

"I'm so sorry, Amelia." I whisper as tears glass my eyes. "I never meant for this. You need to wake up, I need my angel back. I need to see those eyes. I can't breathe when I can't see them."

Taking her hand in mind I sit at her bedside, hanging my head low from the rest of the world and cry like a baby into the blanket that covers her. I did this. It's all my fault and I hope to fucking god she forgive me.

***

My eyes sprung open as a shiver cascaded down my back, the room becoming darker around me the more I tried to focus on the evening light and the hand that smoothed over my hair caused my body to become immobile as it continued. I was too afraid to move, I wasn't sure if I were dreaming and too afraid to turn my head in case I was dreaming. I just lie here and fall into the feeling that's taking over my body.

"Marcus." Her whisper sounded painful through the dryness of her throat. Please god let this be real. I felt my heartbeat in my chest like it had restarted at the sound of my name, the blood in my body rushed with relief as my emotions were once again thick in my throat.

"Marcus."

I slowly turn my head hoping this wasn't some twisted illusion from lack of fluids when everything fell into place the seconded I saw her blues. I was home. The sigh of liberation left me as I stand to move closer. "Hey beautiful, how you feeling?" I murmur.

She just looks at me, searching my face without a word. An uneasy feeling churned my stomach. I run my hand over her hair, silently praying she would forgive me for everything I've done. "I thought I'd lost you, Amelia. I've never been so scared."

Slowly moving her hand from mine she places it on my jaw, wiping the tears with her thumb before her chest convulses with her silent sobs that leave her fragile body.

"Shh, it's ok. You're going to be ok, you're safe now." Carefully I climbed up on the bed beside her and held her close. Reassurance left my lips as she cried hard against me, soaking my shirt as she let out all of the fear and pain she's suffered these last few days. Never again will I leave her. Not now that I've found her.

"I'm not going anywhere baby, I'm right here with you."

Chapter Thirty-Six

Amelia

My body felt foreign to me and it hurt like hell. Tubes and wires trailed from my body to machines behind my head but that wasn't the reasoning of my discomfort. It was the knowledge that somewhere in this hospital lays the man that put me here. It felt as though his eyes were on me even though he wasn't in the room and now he was exposed, I feared for those around me more.

I remember every second of what happened and I know it won't leave me anytime soon as each time I close my eyes I see his lifeless eyes and sickly grin as he towered over me. I gave up my fight for survival once the hammers to my ribs came; blow by blow I felt my bones cracking inside me as more air left my body. Tumbling me to the ground as my legs were taken from under me. I was immobile, lifeless and too exhausted to fight back, and when his solid body straddled mine and pressed his hands around my windpipe I gave up all hope of trying.

But then as I began to fall into a world of bright lights and coloured stars I saw his face. His smile that makes the corners of his eyes crinkle and the hazels that make time stand still when I look into them. His heart that fixed mine and the warmth of his body that holds me closes and makes me feel alive. That's when I knew I couldn't give up, I had to keep on fighting. Fight for that one person that's change everything in my life and brought me out of the darkness. I couldn't let Daniel win and take my heart away from me again now that it had been repaired. So I fought.

"Hey, you're awake." Marcus smiles as he enters the room, easing my apprehension in me the moment his eyes were on me.

"Where did you go?" I ask softly.

"You were sleeping so I made a few calls to keep everyone updated and thought it was best I changed my shirt." He placed the overnight bag on the floor and comes to me.

"So now that everyone is updated are you here to stay with me?" I wanted him as close to me as possible, terrified that Daniel could still come after either of us.

"I'm all yours. I'm not going anywhere." I didn't have to tell Marcus I was scared because he felt it. After I woke I didn't let him go for hours and clung to him like my life depended on it while he whispered reassuring words in my ear.

He kicks off his shoes and climbs up on the bed, carefully trying not to knock me. The high dosage of meds took away the majority of the pain but there were times when it shot through my body leaving my crying out and unable to get comfortable.

"Mum sends her love and said to say she'll be back in the morning along with Lucas who's getting in shortly." I forgot Rosa had come back, I was meant to be meeting her for lunch today and no doubt cry on her shoulder over Marcus. And the thought of Lucas coming back makes me feel more protected than ever. He loves throwing his weight around when it comes to his girls and I expect he'll do just that with the doctors and police officers that continue to harass me with questions. Not long after I woke and cried a river on Marcus with the overwhelming feeling of being alive and having him with me, they bombarded me with questions. Only then it was Marcus who went all cave man and told them they'd had enough from me.

"Is she mad we never got to do our ladies with little food but more wine lunch?" I smile as I rest my head on his chest to listen to his heart.

"Oh yeah, I've not heard the end of it. She no doubt hired topless waiters and everything and is highly disappointed that you went and ruined her afternoon of fun."

The giggle that left me took my breath with the sharp pain that rippled through me torso. "Fuck, don't make me laugh."

"Sorry babe." He murmurs kissing my hair.

My eyes fall heavy with exhaustion while I try to remove the vision of Daniel from my mind once my lids close. Minutes ticked by before I felt the gentle stroke of Marcus's fingers over my cheek as he murmurs, "Amelia, I need to tell you something."

My stomach flopped with dread as my eyes drew open to find his. Worry filling his hazels as he searched my face and I wasn't sure I wanted to hear what he had to say. "Mum called your dad to let him know what had happened. She thought that despite everything he needed to know," his eyes focus on my neck before coming back to me. "I'm sorry baby but he's not coming. He doesn't want to be here."

So he really had abandoned me and cut me off from his life. "O-oh um, that's ok. Thank you for telling me." I whispered, resting my head back down on his chest. After everything my dad and I had been through I still hoped that one day all would be forgiven and that I'd have him in my life again. Move on from all the hurt between us and start over like mum would have wanted. But no, even after the first time I asked him to save me from Daniel and now after finding me again to try and finish me off he still sits and wallows in his own self-pity and misery. Am I really that much of a letdown for looking like my mother that he can't bear the thought of me?

Much to my own annoyance I couldn't contain my emotions any longer and the tears soon burst from my eyes. I cried hard. I cried for everything that had happened and everything that never did. I cried for me. For my family old and new and for the man holding me as he shelters my body. I then cried because I didn't know why I was crying, all the while Marcus cradled me and spoke sweet words of love. Which only caused more tears because he was being way too nice and I couldn't take all the overwhelming feelings that funnelled through my body.

My overactive state left me in pain and a sweaty mess, making the nurse come check over me and boosting me with more painkillers. I couldn't help to smile at the eye-fuck she gave Marcus and the blush that hit her cheeks once he thanked her for her help.

"Marcus, can you freshen me up please? I feel disgusting." I request as my post sobs still shuddered through my body as I spoke.

He's been my permanent male nurse since the minute I woke up, fetching me water, running around after doctors and now carefully removing my hospital gown to clean me- much to the nurses disapproval. I wasn't allowed to move too much in case of rupturing the stitches in my belly but I couldn't lay here in my own dried blood any longer.

My torso was a web of blues and reds from the bruises and I could see Marcus retreating from me once I lay in just my panties. His eyes full of remorse and anger as they darted to the floor.

"I was so afraid of losing you, Amelia," he says quietly. "If I knew this was going to happen I'd never of pushed you away. I just saw red when I walked into to your office and my fucked up mind thought I was back in the past. Please forgive me. I never wanted to hurt you. I never meant this; I'll never push you away again, I swear."

Tears filled his eyes as I reached for his hand. Pulling him close with the one arm I could use and kissing his cut knuckles on both his hands. "You never hurt me, Marcus, it was all him. I was afraid of losing you too because I knew what his lies could do, but you came for me and you saved me. That's all that matters. None of this was your fault; please don't let this eat away at you. Ok? This. Wasn't. You."

He nods, sniffing back his tears and dipping the face cloth into the bowl. The coolness of the water on my skin was like I'd fallen into heaven as I laid and watched his angel hands work their magic. Relieving the tightness of my skin and feeding my dry pores with the moisture it desperately craved, caressing and cleaning my tender blood stained body with delicacy trying not to hurt me.

I sniffed his shirt hard before he carefully placed it over my body, pushing only one arm through the sleeve as I couldn't straighten the other before he eased me down on to the mattress, whimpering with pain. Once he finished cleaning up he turn off the main light to the room so the warm glow of the night lamp filled the darkness. We lay silent on the bed, resting my head on Marcus's chest while he plays with my hair, dosing on and off once my body become more relaxed and pain free.

"Tell me something true." I whisper. One of the hardest parts of not being with him was our little games we'd play. Snippets of unimportant information that sometimes had us giggling for hours with how ridiculous it was.

"You're beautiful."

"Oh please," tapping his shoulder. "Your such a liar have you seen my face, I look like I've had a failed round of Botox."

"I'll have you know Miss Weston, I am no liar and when I say you look beautiful it's because you do, now enough of the negativity your failed Botox face will heal. Your turn." he smiled, triumphant I had no come back.

"I've not had an orgasm in nearly three days." I chuckle.

"Me neither and as much as I'd like to help you out on that one I think it's best we wait till you're less sore."

"Oh you're no fun," I say with a sigh. "Your turn, tell me something true."

"I'm going to kiss you," he grinned. "I promise I'll be gentle." And gentle he was. He brushed his lips softly over

330

mine as the tips of our tongues touched. Slow and passionate. It was like everything fell into place with that one kiss. My heart swelled with recognition that I was so afraid of feeling. My mind snowballing with everything that had happened and behind my unshed tears it blinded me with what I saw before me. I knew then but now everything become clear. I wasn't afraid anymore and as long as I had Marcus I knew my demons would be crushed with his power.

"You turn, tell me something true."

"I love you, Marcus." He froze as his eyes flashed to mine, filling his hazels with awe as a slight smile curved his lips.

"What?" he breathes.

"I love you. I've always loved you and I'm sorry I never told you sooner but I was just scared. Scared because when I met you I found me and I've not felt those feelings you were making me feel. So I tried to bury them because I thought that was the right thing to do but I realise now I was wrong. Because by doing that I hurt you and I never wanted that." He goes to speak but I stop him, completely abandoning our game with my admission that now rolls freely from my lips and felt so fucking good to hear myself say the words aloud that I'd wanted to say in weeks.

"You're my everything, Marcus and I want nothing more than to spend every waking minute with you. I want you to hold me when I'm scared, kiss me when I'm sad, care for me when I'm sick and love me forever." I place my hand on his jaw to catch the tear that's fallen and melted my heart. "Will you love me forever, Marcus?"

He's silent for a moment, looking deep into my eyes as he reads me. "When I came back here I only wanted to slip back into a life in which I missed. I never came looking and I certainly didn't expect to fall, but I have. You are the best thing that's ever happened to me, Amelia. You captured me from that very moment; you're in my heart, my soul and forever on my mind. You're with me, around me and within me. I want to protect you and keep you safe. But most of all I promise that I will love you forever and always."

His kiss stole my breath, running his tongue along my bottom lip before slipping it deep into my mouth. My cut lip stung and my face ached from his hungriness but I didn't care. I've missed him so much and this kiss engulfs me hard, sucking the life from me and making my heart fit to burst with the flutters he never fails to provide.

"Say it again."

"I love you." I grinned as I ran my fingers down his cheek. I finally felt free. The very last piece of my heart I was so desperate to try and control had unattached itself and been swept away, leaving me fresh, new and open to be loved. "I loved you then. I love you now. I'll love you always."

His grin was the size of the ocean as the tears still glassed his eyes. "You didn't have to say what your eyes hadn't already told me, but you have no idea what that means hearing you say that."

"I'm sorry I took so long to say it."

"It doesn't matter. I love you, Amelia with all my heart, I will fight the world for you and I promise to take care of you always."

He kisses me again, wiping my own tears in return as his thumb strokes over my cheek. I stare into his eyes and fall into the world of just us. I still fall for this man every day and want nothing more than to spend my future with him. Marcus never fails to ignite new promises and passion. He's proven to me that a life of love does exist and that no two men are the same. Every day I'm his queen, the way he tends and cares for me is overwhelming, the way I can open up to him is nothing like I've ever experienced. He knows me all the way through to the inside of my heart and soul and I'm no longer afraid to bare all. I'm no longer afraid to fall and no longer afraid to love. He's changed me in many ways, I love him unconditionally and I no longer have to bottle up the good times and keep them for the times I need to replay them. Because every second of the day that this man is glued to me is more than just a good time. He's my first true love, my missing piece of the puzzle I've been searching for all these years and I will be forever thankful that I was found by him.

Epilogue

Amelia

Three Months later

I stretch my overly satisfied body and grin aware of what was happening on the other side of the door. I forgot to text Megan back earlier and I knew she'd be round to check I was ok.

"Are you two fucking? Because as much as I love sex, I really don't want the memories of Marcus's nakedness in my mind, especially as I can't touch."

Marcus quickly shoots up from his doze and covers himself with the sheets as Megan stands in the bedroom doorway covering her eyes. "Megan, what the fuck!" He shrieks in panic as I lay there giggling. Yeah I forgot to tell him she has my new key.

"Didn't you get my text? I sent you both one hours ago."

"We were otherwise engaged babe. And you can uncover your eyes now."

She lifts her hands down and blinks with a smile, looking at us before locking her eyes on Marcus. "Holy shit your abs get better by the second. What else is going on under those sheets?" she winks.

"What do you want, Megan?" Marcus chuckles with a hint of red in his cheeks. Like always Megan makes herself completely at home and crawls up the mattress to lie on her belly between us like a child in mummy and daddy's bed.

"Hi," she whispers with a shit ass grin. I roll my eyes and reach for my phone and read her text out aloud.

"Fuck yeah. Beach party and campfire night. Bring booze and shirtless man. See you in a few hours you horny kitten." I place the phone on my tummy and tilt my head with a cocked brow.

"What? It's Saturday, it's still warm out and it needs to be filled with over muscled men dripping in sea water. Just because you have Mr Man Candy here doesn't mean I have to stop looking." She tips her head to Marcus with a raised brow. "I sent you a text too."

He grunts and reaches down taking his phone from his jeans pocket he abandoned earlier and reads out her text. "Put Amelia down and get her to answer her phone you ass-wipe."

"I wouldn't have had to call you that if ginger here answered her messages."

"And who do you suppose we bring to this beach campfire thing?" Marcus says scratching his belly. "I only know Andrew as Jack and Nathan are both working at Rubies."

"Andrew will be fine." She says with a glimmer of something in her eye. I look at Marcus who sighs with an eye roll as Megan looks on, battering her lashes with plead.

"Fine, we'll come down to the beach, but no heavy drinking, I'm still recovering."

"Ugh, please. Recovering from hot sex more like." She replies before leaning into Marcus and whispering. "You can get up now, Marcus. I promise I won't look at your nakedness."

"Goodbye, Megan." He says dryly.

"Please, just sneaky peak?"

We both giggle as he shakes his head in amusement. "I'm not leaving this bed till you leave this fucking room."

"Ugh, no fun."

I was in hospital just over a week and once I was up for visitors I had everyone running round after me like mother hens. Lucas had arrived and like I predicted, threw his weight around demanding answers and if that wasn't enough, I later had to calm Marcus down once he found out the trial against Daniel won't be for a few more months. Nadia sent us a long letter of apology and dropped the lawsuit against Marcus for assault on her employee. Only to be slapped in the face with one from Marcus for failing the correct protocol when hiring staff with fraudulent personal details.

My recovery hasn't been an easy as I hoped. My wounds healed quickly but it was the aftermath I struggled with. Stepping into my house brought back all the haunts and everywhere seemed to be laced with Daniel's presence causing me to have panic attacks and not being able to go back there. I've officially moved in with Marcus and he has now set up his business here in Spring Rose while Rosa commutes to and from the city so Marcus can stay with me until I'm fully recovered.

Even though in one sense I'm in a better place than what I was years ago, I often felt like I'd fallen back into the dark world. Without warning my mind would be overshadowed with unpleasant memories of the evil and my nightmares were just as vivid as I remember which resulted into more appointments with my therapist. I was just thankful I had more people around me that understood my emotional state.

"Are you sure you feel up to this dear?" Rosa questioned as I stuff my thick cardigan into my beach bag. The season was heading into late autumn and although it was still warm during the day at night the sea breeze got to your bones.

"Yes, I'm fine Rosa. I've packed for all weathers and I'm excited to hit the beach. I feel like I've not been out in days."

"That's because we haven't babe." Marcus winks finishing his coffee.

We finished packing the final bit's that Megan ordered us to bring and placed the bags in the car. It felt great to be out the house, the weather has been unpredictable with storms and high winds the last few days but now the sky is clear as the late afternoon sun warms my skin.

Rosa went on ahead as Marcus had to stop off at The Grand to check on a few things whilst I waited in the foyer chatting to Felicity. I'm not back working full time yet as the long hours exhaust me, but I try and do as much work as my body will let me. By the time we left it was dusk once we headed to meet the others.

"Marcus, why are we heading to Marbles Cove? I thought we we're meeting Megan?"

"We are but I asked her to meet up here. I thought our own private party would be better."

"You mean you're letting, Megan invade your personal beach space? You do know she'll be here all the time now?"

"There's always an injunction." He chuckles.

I couldn't stop the smile that hit my lips once I got out of the car. The pathway down to the beach was lit by lanterns as the beach glowed with its own light. At the far end of the beach was a camp fire but it was the centre that caught my attention. A huge outline of lanterns in the shape of a heart filled the sand. It was beautiful.

"What is all this?" I look to Marcus who's smiling.

"Well I still remember the look in your eyes the first time I took you to the beach. Your face was full of awe with the lanterns amongst the dunes and I wanted to experience that again, only this time I brought it to Marbles Cove, with friends."

God, could he get any more adorable.

We made our way further onto the beach as Megan come bounding up towards us, hair flicking out behind her. "So um, here's the thing. I brought loads of booze like you told me not to and I also found this guy that won't stop asking after you. He's waiting to meet you."

My eyes darted from hers to scan the sand as I clock eyes on Mr Beautiful himself. I've not seen him since I left the hospital and he seems to be spending more time here now than he did in L.A. "What are you doing here?"

"Hey, Ginger Spice." He beams lifting me into a hug. "Well I had a few days off and I thought rather spend it there checking out women, I'd spend it *here* checking out woman."

"Lucas, sweetie I like the sound of that, maybe I could help you out if you get bored. I'm thinking of dating younger men."

"Mum!" Marcus calls to a flirtatious Rosa.

Drinks and amusement flowed within the group along with the toasted marshmallows dipped in chocolate spread that Lucas and Megan fought over, and burgers that Andrew and Marcus cooked. Like their childish games they always played, Lucas chases Megan around the beach before catching hold of her and running into the water, throwing her in deep as she screamed in enjoyment. I can't wait till Lucas moves here permanent as then my new family will be complete.

"Can you remember the last time we danced on the beach?" Marcus murmurs as I hold him close and dance to the music from the portable stereo.

"Yeah," I chuckled. "You told me you loved me and I freaked out and left. I won't be doing that again."

"Glad to hear it." He smiles looking into my eyes, a look that was full of devotion and commitment. A look that went on so long it made me a little uneasy.

"You're blushing, Miss Weston."

"You're staring, Mr Matthews."

"I'm staring because you're beautiful."

My blushing quickly deepened and a rush of heat charged through me. My breath hitched and my hand covered my mouth when he pulled away from me to get down on one knee whilst I heard the gasps a squeals from those around us. In my head I was asking him what the hell he was doing but the words wouldn't leave my lips.

"Marcus."

"Amelia Grace Weston, I love you unconditionally and fall in love with you more each day. You're beautiful, sexy, incredibly strong and I'm nervous as shit right now but that said..." he stops and opens the small red box to reveal a stunning diamond ring that sparkles in the nightlight. "Amelia, will you marry me?"

Tears flooded my eyes to blur my vision. My heart felt like it was going to explode as it pounded in my chest. I knew my answer the moment he started to speak and I knew that my love for this man was unconditional and that I wanted each and every day spent with him.

"Yes!" I squeal, kneeling down to join him as he slips the ring over my finger.

I kiss him hard forcing him back to lie on the sand as I continued my invasion on his mouth. "I love you, Marcus Matthews." I smile against his lips. "I love you so much."

"I love you too and when I said I wanted to spend every minute with you I meant it. I can't see a future without you and a family."

"You want kids?" I beamed.

"Why not, I can just see little Ginger Spices running around."

"Hey, that's my tagline fucknut, find your own." Lucas shouts, as Rosa pops open the champagne. Now I know what all the secrecy was between these two the last few days.

"You feeling ok?"

Someone once gave me a box full of darkness and after years of hurt and suffering it's made me realise-as crazy as it sounds, that it was a gift. Because if I didn't have that darkness I wouldn't of found my light. Marcus came into

341

my world when I was at my weakest and he's the reason why I'm now at my strongest. I didn't expect to be that girl in the past and I certainly didn't expect to become the woman I am now, and it's all thanks to him. He's changed me for the better and never fails to take my breath away. He has taught me many things I've fought for years. He taught me to trust again, to not be afraid. Taught me to open my heart and taught me that I do deserve a second chance and a happy-ever-after. But most of all he has taught me the greatest thing anyone could provide. He has taught me that falling in love isn't scary after all.

"I've never felt more alive."

The End.

Playlist

Katy Perry - Last Friday night
Ed Sheeran - Kiss me
Celtic Woman - Amazing Grace
Leona Lewis - Come Alive
Bruno Mars - Just the way you are
John legend - You and I
Leona Lewis - Angel
Ne-Yo - Let me love you (Until you learn to love yourself)
Matt Cardle - Amazing
Westlife - The Rose
Christina Aguilera - Bound To You
Pink - Try
Beyonce - Halo
Leona Lewis - Can't breathe
Rihanna - Cold Case Love
Goo Goo Dolls - Without you here
Jennifer Hudson - Giving myself

Coast - Oceans

Acknowledgments

When I first had the image of two characters in my mind I knew they weren't going away any time soon. Marcus and Amelia will forever hold a special place in my heart and I hope their story will touch the hearts of many. They took over my life in a way I can't explain, they literally become my every thought and when I first started writing I had no idea it would lead to this. I have achieved something I never thought I could and I couldn't have done it without those involved, so thank you!

Mum and Dad. Who would have thought that this was ever possible?

As you know the journey hasn't been easy but I got there in the end. Words cannot describe how incredible you both are. Thank you for putting up with me, and honestly the endless hours I spent being unsociable was really nothing personal. XX

To the other part of Twitch (You know who you are) Well let's face it, the stories had to come alive at some point right? I knew our Friday nights would pay off at some point! Thank you for being my shoulder to cry on when I had the meltdowns and there will no doubt be many more to come, just to warn you. Love you long time Xx

Dotty King. I simply cannot thank you enough. Without you, this wouldn't have been possible. Thank you for your honesty, your time and putting up with my freak out moments. Your support, guidance and knowledge has helped me bring this book to life. I wouldn't of known where to start (other than with a blank page) and just by chance and the mention of writing you become my lifeline. You are a mind of information and a joy to work with. Xx

Amanda Wylie. What's that saying…We'll be best friends forever because you already know too much?! Thank you for being ridiculously awesome and the number one bestie I've ever had. Who would've thought that a random comment on social media would develop into the crazy beautiful friendship that we have. Xx

P.S - you still have some blues in my fridge, ha ha!

Sharon. For your input on the naming of Primrose Lodge. I know what a difficult task that was for you whilst on your lunch hour. Xx

Special thanks to-

Najla Qamber Designs.

Lindee Robinson Photography.

Karen, White Hot Ebook Formatting.

You ladies have put up with so many of my questions I even got annoyed with myself at times! That said, all this wouldn't have been possible without your help, so THANK YOU!!

About the Author

I have lived in the southwest my entire life just on the edge of Dartmoor where the moorland goes on for days. It's beautiful, breathtaking and occasionally rather wet. I have a love/hate relationship with chocolate and the weekends are not the same without a Vodka in hand.

I have a loving family that mean the world to me and a hyperactive dog that still thinks she's a puppy and will sit on your feet if you stand still for more than a second.

Music is my lifeline, writing is my therapy and a mind full of beautiful men are always welcoming.

XXX

Printed in Great Britain
by Amazon